FAST TRACK

MORE TITLES BY JULIE GARWOOD

Hotshot

Sweet Talk

The Ideal Man

Sizzle

Fire and Ice

Shadow Music

Shadow Dance

Slow Burn

Murder List

Killjoy

Mercy

Heartbreaker

Ransom

Come the Spring

The Clayborne Brides

The Wedding

For the Roses

Prince Charming

Saving Grace

Castles

The Secret

The Prize

The Gift

Guardian Angel

The Bride

The Lion's Lady

Honor's Splendour

Rebellious Desire

Gentle Warrior

JULIE GARWOOD

FAST TRACK

DUTTON
est. 1852

DUTTON
→ est. 1852 ←

Published by the Penguin Group
Penguin Group (USA) LLC
375 Hudson Street
New York, New York 10014

USA | Canada | UK | Ireland | Australia | New Zealand | India | South Africa | China
penguin.com
A Penguin Random House Company

LIBRARY OF CONGRESS CATALOGING-IN-PUBLICATION DATA
has been applied for.

ISBN 978-0-525-95445-3

Printed in the United States of America
1   3   5   7   9   10   8   6   4   2

This book is a work of fiction. Names, characters, places, and incidents either are the product of the author's imagination or are used fictitiously, and any resemblance to actual persons, living or dead, business establishments, events, or locales is entirely coincidental.

For Marlow Raye Garwood,
our newest pride and joy

May you always have
A sunbeam to warm you,
A moonbeam to charm you,
A sheltering angel so nothing can harm you.

An Irish Blessing

FAST TRACK

PROLOGUE

Cordelia Kane met her Prince Charming when she was just five years old.

Cordelia, called Cordie by her father since she was a baby, hadn't wanted to go to school when she turned five, but her father wouldn't let her stay home anymore. He insisted she give school a try. He was positive she would like it. As it turned out, he was right. On her first day in kindergarten at the exclusive Briarwood School she made two new friends, Sophie Rose and Regan Madison.

Cordie saw Sophie that first morning crossing the parking lot and was sure the girl had just stepped out of a fairy tale. Her long white-blond hair bounced as she walked, and she had a twinkle in her eyes. Regan arrived shortly after. She was very pretty, too, with thick brown hair and freckles on her nose that Cordie wished she had. It didn't take long for the girls to form a bond. All it took was one incident on the playground. A second-grade bully tried to take Cordie's hair barrettes from her, and Regan and Sophie immediately came to her defense. Sophie was outraged on Cordie's behalf, but it was Regan who proved to be the brave one. She stood up to the bully and wouldn't back down. From that moment on the girls became inseparable. Where one went the others followed.

Cordie's new friends came from homes that were very different from hers. Regan and Sophie were driven to school by chauffeurs in limos and town cars. Cordie's father drove her to school in his old, reliable pickup truck. Regan and Sophie had attended prestigious preschools for two years before starting at Briarwood. Cordie hadn't gone to preschool, yet when she started kindergarten, she already knew how to read. Her father had taught her, sitting down with her every night after dinner and her bath.

Reading wasn't the only thing her father taught her. While other children worked on arts and crafts and played games like hide-and-seek, Cordie spent her days with her father in his automotive shop learning all about cars. He loved working on what he called clunkers, and because she wanted to please him, she paid attention to what he was doing and managed to get grease on her clothes almost daily. Every night before they went home they played a game. He would lift the hood of a car, then pick her up in his arms and point to something in or around the engine. It was her task to tell him what the part was called and what its job was. As she got older, she got better and quicker. Her favorite thing was to ride along with her father in his tow truck and help stranded people. Sometimes it took only a few minutes to get the engine going; other times he had to tow the car back to his shop. The easiest to fix were dead batteries and worn spark plugs. She knew what both of those were because her father had told her. Like other children, she had coloring books and crayons, but she never used them. She preferred following her father around and being his helper.

Because she didn't have playmates, she was fearful of what school would be like. But once she met Sophie and Regan, all her fears slipped away.

Cordie shared a special connection with Sophie. Both of their mothers had died before the girls were old enough to remember them. Regan was the lucky one. She had a mother, and Cordie and Sophie would have envied their friend except for the fact that her mother was never around. She was always traveling and, even when she was in town, seldom spent time at home. If it weren't for Regan's three brothers, she wouldn't have known any family at all. She might have been the only one of them fortunate enough to have siblings, but that didn't matter to Cordie and Sophie. When they were together, they were sisters.

Since Sophie was the oldest by almost a year, she felt she should be able to boss the other two around, and for a while they let her. Then, as time passed, the girls became competitive with one another in almost everything . . . except soccer. They all joined a team, but Sophie didn't like sweating or getting dirty, so she usually walked down the field or just stood where she was and waited for the ball to come back her way. Regan, the shortest member of the team, was a powerhouse. But then, so was Cordie. The two of them usually scored at least one goal each. They were girly girls who loved ribbons in their hair and ruffles on their skirts, but on the field they were aggressive and out to win.

It was at the end of one of their soccer practices that Cordie met him.

Evan, Regan's driver, had been sent to the airport to fetch a friend of her mother's, so Aiden, Regan's oldest brother, got stuck with soccer carpool. Spencer, the middle brother, decided to ride along with him.

The practice field was out in the middle of nowhere. Aiden took a wrong turn, had to backtrack, and was fifteen minutes late getting to the field. The soccer coach always waited until all the girls had been picked up before leaving, and he was about to put Regan and Sophie and Cordie in his van and take them home when Aiden finally showed up. The SUV he was driving was making a loud noise.

The girls stood together with their backpacks at their feet, squinting against the setting sun at the two figures in the noisy vehicle.

"That's an old car," Sophie said. "Really old."

Cordie nodded. "It's a clunker," she announced with authority.

The car came to a chugging stop, and the two teens got out and started across the field.

"Who are those boys?" Sophie asked.

"My brothers," Regan said. "The big one is Aiden. He's sixteen. Spencer is only fourteen," she added. "I don't know where Walker is. Maybe he stayed home."

Aiden whistled and motioned to Regan. "Let's go," he shouted.

"He sounds mad," Sophie whispered.

Regan shook her head. She lifted her backpack over her shoulder as she said, "He isn't mad. He's just always in a hurry."

Aiden whistled again. Regan picked up the pace and shouted, "Stop whistling. We aren't dogs, Aiden."

Her brother obviously thought her comment hilarious and had a good laugh. She handed him her backpack and, following her lead, Sophie and Cordie handed him theirs as well. As they proceeded toward the SUV, Regan introduced her friends. Sophie looked back at the two boys, smiled, and said hello, but when Cordie turned around, she could only stare. Her attention was locked on Aiden. She thought he was the most perfect boy she had ever seen. He looked just like the prince in her favorite story, "Snow White." His hair was almost as dark and his face was just as handsome. He was big, too, bigger than her father. Maybe he really was a prince, she thought.

"How was soccer?" Spencer asked.

"Good," Regan answered.

"It must have been," Aiden said. "You're covered in dirt."

"Cordie's got dirt on her, too," Regan pointed out. "But Sophie doesn't."

Spencer turned to the little blond girl. "Didn't you get to practice today?" he asked, taking in her pristine appearance. She was spotless, and her soccer shoes looked brand-new, as though she'd just taken them out of the box.

"I practiced," she assured him.

"But your—"

Regan explained. "Sophie doesn't like to get dirty."

Spencer glanced at Aiden before asking Sophie, "Then why do you play soccer?"

"I like soccer," she answered.

Regan nodded. "She does."

Aiden laughed. "You're being logical, Spencer."

"And?" his brother asked.

"They aren't."

They reached the faded blue SUV. Aiden tossed the girls' backpacks in the back while Spencer opened the door for them to get inside. "Put your seat belts on," he instructed.

"Why are you driving this car?" Regan asked.

"I borrowed it," Aiden said. "It's a loaner while my car is being serviced. It's all they had."

He got behind the wheel, put the key in the ignition, and turned it. The engine sputtered, then died. He tried again. The same thing happened. Then again and again while he pumped the gas pedal.

He felt a hand on his shoulder. When he turned, he saw that Cordie had unhooked her seat belt and was sitting on the edge of the seat watching him. Before he could tell her to put her seat belt back on, she said, "You should stop doing that. You're probably flooding it."

"It?" Spencer asked.

"The engine." Didn't he know anything? she wondered. "He's flooding the engine," she explained slowly so he would understand.

She remembered what her father often said. If he had a dollar for every call he got about a car that wouldn't start because the driver had flooded the engine, why, he'd have a whole lot of dollars.

Aiden was so surprised by the quiet authority in her voice that it took him a few seconds to react.

"I'm not flooding it," he said.

She looked him in the eyes and replied, "Yes, you are. If you keep doing that, you'll have to wait a long time before you can try again, and you know what? You'll probably flood it again." She patted his shoulder as though she was trying to console him and added, "It's because you don't know what you're doing. If you want, I could show you."

Having given her opinion, she scooted back, clicked her seat belt on, and offered her friends some of the fruity snacks she had in her pocket. Within seconds the girls were whispering and giggling. The topic was Halloween and what costumes they were going to wear to school for the party. Regan announced she was going as a scary witch, and Sophie couldn't quite decide but was leaning toward a ballerina.

"Are you still going to be Cinderella?" Sophie asked Cordie.

Cordie stopped to think for a second and then looked up at Aiden before answering. "I've changed my mind," she answered. "I'm going to be Snow White."

Ignoring the chatter in the backseat, Aiden asked Spencer if he remembered passing any filling stations on the way to the field.

"I wasn't looking. Do you know anything about cars?"

"No," Aiden said. "And neither do you." He tried to start the engine again a couple of times before giving up. "Damn," he whispered. "Why in God's name do they have soccer practice all the way out here?"

"Beats me. One of us should start walking, I guess. It's probably a couple of miles to the nearest house. I'll go. I'll knock on doors until someone lets me use their phone. Unless . . ."

"Unless what?"

Spencer looked over the seat at the girls. "Never mind."

"Unless what?" Aiden asked.

"Unless we ask the kid," he whispered.

"You want me to ask a five-year-old how to fix the damn car?" Aiden asked with a hint of sarcasm.

"No," Spencer said. "I'll ask her."

He turned to the girls. "Now, Cordie . . ."

"Her name's Cordelia, but everyone calls her Cordie." Regan volunteered that information.

"Cordelia's a pretty name," Aiden said.

Cordie hadn't liked her name, but when he told her it was pretty, she changed her mind in an instant. She decided she wanted everyone to call her Cordelia.

"Did you say you could tell Aiden how to get the car started?" Spencer asked.

"I maybe could," she said. She sat forward again. "It's easy. All you have to do is put your foot on the gas pedal and push down. Hold it there. You don't push up and down like you were doing. Then turn the key on and leave it on. You keep turning it off and on, and that's wrong. Everything you did was wrong," she happily informed him. Then she patted him again and added, "Don't worry, Aiden. The engine will maybe start."

"Maybe, huh? Okay, I'll give it a try." He followed her instructions, smiling inside over the fact that he was listening to a five-year-old, but after several seconds with nothing happening, he started to ease off the pedal.

She shouted in his ear. "No. Wait!"

He kept his foot pressed to the floor, and the engine coughed a couple of times, then gained momentum and came to life.

Aiden turned to look at Cordie and was met with a broad, satisfied grin. He straightened in his seat and put the car in gear. As they pulled away from the soccer fields, he lowered his voice so that only Spencer would hear. "Are we going to admit that a five-year-old—"

Spencer interrupted. "We tell no one."

In his rearview mirror Aiden could see Sophie and Regan still chattering away, but Cordie was smiling back at him with the clearest blue eyes he had ever seen. He shook his head and laughed. "Who would believe us?"

ONE

Some deathbed confessions are expected, others surprising, but this one . . . well, this one was a real doozy.

It was Andrew Kane's third heart attack, and he wasn't going to come back this time. Too much damage had been done to the anterior wall to hope for a recovery. He knew it, and so did his daughter, Cordie, who sat by his side in the critical care unit and prayed for a miracle.

Her father was hooked to a plethora of machines by a series of tubes and IVs. The constant beep from the heart monitor was a comfort to Cordie because it assured her that, even though his eyes were closed and his breathing was shallow, he was still alive. She wouldn't leave him, not even for a minute, fearing he would take his last breath alone in the cold, sterile environment while machines sounded his passing with wailing alarms.

Cordie's life had come to a screeching halt at eleven o'clock Friday night when she got the news. She had just arrived home from a charity event at St. Matthew's High School for Boys, and she was exhausted. Her day had started at six fifteen in the morning when she left her brownstone to go to work. After teaching three chemistry classes and two biology classes, she graded papers during study period, supervised two lab experiments, broke up a fight, and filled in for a math teacher who was home with stomach flu. Then, once the students had been dismissed for the day, she, along with most of the other underpaid teachers, helped transform the gymnasium into a Monte Carlo atmosphere for the annual charity auction. The remainder of the evening was spent serving soft drinks and smiling at donors until her face felt frozen.

She had been teaching at St. Matthew's for three years while she finished her PhD. The school was located on the edge of Chicago's South Side, a rough area of the city, to be sure, but thus far she hadn't had any real trouble. A ten-foot-high wrought iron fence that had been there since the school was built surrounded the property and the parking area, and she had to drive only two blocks from the highway exit to get to it. There was always a guard at the gate. An anonymous benefactor had made a substantial contribution to the school with the condition that there would be a guard on duty at all times, and ever since the principal had hired the highly recommended security firm, the number of slashed tires and smashed windshields had plummeted.

Although her father wouldn't admit it, Cordie suspected he was the benefactor. When she started working at the school, he became a staunch supporter. He even took over the auto shop classes when the regular instructor quit in the middle of the semester. The boys could be difficult. Most of them were high risk, but her father didn't have any problem controlling them. He'd grown up in New Jersey and, even now, after all these years living in Chicago, still had a bit of a Jersey accent and a tough-guy facade. He treated the boys with respect, and they responded in kind. His gruff, no-nonsense attitude and his enthusiasm won them over. The fact that he had built a national chain of auto repair shops from the ground up didn't hurt. In the eyes of his otherwise cynical students, it gave him credibility. While he was teaching the class, attendance was one hundred percent.

She knew it couldn't have been easy for him raising her alone. It had always been just the two of them. There weren't any relatives on either side of the family. Her mother had died when Cordie was a baby, so of course she didn't have any memories of her. Her father told her she looked like her mother, but he never shared any stories about her. Cordie believed it was too painful for him to talk about losing the love of his life.

She wasn't ready to lose him. He was her dad. He had always been . . . indestructible. Until his first heart attack six months ago, he had never been sick, never missed a day of work. Cordie depended on him for strength when times were difficult, and he was always there for her. Always.

When she had first entered the ICU room, the shock nearly undid her. A priest was standing over him administering the last rites. She barely recognized her father, and she stood there paralyzed with fear. He was a big man, almost six feet, with a muscular frame, but he looked so much smaller in the hospital bed, so weak and vulnerable.

Now sitting next to him, she was overwhelmed with the need to help him. Tears streamed down her cheeks, and she impatiently wiped them away. It took several minutes for her to gain control of her emotions. If he opened his eyes, she didn't want him to see her crying.

A senior cardiology resident came in to check on her father and assured her that he was resting comfortably. He couldn't tell her how long it would be before his heart stopped beating.

"The heart is an amazing organ," he told her.

"Then he could get better," she whispered, clinging to the possibility.

Snatching her hope away, he shook his head. "No," he said. "Dr. Platte explained the severity—"

She interrupted. "Yes, he explained."

"The damage—"

"I know," she interrupted again. "He's dying."

She couldn't let herself believe it, though. Oh God, please don't let him die.

She knew she wasn't being rational, pleading for the impossible. She was a fully grown woman, yet sitting there watching him she felt like a little girl again. And she was so scared.

She took hold of his hand. She wanted him to know she was there and that he wasn't alone. Gradually her panic began to ease. The initial shock wore off, and she was calm once again.

As she sat there hour after hour, she thought about her father's life. He really was a remarkable man. When she was just a toddler, he went back to school to finish his college degree in business. To support them, he worked as a mechanic in a tiny auto shop. By the time she was five years old, he owned that shop and four more. Then he expanded to sixteen shops in neighboring cities. By her tenth birthday, Kane Automotive was nationwide, and her father was a multimillionaire. Last year he'd sold the company, which had grown to more than twelve hundred shops around the country, but he still tinkered in his garage rebuilding old cars just for the love of the work.

There was never a time he wasn't busy. Yet he was always in the front row for any of her school events. He took her to dance classes and piano lessons and never missed a recital. He was at every parent-teacher night as well. And how many times did he put up with all those sleepovers with her two best friends, Regan and Sophie? Three little girls who giggled over everything must have driven him crazy, but he took it all in stride. The countless trips to the art museum, the zoo, the science exhibits, and the children's movies she wanted to see again and again—her dad had the patience of a saint. When he wasn't teaching her how to rebuild an engine or change the oil, he was monitoring her schoolwork. Smiling at the memories, she realized how very blessed she was to have such a great father.

Around two in the morning she dozed off. She awakened with a start when he squeezed her hand.

"Cordie."

She jumped up and moved closer to the bed. She thought his complexion wasn't quite as gray, and he seemed surprisingly alert.

"I love you, Dad," she whispered.

"I love you, too." He took a breath and said, "This one wasn't like the other two. It snuck up on me and grabbed me from behind. It felt like my heart was being squeezed by a vise. Dropped me to the ground."

"Are you in pain now?" Fear made her voice quiver.

"No, no pain at all. I didn't think I would go like this . . . or so soon. I thought I had more time, but I guess everyone thinks that." He closed his eyes, took another shaky breath, and called her name again.

"I'm here," she answered.

"You're going to be okay. You know I don't want to leave you all alone, but you'll be okay."

She thought he needed her assurance. "I know."

"The lockbox at the bank. The papers are there. Jared Newton, my attorney, will help you. You remember him."

"Yes. Please don't worry about me. You taught me how to take care of myself."

Several minutes passed in silence. His grip had loosened on her hand. She watched him struggle for each breath, and she could feel the fear catching hold once more.

She thought he had fallen asleep, but suddenly he spoke again. "It's all in your name. She won't be able to get her hands on it."

What? Was he hallucinating? "Who are you talking about?"

He didn't answer her. "When you fall in love with the right man, I won't get to walk you down the aisle. I'm sorry."

"Don't worry about such things now, Dad."

"Just don't make the same mistakes I made. Don't long for what you can never have. Before you know it, you will have wasted years waiting. And then it's too late. I should have remarried, but I couldn't let her go."

"Do you mean Mother?"

"Yes," he said, his voice weaker now, his eyes closed. "It's all there in the box. I waited too long."

His words came slowly and were whispered between labored breaths. "When you were little I didn't know how to tell you. And when you grew up it didn't seem important. There was never the right time."

She softly stroked his hand. "Tell me now."

"There was no accident . . . Your mother didn't die in a car accident."

Cordie was confused. Why would he lie about that? They never talked about her mother, so why was he focusing on her now? "Then how did she die?"

His last words were faint but unmistakable. "She didn't."

TWO

Cordie was numb with grief and shock. Although her father had had the last rites, the parish priest, Father Patrick Anthony, blessed him again and then sat with her until she was ready to leave the hospital room and allow the body to be taken to Neeson Funeral Home. It took a long while for her to let go of her father's hand . . . to let him go.

It was almost five in the morning by the time she reached her brownstone. She went inside and sat at the kitchen table with a cup of hot tea she didn't remember brewing. If it had been a normal morning, her father would be getting up soon to get dressed for six thirty Mass at St. Peter's. He never missed. Then he'd come back home and go to work on one of his many projects. She had thought he'd slow down after he sold his business, but that only freed him to concentrate on his other interests.

He had moved in with her two weeks ago—a temporary arrangement, he'd insisted—while he looked for a smaller home. He hadn't expected his old house would sell so quickly.

She'd loved having her dad around, and she hadn't been in any hurry for him to leave.

She had to plan a funeral, she thought. There was so much to do she didn't know where to start. She should call people, shouldn't she? She picked up a pen to make a list, then put the pen down. Nothing could be gained by calling her father's friends now. She would wait a couple of hours so she wouldn't disturb their sleep. Not everyone got up at the crack of dawn like her father. She would also follow his instructions and call the attorney first, she decided. She should probably write that down somewhere so she wouldn't forget.

There weren't any relatives to call. The closest thing she had to family were her two best friends. Cordie could have called them from the hospital, but Regan and her husband, Alec, were in London for a conference, and Sophie and her husband, Jack, were on their honeymoon somewhere in Bermuda. Regan and Sophie loved her father almost as much as she did, and his death was going to devastate them.

The senior boys at St. Matthew's High School were going to be upset, too. As tough and streetwise as some of them were, they all had a soft spot for her father. They liked working on cars with him and learning from him. He had also been a father figure of sorts, she thought, remembering all the times after auto class a student would ask him if he could run something past him. Though her father never mentioned it, she had a feeling he got some of them out of trouble with the law.

Her dad was too young to die. He wasn't even fifty yet. A tear slipped down her cheek. She didn't want to call anyone. That would make it real. Once she said the words, she couldn't take them back. Cordie knew she wasn't making a lot of sense and blamed her muddled thinking on exhaustion, so she went upstairs and got ready for bed. After she set the alarm on her cell phone, she curled up on top of her duvet cover and closed her eyes. She would sleep for two hours, then get up and do what needed to be done.

Her mind wouldn't quiet down. She kept replaying the conversation she and her father had had in the hospital. He'd told her that her mother was alive. Cordie didn't know how to process that information. He had also confessed that he had wasted years waiting for her to come back to him. Okay, so she had left him. No, she had left both of them. But why? Where was she now? And why had her father lied about her mother all these years? The answers were in the safe-deposit box, he'd said.

Cordie drifted off to sleep wondering what other secrets her father had had.

During morning Mass the priest told the congregation a beloved parishioner, Andrew Kane, had died and to please keep him in their prayers. Word quickly spread, and by noon Cordie's home was packed with friends, business associates, clergy, neighbors, and enough food to feed the entire parish. Apparently casseroles were a hot item for mourners. She had seven of them in her kitchen by midafternoon. Thankfully, her neighbor and friend Brenda Hagerty took charge of the food, and Brenda's husband, Tom, helped with the crowd.

Jared Newton, the family attorney, drove Cordie to the bank to go through the safe-deposit box. It was stuffed with stock certificates, bonds, and all sorts of other legal papers. There was also a long, narrow box labeled *For Cordie*. Jared made copies of the documents, placed them in his briefcase, and handed the copies and the small box to Cordie. Lifting the lid, she glanced inside and saw a stack of envelopes. She would go through the contents tonight when she was alone.

It had taken them less than an hour to make the trip to the bank, and when they turned the corner at the end of her block, they were stopped by the congested traffic. Cars were double-parked in front of her door, and a steady stream of people headed toward her brownstone, many carrying covered dishes. Cordie was touched by the outpouring of sympathy, but she had no idea where she was going to put everyone. The crowd already spilled out onto the steps and sidewalk.

"Your father was well loved," Jared said. "And these people are here for you, too."

She nodded. "I know."

"I'll drop you off in front and find a place to park," he said. "Cordie, tell me what I can do to help."

"I have to write an obituary."

"Okay, I'll help you with that."

She smiled. "Thank you."

Jared was such a sweet man. He was nice looking, too, she realized. She'd known him for five years, but until this moment she had never taken the time to notice how handsome he was. He had asked her out several times, and she'd always declined. Why had she done that? The answer was quick. Because she'd been chasing a foolish dream. Her father was right. It was time for her to face reality and move on.

She unbuckled her seat belt and opened the car door, but she didn't get out. She sat there thinking.

"Cordie?" Jared asked, wondering why she was hesitating.

She turned to him again. "Are you seeing anyone now?"

The question surprised him. "I was," he said. "But it wasn't going anywhere, so I broke it off. Why do you ask?"

"I was wondering . . . once things calm down, would you like to go to dinner or something?" She couldn't believe she was doing this now with her life so crazy. She knew she wasn't thinking straight, but that didn't seem to matter. She still plunged ahead.

"Yes, I'd like that," he replied.

Okay, she thought. Step one: Move forward.

"I'll see you inside," she said. "I have to make a couple of calls first."

It took her a good fifteen minutes to make her way upstairs. Her father's poker friends were sitting together at the dining room table reminiscing. She stopped to talk to each one of them, then went up to her bedroom and shut the door.

She called Regan first. Her husband answered. "Hi, Alec," she said. "How's the conference going?" She hadn't meant to ask that question, but she needed time to get the reason for her call out, to find the right words. He knew something was wrong the second he heard her voice.

"What's going on?"

She decided not to ease into it. "My father had a heart attack. He didn't make it."

"Oh, Cordie, I'm so sorry."

He wanted details, and she answered each of his questions. As though she were in a trance, her voice was devoid of emotion. Alec was like a brother to her. She didn't have to be strong with him, but his sympathy was bringing all the grief and pain to the surface again, and she couldn't afford to lose control now.

"Regan will be back in an hour," he said. "I'll have her call you just as soon as—"

"No," she blurted. "If I talk to her now, I'll fall apart, and I have a houseful of people . . . and casseroles. Oh God, there are so many casseroles. Will you call Sophie for me? Please."

"Yes, of course I will," he said. "What else can I do?"

"That's all for now."

"Regan and I are going to help you get through this. We'll be on the next flight out of here."

After ending the call, she went to her bathroom and splashed cold water on her face. There was so much to do before she could sit down and take a breath. She descended the stairs and immediately was surrounded by a throng of sympathetic faces. Cordie realized all the offers of help were given with good intentions, and she appreciated each and every one of them, but there were some things she needed to do alone. She had a three o'clock appointment at the funeral home. She eased her way through the crowd so that she could sneak out the back door without anyone noticing or insisting on accompanying her.

To her surprise she found that her father had already taken care of all the arrangements. He'd left precise instructions. He wanted the funeral Mass to take place at St. Matthew's Catholic Church, which was just across the parking lot from the high school where she taught. Some of her father's older friends were going to balk at driving into what they considered a dangerous area of the city, and she would understand if they didn't attend. Nevertheless, she would honor all her father's wishes, even if no one showed up.

She navigated the rest of the day in a fog. She must have listened to a hundred wonderful stories about her father, but after a while they all blended together. His loyal friends had already sainted him.

The box she'd brought home from the bank was on a shelf in her closet. She had every intention of going through it tonight, but by the time she went upstairs, she was so weary she could barely focus. She dressed for bed and slipped under the covers, the sad faces and words of condolence swimming in her head, and she fell asleep knowing that in the morning the ritual would start all over again.

Cordie was in the living room picking up glasses and putting them on a tray to carry to the kitchen when the front door opened and

Sophie and Jack MacAlister walked in. The second Sophie saw her, she started to cry. Cordie put the glasses down and went to her.

As she hugged each of them, she said, "Thank you so much for coming." She realized what she had just said to her dearest friends and shook her head. "I've been saying those words since yesterday morning to everyone who stopped by. I meant to say, 'Thank God you're here.'"

Jack put his arm around her and suggested they go somewhere quiet to talk.

"How about the study?" Cordie suggested. She didn't know if there were people in there or not. She grabbed a couple of tissues from the box on the table, handed them to Sophie, and led the way.

One of her advisors in the science department at the university put his hand on her arm to stop her. He was a gregarious man with a rich baritone voice.

"We're going to take off now," he said. "But I was wondering . . ."

"Yes?"

"Did your father know?"

She understood what he was referring to. "No, I had only just found out."

"Found out what?" Sophie asked.

Cordie remembered her manners and introduced the professor and his wife to her friends. The professor answered Sophie's question.

"Cordie's dissertation was approved. She's now a PhD in bio-chemistry. Her thesis was groundbreaking. As young as Cordie is, to have accomplished such an impressive feat is quite remarkable."

Cordie wasn't comfortable with compliments because she never knew what to say, and so she quickly changed the subject. A few minutes later she walked the professor and his wife to the door, thanked them again for coming, and then went to join Jack and Sophie in the study.

Jack pushed the door closed behind her.

"You look tired, Cordie," Sophie said as she took a seat in the overstuffed leather chair by the window. Jack joined her, sitting next to her on the chair's arm.

Cordie couldn't relax. She leaned against the desk, folded her arms, and took a deep breath. "Tired?" she scoffed. "You're being kind. I look like hell." She wasn't exaggerating. The last time she'd passed a mirror she was shocked to see how pale her complexion was, and the dark circles under her eyes looked as though she'd drawn them there with charcoal.

"Tell me about your dad," Sophie said. "Were you with him when he had the heart attack?"

"No," Cordie answered. She explained what had happened.

By the time she was finished, Sophie was on her second tissue, dabbing the tears from her eyes. "Did he suffer? He didn't, did he?"

"No, he didn't," Cordie assured her. "The doctors gave him medication to take care of the pain. I sat with him, and I would have known if he had any discomfort."

"I'm sorry I wasn't there for you," Sophie whispered.

"It's okay. You're here now."

"I loved your dad."

"I know you did. He loved you, too."

"What needs to be done?" Jack asked. "Put us to work."

One of the neighbors knocked on the door and looked in. "Cordie, the priest is here to talk to you about the funeral Mass, and there are two policemen at the door. They're wanting something done about the cars blocking the street."

"I'll talk to the police," Jack said, and headed out the door.

Sophie smiled as she watched him leave. "It's nice to have an FBI agent for a husband. Certainly comes in handy sometimes." Standing, she removed her sweater and draped it across the back of the chair.

"How about I go in the kitchen and help while you bring the priest in here and talk," she suggested. The look on Cordie's face made her laugh. "Don't worry. I won't cook. I'll wash dishes or something."

The last time Sophie made pasta in Cordie's kitchen it took an hour to get the gummy noodles off the burners. The food was actually pretty good, but the entire kitchen was a mess.

Cordie didn't have another minute alone with her friends the rest of the day. It was heartwarming that so many people wanted to pay their respects and talk about their friendship with her father, and she felt the least she could do was give each of them her time and attention.

By nine o'clock that evening, the last of the guests had left. Sophie and Cordie were sitting at the kitchen table, and Jack, with his sleeves rolled up to his elbows, was washing the pans in the sink when Regan and her husband, Alec, arrived.

Alec looked rested, but then he could sleep anywhere, according to Regan. He had slept all the way from London to Chicago. Regan, on the other hand, looked wiped out.

"You've had a long trip," Cordie said. "You should go home to bed."

Regan shook her head. "I'm fine, and we won't stay long. I just wanted to see you, to make sure you're okay."

Alec wrapped his arm around Regan and pulled her into his side. Cordie watched her lean into him. The way they looked at each other was so sweet, so loving. It was the same way Jack looked at Sophie. Her best friends had found their soul mates, and she was truly happy for them.

It was amazing, she thought, how fate worked in such mysterious ways when it came to love. Alec Buchanan had come into Regan's life under the most unexpected circumstances. Regan had become the target of a madman, and it was Alec, a Chicago detective, who was given the responsibility of protecting her. By the time the traumatic event was over, the two knew they were meant to be together. In a short time, they married and moved away so that Alec could join the FBI. Cordie and Sophie missed their friend terribly, and when they got the news that Alec would be assigned to two offices, Chicago and Boston, they were ecstatic. The trio would be back together again. Fate wasn't through with them yet, however. The moment Regan met Alec's new Chicago partner, Agent Jack MacAlister, she knew he would be a match for her vivacious friend Sophie. And she was right. They were crazy about each other.

Her friends had found true and lasting love, and up until the night her father died Cordie believed she, too, could have happily ever after with the man of her dreams, but no longer. She had been a fool long enough. It was time to grow up.

"When is Aiden getting in?" Alec asked Cordie. "Did he say?"

"I don't know. I haven't talked to him."

"You didn't call Aiden?" Regan looked dumbfounded.

"No, I didn't. I didn't call any of your brothers."

Alec was frowning at her, and Cordie understood why. Whenever there was anything going on, good or bad, Cordie always insisted on including Aiden. Had her foolish crush been that transparent? Apparently so, she thought.

She decided to turn their attention. "Are you hungry? There's all sorts of food in the refrigerator."

"I could eat," Alec replied.

"Me, too," Jack said as he dried the last pan and set it on the counter.

Cordie went to the refrigerator and started bringing out covered dishes, but Alec took them from her and turned her toward the living room. "We'll take care of this. Why don't you three go sit down and talk?"

Grateful for the suggestion, Cordie headed to the sofa, dropped down in the center, and put her feet up on the ottoman. Sophie sat on her right and linked her arm in Cordie's, and Regan sat on her left with her arm around Cordie's shoulder. The three friends couldn't be more different—acquaintances usually categorized Sophie as the uninhibited one, Regan as the sensitive one, and Cordie as the scholarly and practical one—yet when they were together, they were an unshakable unit.

"Tell me something happy," Cordie said. "How was Bermuda, Sophie?"

For the next few minutes, Sophie gave her friends a very romantic account of white-sand beaches and warm tropical nights with Jack, listening to the sound of the surf under a starlit sky. When it was her turn, Regan told them all about London. She and Alec had been involved in projects to help at-risk youth in Chicago for a couple of years and were attending a conference in England with representatives from several European countries with similar goals. Her excitement was obvious as she talked about the success of the conference and the new ideas that were shared.

No matter how hard Cordie tried to keep the subjects light and upbeat, the conversation eventually turned to her father.

"Do you realize how remarkable he was?" Sophie asked. "When you were a baby, he was a mechanic, and when he died, he had just sold Kane Automotive for millions of dollars."

"From one little shop to more than twelve hundred across the country," Regan added. "Your dad was amazing."

"Yes, he was."

"Did he know you were with him?" Regan asked. Tears were already flooding her eyes. "In the hospital . . . did he know?"

"Yes, he knew. We talked for a little while, and then he drifted off and was gone. It was very peaceful."

"What did you talk about?" Regan asked.

Cordie didn't want to cry, and so she made light of the question. "He told me where all the bodies were buried."

Regan wasn't amused. "That's not funny."

"Yes, it is," Sophie said, smiling. "Your dad was such a stickler for the rules. I'll bet he never got so much as a speeding ticket in all the years I knew him."

"That's true," Cordie agreed.

"So no surprises?"

Cordie paused and took a breath before answering. "Just one."

THREE

Aiden Hamilton Madison didn't suffer fools easily, and after spending twenty minutes with Lester Chambers, he had had enough, but his brother Spencer had dragged him into this deal and was really pushing it. For that reason Aiden held his patience as long as he could.

Lester Chambers and his cousin, Congressman Mitchell Ray Chambers, had inherited Rock Point, a pristine piece of Oregon land overlooking the ocean, and after lengthy negotiations had agreed to sell the property to the Hamilton Hotel chain for quite a tidy sum. Aiden and his brothers planned to build another one of their exclusive resorts on the site.

There was another property available about 250 miles south of Rock Point, and Aiden much preferred that area of coastline. As CEO of Hamilton Hotels, he made most business decisions, but he'd agreed to let his brother, a partner in the company, make the choice this time. Both Lester and his cousin had verbally agreed to all the terms. Aiden had the papers drawn up, and as far as he was concerned, the deal was done.

The hotel was going to be a godsend to the economically depressed area, and perhaps that was why Spencer had pushed so hard.

Word had already spread that the acclaimed five-star hotel was going to be built near the small, struggling community of Fallsborough, and men and women desperate for work were once again hopeful about the future. Spencer wanted to expand, and this property was slated to become an all-inclusive resort, a luxurious retreat where the stressed-out could go to decompress.

The brothers flew to Fallsborough in one of the company jets. The tiny airfield was in dire need of resurfacing, but Aiden would let Spencer deal with that issue once construction was under way.

A car was waiting for them. It was cold and windy and damp, but neither brother wore a topcoat. On the way to Lester's office, Spencer suggested a bet. Aiden hadn't met Lester or his cousin, but Spencer had. He told Aiden exactly how Lester would introduce his cousin. Aiden took the bet, certain his brother was exaggerating.

When the brothers walked into the lobby of the building where Lester had offices, they were all but ambushed by the local news. A reporter, microphone in hand, and a cameraman a few feet behind chased Aiden to the elevators.

The reporter was a young woman named Kalie. "Is it true?" she asked, stretching her arm so that the microphone was close to Aiden's face.

"Is what true?" he asked.

"You're Aiden Hamilton Madison, aren't you? And standing next to you is Spencer Madison."

Aiden smiled. "Yes, that's true."

She was very nervous. The microphone was shaking. "No, I mean is it true that the Hamilton Hotel is coming here? That you're going to build on Rock Point?"

"That's the plan."

Smiling, she said, "Oh, that's wonderful news. When will you start building? Do you have a target date?"

"No date yet. We've agreed to terms and we're here to get the papers signed. Spencer has the timetable. You should talk to him." He glanced to his left, where his brother had been standing.

"He already went up in the elevator," Kalie explained.

Aiden laughed. Spencer hated doing interviews almost as much as Aiden did. He would have taken off if he'd had the chance and left Spencer to field questions, but he wasn't fast enough this time.

"Now, if you'll excuse me . . ."

"Just one more question, please. How did you find out about Rock Point? This is such a remote area," she explained.

"Mayor Green," he answered. "She waged a relentless campaign to get Spencer to come look."

Kalie thanked him, motioned to the cameraman to stop filming, and then followed Aiden to the elevator. "Will you be staying in town tonight?" she asked.

His answer was abrupt. "No."

"I could take you out for a drink . . ." Her voice was wistful.

He smiled to soften the rejection, then said, "No, thank you." The elevator doors closed before she could ask another question.

The meeting was set for four o'clock. They were fifteen minutes early—Aiden couldn't abide being late for anything—but apparently the Chamberses had a more relaxed notion of meeting schedules.

Spencer grinned when he saw his brother. "What took you so long?"

The question didn't merit an answer. Aiden went to the two-story window and looked out at the landscape. It wasn't a pretty day. The sky was gray, but darker clouds were moving in, and from the way the trees were swaying, he knew the wind was up.

The receptionist, a thirty-year-old single woman, couldn't stop staring at the brothers. They were handsome men, both tall and muscular through the shoulders, impressively lean and fit, with dark hair and patrician features. They wore business suits, designer label, she surmised. Aiden in his dark suit with pale blue shirt and striped tie, and Spencer in a pinstriped suit with a crisp white shirt and red tie. Oh my, were they sexy. She heard herself sigh and was mortified. But they were just so . . . fine.

"Is something wrong?" Spencer asked when she continued to stare at them.

"No, no," she stammered. "I was just noticing what nice suits you're wearing, and I was thinking that both of you look like you belong on Wall Street."

Spencer smiled. "These days that isn't a compliment."

She laughed. "I guess it isn't. I'm sorry you're having to wait. Mr. Chambers should be out any minute now. I've buzzed him three times already."

At twenty minutes after four the double doors suddenly flew open, and Lester came rushing out to greet them. Aiden supposed he was trying to give the impression that he was a very busy man. He waved his hands while he apologized for keeping them waiting, explaining that he was on an urgent call.

"Very urgent," he reiterated as he shook their hands. He ushered them into his office and closed the door. "You boys are getting quite a bargain. I feel like you're stealing Rock Point from me and my cousin. I really do."

Boys? Spencer glanced at Aiden, who didn't show any reaction to Lester's condescension.

"The offer you accepted was more than fair," Aiden told him in a firm, no-nonsense tone of voice.

"Where is your cousin?" Spencer asked.

As if on cue, the doors opened and Congressman Mitchell Ray Chambers strolled inside. He didn't look anything like his cousin.

Lester was short, not quite five-two, with a noticeable paunch and a bald spot on the top of his head. Mitchell had a full head of silver-tipped hair, compliments of his stylist. He was a trim six feet, and his face seemed to be cast in a perpetual smile.

"I'm sorry I'm late," Mitchell began. "I came up the back steps, but I still got caught and asked for autographs. I couldn't say no." Almost as an afterthought he added, "I'm a man of the people."

If he was out to impress Aiden and Spencer, he was failing.

"Let me make the introductions," Lester insisted. "I'd like you to meet my cousin, the very important congressman Mitchell Ray Chambers."

Spencer grinned. He'd just won the bet. Very important indeed.

Lester went to his desk and sat. "I can't tell you how long it's been since Mitchell has been home. At least a year now."

Mitchell frowned. "Nonsense. I represent the good people of Fallsborough. I fly back and forth from Washington all the time."

Lester scoffed. "No, you don't, and the good people of Fallsborough have noticed."

"This isn't the time for complaints," Mitchell snapped. Turning back to Aiden and Spencer, his smile still plastered on his face, he said, "Shall we sit at the conference table? I'm here to negotiate, so let's roll up our sleeves and get down to business."

"Negotiate what?" Lester wanted to know.

"The sale of Rock Point, of course." Crossing the office, he turned one of the swivel chairs from the long conference table and sat down. He swung his right leg over his left and rested his ankle on his knee, then leaned back and waited.

Spencer and Aiden stayed where they were. Since Spencer had talked to both cousins and their attorney multiple times, hammering out all the details, he was the one who had heard both Lester and Mitchell agree to the final price for the land.

"There isn't going to be any negotiation today," Spencer said. "You agreed to the price. It's time to sign the final offer."

"I didn't agree to anything." Mitchell smiled while he told the lie. A true politician, Aiden thought.

"We both agreed," Lester reminded him.

"No, we didn't," Mitchell snapped. He shot his cousin a glare before the smile was back in place.

Lester didn't know when to be quiet. "Our attorney looked over the papers. Everything's in order. Let's just sign them."

"I didn't look the papers over," Mitchell countered.

"Yes, you did. They were sent to you, and you told me you got them."

"Will you keep your mouth . . ." Mitchell took a breath and turned to Spencer. "Have your attorneys had time to read the documents?"

"My brother and I are both attorneys," Spencer explained. He was trying to keep his anger under control, but the congressman was making that a real challenge.

"I agreed to an opening bid," Mitchell announced.

Aiden watched Spencer. He was letting him take the lead and decide the next move. His brother opened his briefcase and put the folder with the contract inside. "What would you consider a fair price, Congressman?"

"At least three times what you offered," he answered with certainty. He sensed a victory and couldn't have been more pleased. "Come on, now. Sit down and let's work out this deal."

"No, that isn't going to happen. You gave your word." Spencer's voice wasn't pleasant now, but hard, angry.

Mitchell shrugged. "I didn't sign anything. Keep that in mind."

Beads of sweat were beginning to form on Lester's forehead. He turned to Spencer. "Let's talk this through. I know how much you want Rock Point. You said yourself it had great potential. You must have walked over that ground a dozen times."

Aiden had heard enough. "We don't work with people whose word is meaningless. We're through here."

Lester's mouth dropped open. "But we . . . we had a solid offer . . . we . . ."

Mitchell didn't say a word while his cousin sputtered his indignation. He simply watched the Madison brothers leave Lester's office. Then he strolled over to the bar and poured himself a drink.

"It was a great offer," Lester muttered. "What have you done?"

"Don't worry," Mitchell said, his voice smug. "They'll be back."

Lester shook his head. "I'm not so sure."

"I'll bet they reach the lobby and turn around. Spencer Madison wants Rock Point, and I'm going to make him pay a premium for it. He'll talk his brother into negotiating. Just you wait and see."

"They seemed angry that you broke your word."

Mitchell shrugged. "They'll get over it. Saying one thing and doing another . . . that's all part of negotiating. As long as you don't sign anything and you're not being recorded . . ."

"Do you hear yourself? A man's word—"

"Can it, Lester. Just let it go. I know what I'm doing."

Mitchell kept his eye on the elevators, waiting for the doors to open and prove him right. The Madisons were probably on their way back up.

Aiden and Spencer had no intention of returning to Chambers's office. As soon as they reached the lobby they were surrounded by a crowd of men and women holding balloons and cheering. The cameraman was there again, standing behind Kalie, the Channel Seven reporter, who stepped forward with a wide smile of greeting. She held the microphone up to Aiden and said, "And here are the new owners of Rock . . ." She stopped when Aiden shook his head. "You didn't purchase the land just yet?"

"No," he answered. He looked directly into the camera as he explained. "Congressman Mitchell Chambers changed his mind. He wanted more money than we originally agreed on. We won't be buying Rock Point."

"It's disappointing," Spencer interjected. "But we're going to move on to another property."

Kalie looked stunned. "Wait," she pleaded as Aiden walked past her. "Are you saying Congressman Mitchell Chambers stopped the sale?"

"Yes, that's what I'm saying," Aiden answered.

"Then the Hamilton Hotel won't be built here?"

"No." His tone was emphatic.

Aiden walked out the door and didn't look back. Spencer followed. The plan was to fly to San Francisco and stay at the Hamilton there while Spencer checked on the remodel he'd begun three months ago, but the plan changed when they received a text from their sister, Regan.

Aiden retrieved his phone from his pocket and looked at the screen.

"Oh no," he said.

"What's wrong?" Spencer asked.

"Cordelia's dad died. Heart attack."

Shocked by the news, Spencer didn't speak for a few seconds. The Madison family had known Cordie and her father for almost twenty years, and Mr. Kane had always been so strong and vigorous.

"Andrew Kane was a good man," he remarked.

"Yes, he was," Aiden agreed. "Cordelia must be devastated."

He immediately called Regan to find out when the funeral was scheduled. His sister was crying. "Cordie's all alone now. Are you coming home? She'll want you and Spencer there."

"Of course we'll be there. We're on our way home now."

Spencer opened the car door, then paused to look up at the building they'd just left. All that time wasted, he thought. The engineering reports, the back-and-forth negotiating with two of the most unpleasant men he'd ever encountered—all for nothing.

"Let's go," Aiden called out impatiently.

Lester Chambers stood at the window and watched the SUV pull onto the main road and drive away. "They're on their way to the airstrip," he said. "And you were so sure they would come right back up here."

Mitchell went to the bar to freshen his drink. He dropped an ice cube into his glass, causing the whiskey to splash all over his hand. He grabbed a napkin to mop up the mess, then took a sip of his drink.

"They're not coming back." Lester continued to stare out the window until the SUV vanished. There was panic in his voice. "It was a damn good offer."

"Stop whining. I know what I'm doing. I know how people think," he boasted. "It's why I make such a great congressman. Believe me. The Madisons will be back. Maybe not today, but soon. I'll give them a week to come begging."

Lester's receptionist rushed into the office. "Sir, one of the secretaries . . . Jenny just mentioned that Channel Seven was in the lobby."

Mitchell let out a loud, long-suffering sigh. "They're here for me. I'll let them wait a little longer before I go down and do the interview."

"No, Jenny said the channel's crew just left but that we should all watch the five-o'clock news."

"They probably got tired of waiting for you," Lester told his cousin.

Mitchell agreed. "I can't be everywhere all the time," he excused himself. He reached for the remote on the desk and turned the television on. It wasn't quite five yet, so Mitchell put the sound on mute and sat on the sofa.

"Did you know Mayor Green is running against you?" Lester asked.

Mitchell snorted. "Of course I knew. She's wasting her time and money. She doesn't stand a chance. I'll bet I get ninety percent of the vote."

"The primary is not that far away," Lester reminded him.

No one was going to take his job away. Mitchell loved being a congressman. He loved the power, the position it garnered, and the respect, though admittedly the public didn't think much of Congress these days, probably because they knew so many of them were corrupt or just inept. There was talk of term limits. Mitchell had promised to push for those if elected, but once he was in office he changed his mind. Besides, no one in Congress was ever going to vote for that, and Mitchell planned to stay in office until he was well into his eighties. The governor had handpicked him for the job, and as long as Mitchell played ball and voted the way the governor wanted, he would remain a congressman.

"You know it was Mayor Green who got Spencer Madison interested in Rock Point," Lester commented.

"So she says."

"Oh, there she is. Turn the sound on. I want to hear what our mayor has to say."

The segment lasted a good ten minutes without a commercial break, which was unheard of. The last footage Kalie showed was Aiden Madison explaining why they wouldn't be building a Hamilton Hotel on Rock Point. He placed the blame squarely on Congressman Chambers's shoulders.

Then the mayor was on again, telling the viewers what the hotel would have meant to the community: the new jobs, the improved schools, the revived economy. All these were gone now. She ended her speech with a promise that things would change once she was elected to Congress.

"Congratulations," Lester said with a snide smirk on his face. "You've just lost your reelection."

FOUR

They would be talking about Andrew Kane's funeral for months to come, maybe even years.

Alec and Jack dropped Regan, Sophie, and Cordie off at the funeral home much earlier than necessary. It had been decided that Regan and Sophie would ride with Cordie in the limousine behind the hearse, and Alec and Jack would meet them at the church.

It was an unseasonably warm day. Cordie wore a simple sleeveless black sheath dress with a square neckline and black heels. She didn't wear much jewelry, just a pair of diamond studs for her ears and a Hermès watch her father had given her for her last birthday. She didn't try to do anything fancy with her hair but left it down. Her natural curls were straightened by its length, just past her shoulders.

Sophie and Regan, who sat on either side of her in the limousine, were also dressed in black.

Regan held on to Cordie's hand. "When we get to the church, I'll take your cardigan and your clutch. Is your phone in there?"

"Yes," Cordie answered.

"Make sure it's turned off."

"I already did."

"I can't believe your father's gone," Regan whispered.

"What did he tell you just before he died?" Sophie asked. "You said there was one surprise, remember?"

If there was a secret, Sophie had to know what it was. She couldn't help herself. She worked for a newspaper and was always looking for the next story. Her dream was to be an investigative reporter, but for now she was in charge of the food section and wrote about new recipes. Regan and Cordie thought the irony was quite funny since Sophie didn't know the first thing about cooking. She had learned how to make one pasta dish that was passable, but that was it.

Smiling, Cordie said, "I also remember telling you that I would explain what the surprise was after the funeral. Today is about his life. Tonight I'll tell you. I promise."

Still fishing for a hint, Sophie said, "It must be a big deal. Otherwise you would have told us. You tell us everything."

Both Regan and Cordie laughed. "That's *you*," Regan said. "Of the three of us, you're the one who can't keep a secret."

The friends fell silent as the somber procession turned off the main thoroughfare and made its way through the streets of run-down apartments and dilapidated houses toward St. Matthew's.

"When we get to the church . . . ," Cordie began, and then hesitated.

"Yes?" Sophie asked.

"Eight of the students my father worked with are going to be the pallbearers. They had a special place in his heart, but I want you to know they can be a little territorial with one another."

"What does that mean?" Sophie asked.

"They're at-risk kids," Regan answered.

"Some are," Cordie agreed. "There might be some pushing and

shoving. You know, boy stuff. Nothing to worry about," she assured them.

"Do you think many students will attend?" Sophie asked.

"No," Cordie answered. "It's a Saturday. They're kids. The last place they want to be is in church. I don't expect—" She stopped abruptly. The limousine had just turned onto Grant Street, and there in front of the church, filling the sidewalk from corner to corner and spilling out into the street, were the students of St. Matthew's High School. It looked as though most of the student body had turned out, and all the boys wore their school uniforms: khaki pants, white shirt, and navy blazer with the school emblem on the pocket. The boys were waiting quietly, their expressions solemn. Each class stood together, with the seniors in front. The second the limousine driver turned the motor off, two students stepped forward to open the door. The taller boy pushed the other aside to get to the handle. A transfer student named Victor won the push and shove. One of Cordie's favorite students, he was a math whiz but thus far hadn't developed a lick of sense. He opened the door, grasped her hand, and yanked her out. Her feet actually left the ground, but fortunately she landed feetfirst on the sidewalk. Sophie and Regan were given assistance as well. It didn't matter if they wanted help or not. Both were hauled out and deposited next to Cordie.

Alec and Jack were waiting on the church steps. When they saw the crowd engulf the women, they rushed down and pushed their way through the teen mob.

"That guy has a gun," one student whispered loud enough for Cordie to hear.

Before she could explain who they were, another student said, "Both of them have guns."

"How come they get to bring guns into the church?"

Cordie whirled around. "They don't get to," she said. "They're FBI agents. It's their job to carry guns. They also have badges."

"Why is the FBI here?" another student asked in a loud whisper. Cordie didn't recognize the voice, but his tone was hostile. "We didn't do anything, and I'm not going anywhere without a warrant."

Cordie explained before more of them could get riled up. "They're my friends," she said. "And they were my father's friends, too." She handed Regan her cardigan and her purse and said, "You and Sophie go inside now. The pallbearers will sit in the front row, so sit behind them."

Sophie nudged Regan. "Let's go."

Jack and Alec didn't follow their wives. They stood where they were, watching the crowd of restless boys. Several teachers were trying to get the students to go inside, but none of them would obey. In fact, they squeezed closer to Cordie until they all but swallowed her up like a swarm of bees around a hive. Jack and Alec immediately went into defensive mode, but Cordie raised her hand to let them know she wasn't in danger. Alec hesitated at first, then, realizing the boys' behavior was protective, not threatening, he motioned to Jack, and the two stepped aside.

Aiden and Spencer arrived and, spotting Alec and Jack, made their way around the throng. Aiden looked in all directions and asked, "Where's Cordelia?"

"In the middle of the crowd," Alec said.

"I don't see her," Aiden said, frowning.

"How is she doing?" Spencer asked.

"Remarkably well," Alec answered.

The muttering from the boys got louder, and then suddenly the mood changed. As though a signal had been given, the pushing and nudging and shoving stopped. The boys straightened to their full heights and stood silent. Parting to allow Cordie to get to the front, they watched the coffin being removed from the hearse. Two men from the funeral home placed the coffin on a rolling gurney, then covered it with a white linen cloth that nearly reached the ground. After carefully placing a long spray of deep-red roses on the coffin, the men began to push the gurney up the gentle incline to the church entrance, where Father Patrick Anthony waited with an altar boy who held a gold crucifix that was considerably taller than he was.

Jerome Smith, the senior class president and her father's constant shadow when he was at school, stepped forward. "Now?" he asked Cordie.

"Yes," she answered.

Seven young men separated from the others and followed Jerome up the steps. They quickly moved to flank each side of the coffin, a couple of them noticeably fighting back tears.

With slow, measured steps, the priest led the silent procession down the main aisle of the church. Cordie walked behind the coffin and was followed by the students of St. Matthew's. The side pews were already filled with mourners, and by the time the boys filed into the pews behind her, the church was packed.

Cordie sat on the end and left room for Jack and Alec to join their wives. As the priest turned to face the mourners and the organist began to play the first hymn, she glanced around at the congregation, and that was when she saw him. Aiden, followed by Spencer, was taking a seat several rows back on the other side of the church. A rush of emotions swept over her. She was happy he was here yet angry at herself for the old feelings that surfaced at the very sight of him. He glanced in her direction, and for a split second their eyes met. He gave her a sympathetic smile, and she smiled in return. The old Cordie would have wanted him sitting next to her, holding her hand, but no longer. Things were different now. She was different now. With renewed resolve she turned around, sat up straight, and focused on the ceremony.

It was a beautiful Mass, and the priest's remarks about her father were heartfelt and quite lovely. At least a dozen people had offered to give eulogies, but if all of them had been allowed to speak, the funeral would have lasted hours, so it was decided that three of her father's closest friends would talk. Their speeches were short—no more than a few minutes each—and focused on what a kind and loyal friend Andrew Kane had been. As the last man was finishing his remarks, Cordie heard a rustling behind her. At first she thought the students were just getting restless, but then she noticed several of them nudging one of the boys and urging him to stand up. He was a sophomore and a transfer from Truman High School. She hadn't had him in class, but based on the number of times he'd served detention, she knew he was one of those kids who liked to skate on the edge.

The boy finally gave in to the prodding and, rising out of his seat, headed toward the pulpit. Uh-oh, Cordie thought, this was not planned. She suddenly felt uneasy. There was no telling what he had in mind. As he stepped up to face the congregation, his hands firmly planted in his pockets, he looked at his feet and shuffled back and forth as though he was searching for something to say, and then he began.

"My name is Jayden Martin, and I've been at St. Matthew's High School since last November when I was . . . you know . . . asked to leave my old school because of a misunderstanding. My favorite class is auto shop, and my favorite teacher is Mr. Kane. I mean he was my favorite teacher until . . . you know . . . he died."

Several students nodded, and Cordie had to force herself not to smile.

Jayden paused for several seconds, and she thought he was finished, but he continued to stand there looking unsure of himself. He suddenly straightened as though he'd just made a very important decision and said, "Mr. Kane told me a story about this kid who wanted a car . . . you know . . . for transportation. He was sixteen, and he had a driver's license, but he didn't have any money to buy a car, so he did something really stupid and stole one." He paused to look around the church to gauge his audience's reaction, and seeing that everyone was intently listening, he continued. "It was a sweet ride, a five-year-old Camry in mint condition, like it just came off the showroom floor. Anyway, this kid took the car from the front of this old guy's house—he had to be almost as old as Mr. Kane—and he drove it around for a couple of miles, but then something happened . . . I don't know . . . maybe his conscience kicked in, and he realized he shouldn't have taken it. I mean, I . . . he could go to prison for stealing a car, right?" Several students nodded in agreement. Because his classmates were hanging on his every word, Jayden relaxed. Draping one arm over the pulpit, he leaned forward as he continued. "So what he did was drive the car over to Mr. Kane's house, and he told him what he had done. Mr. Kane was real angry, and he yelled at the kid for doing something so stupid, but once he calmed down he said he'd help fix it. He had him wipe his fingerprints off the car handle and everywhere else he touched, and he followed him back to the old guy's house." Jayden couldn't keep from grinning a little. "The funny thing was, another car had parked in front of the house, so Mr. Kane had the kid park the Camry across the street. If he hadn't been so scared, he might have waited until the old guy came out to get in his car just to see the look on his face. Would the guy think he had parked it across the street and just forgot? Mr. Kane said he would probably just scratch his head and go on about his business, and I guess he was right because there wasn't anything in the local news. Mr. Kane saved that kid from going to prison. At least, that's what I think." He stopped and looked down at his feet again. When he finally could speak, his voice cracked. "Mr. Kane was okay." With his hands back in his pockets and his head down, he hurried back to the pew.

The church was completely silent. When Cordie took a quick look at the people behind her, all she saw were stunned faces. She took a deep breath and hoped Jayden's flimsily veiled confession would be passed over, but before she could turn around to the altar again, another student was heading to the pulpit. Like Jayden, he recounted another story, allegedly told to him by Mr. Kane, of an anonymous student who, in a fit of anger, broke into the school and vandalized it with a couple of cans of black spray paint. According to his account, after the boy had made the mess and written some pretty foul words on the walls outside the principal's office, he started to think that maybe what he was doing might be a bad idea and he could be in some real trouble. He had heard Mr. Kane had helped another student get out of a bind with the police, so he called him. "Mr. Kane was steaming mad, all right . . . at least that's what he told me," the boy said, "but he got some paint and brushes and helped the student clean it all up." He added, "It took all night."

And on it went. Seven students in all told stories of how they had heard of incidents where Mr. Kane had helped some kid in trouble. When the parade of narrators finally ended, Cordie sat motionless, almost afraid to look around.

"How many felonies are we up to now? Four?" Jack whispered the question.

"Five," Alec corrected.

Cordie knew there were several detectives and policemen in the congregation because her father had been a big financial supporter of the department. They would most likely call some of her father's acts of kindness aiding and abetting, tampering with evidence, obstructing justice, and God only knew what else. If she didn't do something quickly, there was a strong possibility that at least two students would be arrested when the Mass was over.

Father Anthony had just started back to the altar when Cordie sprang to her feet. The priest saw her and went back to his chair. Her mind was racing as she slowly walked up the three steps to the altar and then crossed over to the pulpit. She didn't have the faintest idea what she was going to say until she started speaking.

"My father was proud of the fact that he was Irish, and he used to tell me that the Irish are great storytellers. *He* certainly was," she began. So far, so good. The crowd seemed to be buying it. She went on. "He loved to tell stories about students from the past, and the boys here today . . . like me . . . have all heard his stories so many times now, they've almost made them their own. Of course, you can assume that all those kids my father talked about and some of the things he said they did were greatly exaggerated. He meant his stories to be lessons so that the students would learn from mistakes others had made in the past . . . cautionary tales."

Cordie wasn't quite sure what she said after that. When she went back to her seat, she noticed that Alec and Jack weren't smiling, but there was a definite sparkle in their eyes. They knew exactly what she had just done and why. Like her father, she was protecting the boys.

Somehow Cordie got through the rest of the day, though she couldn't remember most of it. After the funeral and the burial, a large number of well-intentioned and caring people followed her to her home and stayed most of the afternoon. Gradually the guests began to thin out, and by evening most of them had said their good-byes, leaving only her close friends. With her house finally quiet again, she curled up in the corner of her sofa, her bare feet tucked under her. All she wanted to do was close her eyes and sleep.

Spencer and Aiden were still there. They were in a deep conversation with Alec and Jack. The topic was a congressman named Mitchell Ray Chambers, and from the look on Aiden's face, he wasn't a fan. Up until now she had avoided looking at Aiden whenever possible. He was like a magnet, though, drawing her to him. She had had a crush on him for so many years—she refused to call it love—and she knew it would take time to break old habits. She'd been completely infatuated with him, but infatuation wasn't love. She imagined most women who met him quickly became captivated. It wasn't just his looks that drew women to him. Yes, he was one gorgeous man, the epitome of tall, dark, and devastatingly handsome, but it was the power that radiated from him that kept women begging for his attention. And until a couple of days ago, Cordie had been just like all those silly women under Aiden's spell.

Her eyes were open now. Her father's confession had opened them. She had never been in love with Aiden; it had been just a foolish crush. That was all. Fortunately for her, the man was clueless. As brilliant as he was in business matters, he was a neophyte where women were concerned. She knew for a fact that he didn't have any idea how she felt—how she *had* felt—about him. If she weren't his sister's friend, she doubted he would have even given her a second glance. She certainly wasn't his type. From all the women who had hung on his arm in the past, she knew he preferred tall, slightly anorexic blondes. Cordie was the complete opposite. Her hair wasn't blond; it was as black as ink and looked even darker against her fair complexion. At five feet six inches she considered herself average height, though she was a smidge taller than Regan and Sophie. She supposed she was in good shape, but no matter how much she dieted, she couldn't attain the flat-chested skinny-mannequin look. She was what men called curvaceous.

She realized she was staring at Aiden and quickly turned away. God, she had been such an idiot for such a long time.

Sophie nudged her. "Have you eaten anything today?"

The question jarred her. "What? I don't know. Why?"

"Let me fix you something," Regan suggested.

Cordie shook her head. "I'm not hungry, but thanks for offering."

"You're exhausted, aren't you?" Sophie asked. She reached for her coat and put it on. "Come on, Regan. We should all go home and let her get some rest. It's been a long, stressful day. Do you think you'll be able to sleep tonight, Cordie?"

"Maybe one of us should stay over," Regan suggested.

Cordie laughed. "No one is staying with me. I'm fine, really. I'm begging you, please go home. And take those men with you," she added, waving her hand toward Jack, Alec, Spencer, and Aiden.

Hearing her, Aiden turned around. "Those men?" He grinned as he repeated her comment.

"I could be wrong, but I'm getting the feeling that Cordie might want us to leave," Jack said.

Aiden reached for his suit jacket and slipped it on. He looked as though he were about to walk into a boardroom. His suit was a perfect fit, of course. Everything about the man was impeccable. After asking her if there was anything she needed, he and Spencer, insisting that she not walk them to the door, came over to give her a hug. Aiden smelled divine when he wrapped his arms around her, and she tried not to react. She pulled away as quickly as possible.

After they were gone, Sophie and Jack, along with Regan and Alec, prepared to follow, but just as Sophie reached the door, she suddenly stopped, causing Regan to bump into her. Sophie turned to Cordie. "I can't believe I forgot to ask you . . . what was the surprise?"

"There's a surprise?" Jack asked.

"Yes, her father told her something surprising," Regan remembered.

"She promised to tell us tonight," Sophie explained. "So what was it?"

"Maybe she doesn't want to share it just yet," Jack suggested, being diplomatic, but Sophie was already back in the living room waiting for an answer.

Cordie stretched her legs out, then swung her feet down to the floor and sat up. Looking around at the curious faces of her four closest friends, she decided there was no easy way to say it other than to just simply state the facts. "My mother . . . Natalie Kane . . . didn't die in a car crash. She—"

"What?" Sophie exclaimed. "If not in an accident, then how?"

"According to my father, she's not dead," Cordie said.

Sophie pulled her coat off and handed it to Jack as she rushed back to Cordie. Regan dropped her purse on her way across the room.

"Where is she? What happened to her?" Sophie demanded.

"I don't know," Cordie replied.

"Do you think she just up and left you and your father?" Regan asked.

Cordie shrugged. "From what my father said just before he died, I'm pretty sure that's exactly what she did."

"How could any mother . . ." Regan couldn't go on. She was so angry her face turned red.

Her friends had a hundred questions, and Cordie couldn't answer any of them. No, her father didn't give her any other details, and no, she didn't know why he had gone to such lengths to keep the truth from her, especially after she became an adult.

"Are you going to try to find her?" Sophie asked.

"Would you?" Cordie replied.

Sophie started to nod, then stopped. "I don't know. I'd be curious."

"Alec and Jack could locate her for you," Regan offered.

"Of course," Sophie agreed. "They could use their resources at the FBI."

"No, thanks," Cordie said, shaking her head. "I'm not interested in finding her."

"Don't you want to know why she left?" Regan asked.

"No."

Alec walked over to the ottoman and sat facing Cordie. "What do you know about her?" he asked.

"Her name was Natalie Ann Smith, and she was born in Sydney, Australia."

"What else did your father tell you about her?"

"Oh, he didn't tell me anything. I found out her full name and where she was born when I got a copy of my birth certificate so I could get my driver's license."

"He didn't tell you anything about her?" Alec asked.

"He told me she died when I was a baby, and I now know that was a lie, but I'm assuming that's when she left. My father didn't like to talk about her. Every time I mentioned her, he would become upset. After a while I knew not to ask questions."

"Are you absolutely sure you don't want to find her?" Sophie asked again.

"I'm certain."

"But there could be extenuating circumstances—" Sophie began.

Cordie cut her off. "I don't care. She broke my father's heart. I want nothing to do with her."

Cordie left no doubt that the subject was closed and that she was resolute in her decision to let it go, but after she read the letter her mother had left for her father and all the letters he had written that were returned, her attitude drastically changed. She not only wanted to locate the woman who broke her father's heart, she wanted an answer to the question that was gnawing at her: Did Natalie get the life she wanted or—if there was any justice—the life she deserved?

FIVE

Andrew,

This is a difficult letter for me to write. What I have to say is going to upset and perhaps shock you, and I'm sorry about that. You've been working such long hours you haven't had time to notice how unhappy I am. I'm not going to sugarcoat how I feel, though, no matter how much it hurts you.

This marriage was a mistake. I never should have let you talk me into keeping the baby. We both know I wouldn't have married you if I weren't pregnant. Marrying a mechanic was an act of rebellion and terribly foolish. If my family ever found out, they would disown me.

I can't do this anymore. I hate being poor, and as selfish as this seems, I believe I deserve more out of life. You and I are so different. I want adventure, and I want to see the world. I know you love me, Andrew, but it isn't enough.

I want to go home. I'm going to pretend this marriage never happened and start over. I'm going to put all of this behind me, and I don't want any reminders. My home is a continent away, so there should never be any chance encounters.

I'll leave it to you to file for divorce. I don't want anything

from you but my freedom. You and Cordelia are part of my
past now. I don't want to share custody. You can have her.
Please accept my decision and don't come after me.

Natalie

Cordie's heart ached for her father. She couldn't imagine what he must have felt when he read the letter. It was so cold, brutal, unfeeling. It had to have devastated him, and yet he mourned her on his deathbed.

He'd treated the letter as though it was a treasure. He'd wrapped it in tissue, then sealed it in a plastic bag and tucked it in the bottom of the box with his other important papers. His letters to Natalie were there as well. There were four of them, and all had been returned unopened with *Return to Sender* stamped on the front. The address showed her father had sent them to a post office box in Chicago.

If her father hadn't wanted Cordie to read the letters he'd written, he would have destroyed them, she decided. She sat in the middle of her bed, spread the envelopes in front of her, and one by one opened them.

In the first two letters he pleaded with Natalie to come home. He told her he loved her, that he would always love her, and that he was lost without her. In the third letter, sent two years after she'd left him, he notified her he had filed for divorce and had requested full custody of their daughter, Cordelia. He added that, even though he was taking legal action, he still loved her and wanted her to come back to him. He promised to wait because she would always be the love of his life. The fourth letter was verification that the divorce was final.

At first Cordie wanted to find the woman, to look her in the eyes and tell her what she probably already knew, that she was a horrible person for causing her father so much pain, but as therapeutic as it would be, Cordie knew she would never confront her. What would be the point? She gave up on the idea of having a conversation with the woman. She still wanted to find her, though. There were a few questions that needed answers. Had Natalie's life changed for the better or the worse? Had her ridiculous dream of pretending she'd never been married and starting all over worked? Was she being pampered? Cordie most wanted to know if she had any regrets.

There were two other documents in the box with the letters: the marriage certificate and the divorce decree. The marriage certificate showed that Natalie Smith married Andrew Kane in Las Vegas, Nevada. It was dated four months before Cordie was born. The divorce decree was a very basic notice dissolving the marriage. She read them both and then carefully put everything back in the box and closed the lid.

It was after midnight when she finally got into bed. She tossed and turned for another hour before her mind calmed. She kept thinking about her father and how he had thrown his life away waiting. He could have remarried and had a wonderful life if he'd only been open to the idea. Did his love for Natalie become an obsession? Or did he feel, once married, always married?

She didn't have any answers. She couldn't understand how he could continue to love Natalie after reading that terrible letter. *You can have her.* Those were the last words that drifted into Cordie's thoughts before sleep claimed her.

Sunday afternoon was spent grading papers, and Sunday evening was spent falling apart. She had been melancholy all day, but she kept busy so that she wouldn't have time to feel sorry for herself. Not wanting to talk to anyone in her present frame of mind, she let the phone calls go to voice mail and tried to focus on getting organized for school. She was fine, she told herself again and again. She was just feeling a little stressed, nothing more, and certainly nothing to worry about.

But she wasn't fine. She had lost her dad, her only family, the one person who had loved her unconditionally, like a good parent should, and then she'd read that horrible letter from the woman who had to be talked into giving Cordie life and then couldn't wait to be rid of her. *You can have her.* Those words were branded in her mind. And there were her father's desperate pleas in his letters for the love of his life to come back to him. How could her father have loved someone like that?

It was getting late. Cordie collected her papers and books for the next day and slipped them into her satchel, then stood and stretched. The strain of the last few days had taken its toll. The tension in her muscles was working its way upward, and now her head was beginning to throb. Rubbing her temples, she climbed the stairs to her bedroom. A long, hot shower was exactly what she needed.

She let the soothing water flow over her tight muscles, and by the time she stepped out of the shower, the tension had eased and her headache was gone. She washed and dried her hair, then put on a short silk nightgown. She was beginning to feel much better and was proud of herself because she had kept it together all evening. She'd done enough of that in the past few days.

She hadn't been sleeping well lately and hoped tonight would be different. She was so tired now, she thought she might just fall asleep the second her head hit the pillow, but to be sure, she would go down to the kitchen and brew a cup of chamomile tea. Not bothering to put on her slippers, she picked up her silk robe and padded out into the hallway. She was tying the sash on her robe and didn't notice the box of books she'd left sitting on the landing until she tripped into it, lost her balance, and went flying down the stairs. The box careened down the steps with her, and she landed on her backside with books all around her. It was the last straw in a miserable day. She leaned into the banister and burst into tears. She could have broken her neck, and no one would have known until they found her decomposing body days later. Oh Lord, what a depressing thought. She was so caught up in her misery she didn't hear the pounding on the door.

Aiden had just climbed the steps to her front door when he heard a commotion and a loud thud coming from inside. He called her name, but there wasn't any response. About to break in, he realized he hadn't tried the doorknob. He'd assumed it was locked, but it wasn't. He rushed inside and was met with the sight of Cordie sobbing as she pushed books off her and tried to get up from the floor.

"Are you hurt?" His worry made him sound angry.

She wasn't in the mood to be sociable. "Go away."

"Are you hurt?" He repeated the question, though now his voice was calmer.

"No."

He rubbed the back of his neck while he studied her. He wasn't sure what to do. It wasn't like Cordelia to be difficult. She always had it together. But not tonight. He picked up the books and stacked them in the box in the corner of the foyer; then he turned back to her. She was still crying. He wanted to tell her to stop.

"Why are you crying?"

Her first inclination was to glare at him, but she was too weary to give it her best effort. She grabbed the banister and, wincing, pulled herself up.

He moved forward and, before she realized his intent, lifted her into his arms and carried her upstairs.

"Did you know your front door was unlocked? Anyone could

have come in. You live alone, Cordelia. You should make certain your doors are always locked and your alarm is always on," he scolded as they ascended the steps.

"I don't have an alarm."

"You're getting one," he snapped.

Aiden's mind raced with all the terrible things that could have happened to her, and he was furious about her cavalier attitude toward her safety. There was only one bedroom door open and he headed there. He could have put her down, but he didn't. She weighed next to nothing in his arms. He sat on the side of the bed with her in his lap, his arms wrapped around her as he waited for her tears to stop flowing. Her head was down on his shoulder, and she was so soft cuddled against him. He had the sudden urge to get the hell away from her. He was reacting to her in a way he didn't like.

She finally stopped crying and leaned back so she could look into his eyes. "Why are you here?"

"I got stuck . . ." He stopped before he hurt her feelings with the truth. "Regan was worried about you. You weren't answering your phone," he explained. "She knew I was out, so she called my cell and asked me to stop by and check on you, and it's a damned good thing I did."

"Why? As you can see, I'm perfectly fine." She sniffed.

Aiden said, "You were sprawled at the bottom of your steps."

"I was sitting, not sprawling," she corrected.

"Wearing this flimsy see-through nightgown."

"You can't possibly see through this material." She looked down and saw that her robe was open, exposing a fair amount of her breasts because of the gown's low neckline. "Oh," she said as she quickly pulled the robe closed. She glanced up and met Aiden's eyes. He was looking at her in a way he'd never done before, as though he was seeing her for the very first time as a woman. A warm, tingling sensation coursed through her body.

"Let go of me and go home. I'm fine, I promise. Tell Regan I'll call her tomorrow, and thank you, Aiden, for taking time to check on me."

Her arms were still around his neck. She leaned up and kissed him on his cheek, then started to move away, but he didn't loosen his hold. He continued to stare into her eyes as though he was searching for something inside her.

The strangest thing happened then. Maybe it was just curiosity to find out what it would feel like, or maybe it was just plain lust on her part. She kissed him again, this time on the lips. He didn't pull away. He nudged her chin down and gently kissed her back. Then, taking her face in his hands, he deepened the kiss, passion igniting when his tongue swept inside her mouth. He was so incredibly hot and demanding, overwhelming her. He made love to her with his mouth while he caressed her. His hand cupped her breast and he groaned.

Aiden was lost in the moment. It was only when he felt her tremble that he came to his senses. He pulled back, forcing her to let go of him, then lifted her off his lap and dropped her onto the bed.

Cordie was so flustered she didn't know what to say or do. She could see he was upset. He walked to the door, turned back to her, and said, "I'll lock up. You get some sleep."

And he was gone.

She sat there a long while trying to make sense of what had just happened. She'd ruined everything. She was embarrassed and mortified. What must he think of her? She'd all but attacked the man. How could she ever face him again? Maybe she was overreacting. It had just been a few kisses—long, intense, unbelievably arousing kisses that all but turned her inside out—but they meant nothing.

After she calmed down she came up with a plan should she run into him anytime soon. She would behave like an adult. Yes, they had shared an intimate moment, but it was still possible to go back to the way things used to be. He would ignore her, and she would do her best to ignore him.

Monday Cordie was back at work. She was busy, but Aiden kept popping into her thoughts. As the days progressed, it became easier to push him to the back of her mind. Each night she went through one of the boxes her father had packed when he'd sold his house. She assumed it would be easy to find more information about her mother, thinking that there had to be some papers or photos stashed away in one of the boxes. But she was wrong about that.

The last three weeks of school were hectic, and the search to learn more about Natalie was put on hold. She made a copy of the horrid letter and took it with her when she met her friends for dinner at the Hamilton Hotel. She had tried to get them to eat somewhere else because she didn't want to chance running into Aiden, who lived in the penthouse at the top of the hotel. He traveled so much he was rarely there, but still, she didn't want to risk it.

Then, during a phone conversation with Sophie, after Cordie had suggested two different restaurants, Sophie mentioned that Jack and Alec were going to be at the hotel playing poker with a couple of the Vice detectives from the Chicago Police Department.

"It's their monthly poker game," she said. "Jack thinks he has a chance of winning a hand or two since Aiden is still in San Francisco. Whenever Aiden plays, he wins."

Cordie relaxed. She was worried she wouldn't be able to control her reaction to him, and she had decided the only way she could move on with her life was to stay as far away from him as possible. She was more determined than ever not to turn into her father and waste her life hoping for the impossible.

After a stressful day rushing from one meeting to another, then enduring a frustrating session with the principal of St. Matthew's, Cordie was ready for a glass of wine.

Regan had reserved one of the smaller private dining rooms at the Hamilton so they wouldn't be disturbed. The room was just off the bar, and with the doors closed it was nearly soundproof, a perfect place to share secrets and gossip. They could laugh as loud as they wanted and not worry about bothering other diners. On the other side of the bar, tucked into an alcove, was the door to another dining room, one the men used for poker games. It was isolated from the rest of the hotel but close enough to the bar to get beer and anything else they wanted.

Cordie was supposed to meet her friends at seven thirty, and she hadn't had time to go home and change her clothes. Dressed in a cream-colored pencil skirt, a deep-blue silk blouse, and nude high heels, she had looked very businesslike all day in her meetings, but she would have preferred to be wearing something more comfortable when she was with her friends. Her hair was driving her crazy hanging in her face, so she put it up in a ponytail. The long mass swung back and forth as she rushed through the shiny brass revolving doors into the Hamilton.

Cordie loved the hotel. There was a quiet elegance about the place. It had a contemporary feel with the shiny marble floors and granite pillars, yet the furnishings were old-world. The soothing colors and the comfortable seating areas made guests want to linger. She knew the Hamilton like the back of her hand; she had visited it at least once a week when Regan lived there before she got married.

Cordie realized she was practically running across the lobby and forced herself to slow down. A man dressed in a business suit and tie tried to engage her in conversation as she entered the bar. She smiled at him and shook her head to his invitation to buy her a drink. She walked past him and opened the door to the dining room but was blocked from going any farther. Aiden was standing just inside the doorway talking to Alec and Jack. He grabbed her by the shoulders to stop her from rolling over him.

She wasn't happy to see him and said the first thought that came into her mind. "Why aren't you in San Francisco?" Her tone was accusatory, which she realized wouldn't make a lick of sense to him. Before he could ask her what was wrong with her, she blurted, "Are you playing poker tonight?"

"Yes, I thought I would." Aiden smiled then because he heard Jack groan. Glancing at him, he said, "Relax, MacAlister. You might win a hand. You never know. Miracles do happen."

Cordie was distracted by his wonderful smile. It was so sexy. He was such a beautiful man. His eyes turned warm and tender when he was happy. Smiling was a rarity to him, though. He was usually very serious about everything, especially when he was working on his next hotel deal. There was no question Aiden was a workaholic, yet somehow he made a bit of time for rugby, poker, and women . . . skinny blond women.

That reminder helped her get her head back together. Aiden still had hold of her. Wanting to distance herself from him, she gently pushed his hands away, took a step back, and then walked around him to get to the table. She noticed Alec was watching her, his expression puzzled.

"What has you frowning, Alec?" she asked.

"Not frowning," he countered. "Just observing."

Regan pulled out a chair for her. "Sit. We have lots to talk about."

Sophie sat across from Cordie at the small round table. "It's all good news," she said. "Except for Jack." She looked up at her husband and smiled. "He hates Chicago winters."

"And?" Cordie prodded.

"We're staying in Chicago. That's where the Bureau wants him. He and Alec were both promoted and will continue to work together."

"Here in Chicago," Regan supplied. "They're both assigned here indefinitely. No more back-and-forth to Boston for Alec and me."

"That's wonderful news," Cordie said. "But what about your town house in Boston?"

"Actually, Alec's brother Nick still owns it," Regan said. "Alec didn't do the paperwork. Neither one of us has had time, and Nick wasn't in any hurry. He's going to put it on the market next month."

"I love that town house," Cordie said. She had stayed there a couple of times with Regan when Alec was out on assignment. The town house had been completely remodeled and was located in a coveted neighborhood. She loved Boston, too, almost as much as she loved her hometown.

"For a while we thought Alec's brother Michael might buy it, but he decided not to. I'm not sure why."

"He's based in San Diego," Alec said. "And these days he rarely gets back to Boston. The town house would sit empty for months at a time."

"But when he leaves the Navy SEALs . . . ," Regan began.

"I don't think he plans to leave anytime soon, sweetheart," Alec said.

"Cordelia?" Aiden called her name, then walked up behind her and put his hands on her shoulders.

"Yes?"

"How are you doing?"

"I'm fine. Thanks for asking."

He tugged on her ponytail. She reached up to swat his hand away.

"Do you need anything?" he asked.

She shook her head. His hands were still on her shoulders, but his attention had moved on. "Are we going to play poker or not?" After asking the question, he squeezed Cordie's shoulders, then turned and walked out of the room. His attitude toward her was so casual; apparently he'd forgotten all about kissing her. She wished she could do the same.

"I'm playing," Jack said. He rounded the table and bent down to kiss Sophie. Alec also kissed his wife, then whispered something that made her laugh.

Cordie watched the two couples, and for the first time since both of her friends had married, she felt like a fifth wheel. What had happened to her self-confidence? It seemed to have vanished. Since her father's death she'd been on autopilot, but now the numbness was wearing off and she was beginning to feel again. There was so much to process and try to understand. Terrified that she was heading down the same desolate road her father had chosen, she was questioning everything about her life and the choices she had made. She didn't know where she belonged anymore. Her life seemed so empty now. Was she just feeling sorry for herself? Maybe, she decided. She'd admit she was a bit depressed, but who wouldn't be after reading those heartbreaking letters her father had written to her mother begging her to come back to him?

A waiter appeared to take their drink orders. Cordie had thought she would drink wine, and a lot of it, but now that she was with her friends and starting to relax, she decided she wanted iced tea. Sophie and Regan ordered the same thing.

"We're such sophisticated drinkers," Regan said with a laugh. "We should have ordered champagne to celebrate the fact that we're all going to stay in Chicago. For a while there I thought Jack and Sophie were going to be transferred to Phoenix, and Alec and I were going to be transferred to Boston permanently, but it all worked out. All of us will be together in the city we love. Even Aiden and Spencer will be home more often."

"Aiden and Spencer?" Cordie asked.

"Spencer told me, once Aiden gets the hotel in Florida up and running, he plans to cut way back on travel. In the past year he's flown all over the world, to Hong Kong, Paris, London, Melbourne, and Sydney, and all over the United States. I hope he'll slow down, but I won't believe it until I see it. He practically lives on the Gulfstream."

"The Gulfstream is a beautiful jet," Cordie said. "The bedroom's nicer than mine."

"Is Aiden still staying on the top floor of the hotel when he's in town?" Sophie asked. "If he's around more, maybe he'll buy a place of his own."

"It's doubtful," Regan answered. "The penthouse seems to work for him. Aiden really hates clutter, and the penthouse is sleek, clutter-free."

"It's beautiful but sterile," Sophie said. "Very impersonal."

"I can understand the appeal. I live in a clutter-free environment," Cordie said.

Regan and Sophie laughed. "Maybe in your dreams," Regan said. "You're always surrounded by clutter."

"Not at work," Cordie insisted. "Chemistry is a precise science, and if I weren't organized in the lab, it would be a disaster. It's just that, when I'm home, I want to relax. Besides, the clutter is mostly books," she said.

"And scarves and shoes and keys and—" Sophie added.

Cordie interrupted. "It isn't that bad," she said. "And we weren't talking about me. You were catching us up on your brothers. What's going on with Spencer? Is he going to stay in Chicago?"

"For now," Regan answered.

"And Walker?" Sophie asked. "I know he's still racing cars all over Europe, but when he retires, will he come back to Chicago?"

"That's a whole other story," Regan said. "And not a happy one."

"What's going on?" Cordie asked.

"According to Spencer, our brother Walker still hasn't grown up. I agree with him," she said. "Walker is seven years older than I am, but he still acts like an impulsive teenager. There are two lawsuits against him, both involving women he jilted. The women's lawyers are trying to get their greedy fingers on the hotels. It won't happen," she rushed to add. "Still, it's a worry Aiden doesn't need. He just settled another suit for Walker, and we had to pay quite a lot of money. Even though it was ruled an accident, Walker was responsible. There weren't any life-threatening injuries, but it's only a matter of time before something catastrophic happens. I wish Walker would figure out his life."

"I wish I could figure out mine." Cordie didn't realize she'd said the thought out loud until Sophie asked her to explain what she meant. She was saved from having to answer when the waiter interrupted to take their dinner orders. Because they had dined at the hotel so many times, they didn't have to look at the menu. Sophie and Regan ordered a Caesar salad with chicken, and Cordie was in the mood for salmon.

She waited until the waiter left the room and then said, "Natalie Kane, my mother—though calling her 'mother' gives me the willies—left my father a farewell letter." Her voice was filled with sadness as she added, "He kept it all these years. He wrote several letters to her, too, but they were all returned unopened. Those letters were in the lockbox along with the marriage certificate and divorce decree."

"Did you open your dad's letters and read them?" Sophie asked.

"Yes, I did. He left them, so he must have wanted me to read them. They were heartrending pleas for her to come home."

"What did she say in her farewell letter? Did she give a reason why she was leaving him?" Sophie asked.

"And Cordie," Regan reminded her. "She left her baby, too."

Cordie reached under the table for her purse and set it on her lap as she fished out a folded piece of paper. "I made a copy of her letter because I knew you both would want to read it."

"What about your father's letters?" Regan asked.

Cordie shook her head. "I don't want you to read them."

Sophie understood. "You think it might color our opinion of your dad?"

"I don't want you to feel sorry for him. I want you to remember him as a strong, loving father. Natalie was his weakness. Too late he realized he'd thrown his life away waiting for her."

"Where did he send these letters?" Regan asked.

"The address on the envelopes was a post office box here in Chicago. He must have thought they would be sent on to her. Maybe that's what she told him."

Sophie read the letter first, and by the time she'd finished, her cheeks were bright pink. She was irate on Cordie's behalf. "She's going to pretend the marriage never happened and start over? Who does that?"

"Apparently Natalie Kane does," Cordie said.

Regan finished reading the letter and handed it to Cordie, but before she could put it back in her purse, Regan grabbed it again and reread it.

"I can't believe 'You can have her.' Shame on her. What kind of a mother . . ." She was sputtering and couldn't finish her thought.

"I'm glad she didn't stay around to raise you, Cordie. After reading this letter I have to say that Natalie Kane is a cold, unfeeling bitch."

Regan agreed. "If she was going through some kind of mental issue, she had years to get her head straight and come back to her family."

"No, she didn't have mental issues. She just didn't like being poor or being married to a mechanic. Remember what she wrote? If her family knew, they'd disown her."

They continued to discuss the letter and Natalie's motives all through dinner, though Cordie didn't eat much because the topic made her stomach queasy.

"How does a mother walk away from her baby?" she asked.

"I wonder how she would feel if she knew your father left millions of dollars. From a humble mechanic to the owner of thousands of auto shops," Sophie said.

"Money wasn't important to my father, but getting Natalie back was all that mattered. That's why he became so driven."

"Even though he was worth a huge fortune, he lived like an ordinary man," Regan said.

"On his deathbed he warned me not to follow in his footsteps. I guess he finally realized all the years he wasted pining away for her." She sighed then and said, "He taught me a lesson. I don't want to chase a dream anymore."

"What do you mean?" Sophie asked.

"I'm not wasting another minute on any man."

Sophie frowned. "When have you wasted a minute on a man? Men chase you, Cordie. It's not the other way around."

"I've changed my mind. I've decided I'm going to find her." Cordie made the announcement and waited for a reaction.

"Why?" Regan asked. "What do you hope to gain?"

"I want to know how her life turned out. Did she find what she was looking for? Did the end justify the means?"

"She broke your father's heart," Sophie said. "I hope she's miserable. And poor," she added with a nod. "I really hope she's poor."

"When you find her, will you walk up to her and introduce yourself?" Regan asked.

Cordie pushed her chair back and stood. "No, I don't want to meet her. I just want to see her with her family. I have no desire to interact with her."

"Then hire an investigator to find her and get the information you want," Sophie suggested.

"No, I have to go," she said, and before Sophie could continue to argue, she asked, "Whose turn is it to pay?"

"Mine," Regan said. "And I already took care of the bill, including gratuity."

"Are you sure it was your turn?" Cordie asked. "I seem to remember—"

"I don't want you to find your mother," Sophie blurted.

"You wanted me to before you read the letter, and don't call her my mother. She left when I was a baby. She doesn't deserve to be called that."

"I worry you'll get hurt, Cordie. You just lost your father. You don't need any more pain."

"I have to do this, Sophie."

Regan could detect an argument brewing and decided to deflect her friends' attention. "Is that a new blouse, Cordie?"

"No, I just haven't worn it in a while."

"Oh, I forgot to ask, how did your meeting with Sister Delores go?"

"Not well at all. She likes to have her way."

"That's why she's the principal," Regan said. "She has to be tough."

"I told her a long while ago that I wouldn't be signing a new contract, but she's determined to get me to change my mind. I'm not going to, though. I want to take some time off from teaching."

"But you're a wonderful teacher. The boys love you," Regan protested.

"I'm determined to make some changes in my life," Cordie explained.

"What kind of changes?" Sophie asked, frowning.

"I don't know yet . . . just something . . . different."

"Come on," Sophie said. "We all ate healthy dinners, so let's go in the bar, order cold beer and potato chips, and Regan and I will help you figure out what you want to change."

Cordie followed Sophie out the door. "Since when do you drink beer?"

"Since I married Jack. I'm taking on all his bad habits."

Cordie laughed. "Beer and chips. Best dessert ever."

"Are you sure you want to go to the bar?" Regan asked. "If the guys from Vice are in there, they won't leave Cordie alone. Both Woods and Zahner are smitten. Alec told me they think she looks like a sexy movie star."

The hotel bar was filled with businessmen. There wasn't a single woman in sight. Every eye was on the three of them as they made their way around the tables to get to the far side of the long mahogany bar. It was like walking a gauntlet of admiring stares, Cordie thought, but she didn't mind. By the time she got to the end of the bar, her self-esteem had gotten quite a boost.

She could hear laughter coming from the poker room next to them. The door opened and Detective Zahner walked out carrying an empty bowl. To say he was scary looking was an understatement. He was the kind of man who made most intelligent people nervous and ready to bolt. He was big and muscular like a professional wrestler, and both his arms and neck were covered in faded tattoos. His hair was long and in desperate need of a comb, but it was the look in his eyes when he was angry that scared the bejesus out of his targets. The only man who rivaled Zahner in terror tactics was Regan's husband, Alec, when he worked undercover. To Cordie, however, Zahner was a big teddy bear. He spotted her leaning against the bar and headed toward her, his wide grin making him appear a bit maniacal.

After kissing Sophie and Regan on the cheek, he turned his full attention to Cordie. He kissed her on her cheek before wrapping her in a bear hug.

"When are you going to realize how good we'd be together?" he asked, his voice crooning like a seventies blues singer's.

"I don't want to ruin what we have," she told him, smiling. "You're a tease, Zahner."

He pressed in on her, leaned down, and whispered, "Let me take you home and show you—"

"What the hell? Get off her, Zahner." Aiden gave the order from the doorway. He strode over, fully intending to pull Zahner away from Cordelia, but the detective was in the mood to cooperate. He stepped back, winked at her, then frowned at Aiden.

Aiden wasn't through acting possessive. "Cordelia, don't encourage him," he snapped.

Regan and Sophie were looking at Aiden as though they thought he'd lost his mind.

"What's the matter with you?" Regan asked.

Aiden didn't answer. To be honest, he didn't know why he'd gotten so angry when he'd seen Zahner draped all over Cordelia. Maybe he was being more protective of her because she was so vulnerable since her father's death. She was all alone and needed some-one to watch over her. Kissing her had absolutely nothing to do with his reaction. That's what he told himself, anyway.

"You sound like a jealous husband," Zahner remarked.

Ignoring the comment, Aiden said, "Are you playing the next hand, or are you out of money?"

"I'm playing," Zahner replied. "My luck's bound to change. I figure I'm due for a win." He grabbed the bowl the bartender had refilled with cashews, turned to Cordie, said, "See you later, sweet-heart," and strolled back into the poker room. Aiden followed and pulled the door closed behind him.

"What was that all about?" Sophie asked. "If I didn't know bet-ter, I'd say Aiden was jealous."

"No," Regan said. "It's just Aiden being Aiden."

"He's never going to change," Cordie said.

"Who wants to go to the ladies' room?" Sophie asked.

Regan raised her hand. "Me."

"Go ahead, I'll order the beers," Cordie offered.

The second her friends were out of sight, Cordie sat down on a barstool and reached for her phone. She texted Alec and asked him for his brother Nick's cell phone number. She could have gotten the num-ber from Regan, but that would have led to twenty questions, and Cordie wasn't ready to explain her plans for her future just yet.

The following morning she called Nick, negotiated the price, and purchased his town house in Boston.

SIX

Congressman Mitchell Ray Chambers's poll numbers were abysmal, and it was all Aiden Madison's fault. If he'd played ball and given the congressman what he wanted for the land, a Hamilton Hotel would be in the district's future, but Madison got all bent out of shape because the congressman had given his word and then broken it. It was such a ridiculously stupid reason to walk away from a multimillion-dollar venture.

It was obvious that Spencer Madison was the one who really wanted the hotel. He was only following his brother's lead when he walked out of the meeting, and Chambers was convinced that once Aiden was out of the picture, Spencer would be willing to negotiate and move forward on the project. It really was prime property, after all.

The hotel wouldn't have been important to the congressman if it weren't for the fact that the mayor of Fallsborough had gone after the Madisons and boasted to everyone in the district that the hotel would bring jobs and money. She'd also told them that their congressman, Chambers, had blown the deal and with it all their hopes and dreams for a better tomorrow. In public the mayor may have acted all distraught about the lost deal, but since she planned to run against him in the next primary, she privately had to be jumping for joy at the windfall that had just come her way.

Although he gave it his best shot, he couldn't put a positive spin on what had happened. The only solution he could come up with to charm the voters back into his pocket was to find a way around Aiden Madison.

SEVEN

Cordie called Sophie and Regan and asked them to meet her at the Palms for lunch. She explained that she had something important to tell them.

Cordie was early, Regan was on time, and Sophie was fifteen minutes late as usual. Cordie had asked for a booth near the back so they would have a little privacy. The three friends met often at this restaurant, one of their favorites, especially when there was news to share. They knew the waitstaff by name and didn't need to place their drink orders after they were seated. Adam, their waiter, immediately appeared with three iced teas and recited the specials. They all agreed on a spinach salad with chicken, strawberries, and feta.

The moment Adam stepped away, Sophie turned to Cordie. "Okay, what's going on?"

"You look beat. Aren't you sleeping?" Regan asked, her concern evident in her expression.

"I was up most of the night on the Internet doing research," Cordie said. "I'll explain why in a minute." She was suddenly feeling tongue-tied as she stared across the table at the two dearest friends she could ever have.

"Tell us what's wrong," Sophie said. "You're worrying me."

"Regan, have you talked to your brother-in-law today?" Cordie asked.

"Which brother-in-law?"

"Nick."

"No, why?"

"I called him and bought his town house. I'm going to move to Boston."

There were at least twenty seconds of stunned silence, then an explosion of emotion.

"No way," Sophie came close to shouting. "You can't leave Chicago. We're all staying here, remember?"

"No, you and your husbands are staying here. I need a change," Cordie explained. "I need to shake up my life . . . try new things . . . take risks . . . and move."

"You love Chicago," Regan reminded her.

"Yes, I do. I love Boston, too."

Regan became teary-eyed. "No, this is wrong," she said. "After the death of a loved one, you shouldn't be making any rash decisions for at least a year. I read that somewhere."

"I think that might apply to widows," Cordie said. "And this isn't a rash decision. I've always loved your brother-in-law's town house, and I'm ready for a change."

A long minute passed. Regan was digging through her purse looking for a tissue.

"Please don't cry," Cordie begged.

"I'm trying not to," Regan said. "Why not mull this over for a couple of months? Then decide on any changes."

Cordie shook her head. "I need your support on this. Boston isn't that far away. It's a direct flight. You can come see me all the time."

Sophie and Regan continued to argue with her for another fifteen minutes. When they finally realized their protests were getting nowhere, they relented. "I know you love Boston," Regan said. "But what will you do for work?"

"Like she has to work. She's a multi-multimillionaire," Sophie reminded her.

"Yes, I do need to work," Cordie said. "I'm going to put some feelers out. I'll find something I like."

"Teaching again?"

"Maybe . . . or maybe something different."

"Alec's family will help you get settled and introduce you to people. You won't be all alone."

"What about your brownstone here?" Sophie asked.

"I'm going to sell it."

"But you just finished renovating it, and selling it makes it all seem so final," Regan said.

Searching for any argument she could think of, Sophie rushed out, "What if you move and then realize you've made a mistake?"

"Then I'll move back," Cordie said, trying to sound cheerful even though the conversation was depressing her. What if she was making a mistake? What then? She couldn't come back to Chicago. "I love Nick's town house, and I love Boston. And both of you will come often, won't you?"

"Yes, of course we will," Regan promised. A tear slipped down her cheek.

"When is this going to happen?" Sophie asked.

"In a couple of months," Cordie explained. "Depending on the work that needs to be done. I'm going to make a few minor changes and paint all the rooms. Maybe even refinish the hardwood floors. Nick thinks I should. I'm going to fly out next weekend and sign all the papers."

"Are you going to stay at the Boston Hamilton?" Sophie asked.

"No, Nick and Laurant insisted I stay with them. It will be fun to see their kids."

Cordie and Sophie knew all of Alec's family and kept in touch with his five brothers and two sisters through Facebook. Alec's parents, who lived on Nathan's Bay, an island accessible by bridge north of Boston, were warm, hospitable people and always insisted that Cordie come for a visit when she was in the area. Cordie imagined she'd spend a lot of time on the island next summer.

"It'll be okay," she said. "I promise."

She was doing her very best to sound enthused. She should be excited about the future, shouldn't she? It was a brand-new beginning. Why, then, did she want to cry?

The next two weeks were crazy busy. Cordie flew to Boston, loaded down with presents for Nick and Laurant's two young children, and ended up spending three nights with the family while all the papers were being prepared. She paid cash for the town house by simply transferring funds, and she didn't feel quite as nervous about the move once she went through the house because she remembered why she loved it so much. All the wonderful architectural details gave the place a classic timelessness, which was exactly what appealed to her. By the time she left Boston she was convinced she would be happy in her new home.

Once back in Chicago she tackled the task of getting her house ready to sell. She finished going through all her father's boxes, and when she was done, she was all the more frustrated because she couldn't find any information about Natalie, especially since her father had been such a pack rat. He had kept all of Cordie's grade school and high school papers and art projects in three boxes labeled *Keepsakes,* and she knew that if he kept every single one of her drawings and test papers, he certainly would have kept mementos of his marriage. And where were all the photos? Surely he would have kept those in a safe place, but where? Was there another safe-deposit box at the bank, or did the law firm that managed her father's affairs have a folder with her dad's personal items? Doubtful, but she would still ask.

Monday morning she called her father's lawyer, Jared, at his law firm and asked him for his help locating information about Natalie Kane, formerly Natalie Smith.

Jared was happy to hear from her. "This firm didn't start representing your father until he opened his first automotive repair shop. That being said, I'll be happy to go through the files and see what I can find. Are you looking for anything in particular?"

"No, just anything and everything having to do with her. I can't find any photos or mementos, and I know there have to be some . . . somewhere. I thought maybe he had the firm hold on to them . . . maybe when he moved into the house from the apartment," she said. "I'll be surprised if you find anything, but I'd appreciate it if you would look."

"To be honest, I can't imagine there's anything here. She died before your father hired the firm. Isn't that right? And you were just a baby back then."

Jared didn't know the truth about her mother, but then why would he? Her father had kept the secret until his deathbed. Cordie decided she didn't want to explain. Let him continue to think that Natalie had died years ago.

"Yes, that's right."

"Okay, I'll see what I can find."

They chatted a bit longer, and by the end of the call Jared had talked her into going to dinner with him that evening. He picked her up at seven thirty, and they drove to an Italian bistro a few blocks from her house. As they sat at a table with a red-checkered tablecloth sipping glasses of rich red wine, Cordie was relieved that Jared kept the conversation light and relaxed, but by the time the dinner was over and they were waiting for the check, Jared's demeanor changed. He looked very serious when she told him about her upcoming move to Boston, and he cautioned her against making any more decisions in her current state of mind.

"Exactly what is my current state of mind?" she asked, trying not to take offense.

"You're in mourning," he reminded her. He reached across the table and took hold of her hand. "Wait to put your home on the market. Don't do anything that can't be reversed. You could wake up one morning and realize you've made a mistake."

Sophie and Regan had given her the same argument. Like Jared, they didn't know the real reason she wanted to leave Chicago, and she wasn't about to tell them.

"It's sweet that you're worrying about me, but moving to Boston is something I really want to do. I think I'll be okay there," she added.

"Maybe I'll come see you in Boston."

"I'd like that."

She meant what she said. She really did like Jared. Although she knew he would disagree, there just wasn't any chemistry between them now, but who knew what the future held? Could something like that grow from friendship?

Later he walked her to her door and kissed her good night. He didn't press to come inside, and she was thankful she didn't have to say no. As old-fashioned as it made her, she didn't sleep around. When infatuated with one man, it was impossible to substitute another. At least for her, anyway. Once she was settled in Boston, she would be able to get Aiden out of her head, and then she would change pretty much everything else about her life. She didn't plan to become promiscuous—that thought made her smile—just not so reserved. It was getting easier to pretend nothing had happened with Aiden. Obviously their kiss hadn't meant anything to him, and that helped her put it all in perspective. Still, until her move to Boston, she would do her best to avoid him.

The next week was spent painting bedrooms and closets and thinning out clothes and clutter to get the house ready to put on the market. By Sunday evening all the bedrooms had been turned into showrooms that could grace any home magazine cover.

Jared called to tell her he hadn't been able to find anything in the firm's records relating to Natalie Kane or Smith. Cordie had known it was a long shot but was still a little disappointed.

She had donated all her father's clothes, and of all the boxes he had brought with him to her house, there were only three left, the ones that had *Keepsakes* printed across the tops in black Magic Marker. She had sifted through the contents once already, but feeling nostalgic, she decided to go through them again. She sat on the floor and lifted the lid on the first box. Her father had saved nearly every paper she'd brought home and had everything organized in folders labeled by grade. She laughed as she looked at some of her art projects. Nearly every one of them had something to do with cars.

In the second box, nestled between the sixth- and seventh-grade folders, was a plain white legal-size envelope. It was stuck to the back of the sixth-grade folder. The first time she'd gone through the boxes she'd flipped through the folders assuming everything in them was her schoolwork. She hadn't bothered to pull out any of the papers.

She opened the large envelope and emptied the contents onto the floor. And there they were. Not many mementos, but a few. A faded black-and-white photo of the first Kane Automotive Shop, and another photo of her father's truck with *Kane Automotive* painted on the side.

She thought it must have been his first truck. There was one other photograph of a stretch of beach and a beautiful sunset on the water. In the distance she could see several people standing on the beach, but they were all turned away from the camera, looking at the horizon. Next she found two flyers for art exhibits, a couple of ticket stubs for a rock concert, and a wedding invitation without an envelope. Hillary Swanson was marrying Jonathan Black at the First Presbyterian Church on Second Street. The wedding date was exactly six months before Natalie married Cordie's father in Las Vegas. Under the invitation was a birthday card. It was signed, *Love, Natalie.* A pang of sorrow stabbed at her heart, imagining her father's happiness at receiving the card, unaware of the insincerity . . . or the grief that was coming. There was a smaller envelope. She opened it, and inside she found a flyer from Las Vegas with a picture of the Forever Wedding Chapel, where she assumed her father and Natalie had gotten married, a matchbook from a Vegas restaurant, a chip from a casino, and a small square of tissue paper. She unfolded the tissue and revealed a simple gold wedding band.

That was it? This was all her father had saved from his marriage? There wasn't a single photo of Natalie. Had he not taken any, or had he destroyed them in a fit of anger? Reading the farewell letter would have done it, she thought.

Now wasn't the time to delve into her father's motives, she decided.

She had enough information to call in the big guns to pinpoint Natalie's exact location. Alec and Jack would do anything for her, and she didn't think it would take them any time at all to get Natalie's address.

She lured them over to her house with pizza and beer. Their wives came with them, of course, and while Regan and Sophie made salads, Cordie let Alec and Jack read the letter her mother had left for her father. She shouldn't have been embarrassed, but she was, and she couldn't understand why. *You can have her.* Maybe that was why. Maybe being tossed aside as though she had absolutely no value to her mother was the reason.

The doorbell rang, and she went to collect the pizzas from the deliveryman, thankful to have an excuse to leave the room. When she returned, they had finished reading, but neither Jack nor Alec commented on the letter. They followed her to the kitchen, where she put the pizzas on the table and quickly got out of the way.

"Wait," Sophie said. "You should eat the salad first."

Jack just smiled at her and took a large wedge of pizza. Alec dragged out a chair and sat across from him. He pulled the pizza box toward him and reached for a slice. Cordie handed them each a beer and distributed napkins as though she was dealing cards.

"So here's what I know," she began. "Her full name was Natalie Ann Smith. She was born in Sydney, Australia, and I assume she went back there."

"What other information do you have on her?" Jack asked.

She handed him copies she had made of her father's marriage certificate, the divorce decree, the flyer from the Las Vegas chapel, and the Swanson-and-Black wedding invitation.

"That's all there is," Cordie said. "Tell me where to start."

"We can check government records, and how about we track down Hillary and Jonathan Black?" Jack suggested. "We have the date they were married, and it's public record . . ."

"They could have moved away," Sophie warned.

Jack smiled at his wife. "We'll find them."

"And the invitation might have been for Cordie's dad before he met Natalie Smith," Regan said. "They might not even know Natalie."

"Cordie won't know until she talks to them," Jack said.

"I've been on the Internet," Cordie said. "I pulled up the phone directory for Sydney. Do you have any idea how many Smiths are listed? It'll take me a year to go through all of them," she exaggerated.

"I know a guy," Alec said.

"Where?" Jack asked.

"Australia."

"That's a big place. Where exactly in Australia?"

"Perth . . . or maybe Sydney," Alec answered. "He moves around a lot."

"Interpol?" Jack guessed.

"Something like that. He's based out of London."

"Who is he?"

"Liam Scott," he answered. "I did a favor for him a couple of years ago. He'll help Cordie."

"One of us will call you tomorrow with the information on the Blacks," Jack told her.

They came through just the way she knew they would. Alec called her at nine fifteen the following morning with the address and phone number for the Blacks. Cordie thought about calling first to set up the meeting but decided face-to-face without any warning would be better. Fortunately she wouldn't have to drive far. They lived in a suburb just north of the city.

It was a beautiful sunny morning for a drive. And hot. She wore a short white skirt and navy blouse with sandals, but she had her workout clothes in her gym bag in the trunk of her car for her kickboxing class. Regan had signed up both of them for the class, insisting Cordie would love the exercise once she got into it. It was offered twice a week. They normally went on Saturday, but because of a conflict they were going today instead.

The Blacks lived in an older neighborhood of cookie-cutter ranch houses. She found their house number stenciled on the curb and pulled into the narrow driveway. A dog barked when she rang the bell, and she stepped back and waited. A moment later a woman with curly gray hair opened the door. When she saw Cordie, her hand flew to her throat and she gasped. "Oh my God, you have to be her daughter. You're the spitting image. I swear you're identical. You could be her twin if she were twenty years younger," she stammered.

"I look like Natalie?" Cordie asked.

The woman looked confused. "Who?"

Cordie shook her head and smiled. "I think we should start over. Are you Hillary Black?"

"Yes, I am," she said. "And I know who you are. You're Simone Taylor's daughter."

EIGHT

C ordie was fit to be tied.

"It was all a lie, a big, fat, horrible lie," she ranted as she paced around Regan's office. "There is no Natalie Smith. Never was. It was just the name on a fake driver's license she bought from Hillary for twenty-five dollars so she could go into bars and drink. That's how they met. Hillary had a nice little sideline going while she was in college. She printed counterfeit driver's licenses for extra money. Lovely, right?" Hands on hips, she turned to Regan. "Hillary bragged that she was really good at it, too; said it was difficult to tell the difference between the fake and real licenses."

She paused to take a breath and then continued. "According to Hillary—and God only knows if she's telling the truth or not—Natalie's real name is Simone. Simone Taylor. Want to hear something else? Simone was nineteen years old when Hillary met her, and wild, really wild. Men were crazy about her, Hillary told me."

The pacing started again. Regan sat at her desk watching her friend and waiting for an opportunity to ask questions. She had never seen Cordie so upset, so out of control. Her friend's cheeks were flushed, and she was sputtering.

"Did you ask Hillary if she knew your father?" She pushed her chair back and stood.

"Yes and no," Cordie answered. "I asked her if she had ever met Andrew Kane, but I didn't tell her he was my father. She said no, she had never met him. You know what was really odd? She never asked my name. I tried to introduce myself, but she interrupted to tell a story about Simone. She talked so fast I could barely keep up. Oh, and she said she could tell by looking at me that my mother had married well. How strange was that?"

"Did you have hundred-dollar bills pinned to your shirt again?" Alec asked the question as he walked into the office.

Cordie knew she needed to take a second to calm down and collect her thoughts. She tugged the scarf from her neck, haphazardly folded it, and tossed it on the desk. It slid to the floor, but she didn't notice. Her sunglasses were on top of her head. She pulled them off and dropped them into her purse, which was perched precariously on the edge of a chair. When she glanced through the double French doors of Regan's office, she noticed Aiden in the outer room. He was leaning against the reception desk with one ankle crossed over the other, and he had his phone to his ear. His frown indicated he wasn't pleased with what he was hearing. His side of the conversation was short and not very cordial. She heard him emphatically say, "No," and nothing else. By the time he finished the call he looked as though he wanted to throw the phone across the room. Turning to the desk, he picked up a stack of papers, walked into Regan's office, and dropped them in front of her.

He seemed preoccupied when he said, "Here are the forms you wanted. They need to be filled out, signed, and sent over to the accountants as soon as possible."

"Everything is as soon as possible with you," Regan said. "We're in the middle of something," she added. "We were talking about

Cordie's mother . . . I mean the mother who gave birth . . ." She was making a muddle of explaining.

"He's all caught up," Alec said.

"What do you mean, he's caught up?" Cordie asked.

Alec went to the desk, sat, and turned on the computer. "Remember I called you on your cell right after you left the Blacks' house?"

Cordie nodded. "I had just gotten back into my car after my lovely visit with Hillary, who told me all sorts of fun stories about her wild friend, my mother dearest, and I was reeling, so you can imagine my state of mind."

"Regan told me where you were going," Alec said. "And I was curious to know how it went."

Cordie recalled the phone conversation. She had been practically incoherent when she answered, and Alec had to calm her down before she could explain what she had found out. "I was very upset, and I might have raised my voice."

Alec laughed. "Might have?"

Cordie turned to Aiden. "Alec caught you up on my exciting life, then?"

Aiden picked up her scarf and moved her purse so it wouldn't fall on the floor. "Alec was in my office when he called you. He had you on speaker."

Oh God. "So you heard every word?" she asked, mortified. She didn't mind or care that Alec had listened to her tirade. Aiden was another story. She still stupidly cared what he thought. Have to work on that, she told herself. She would add that to her list of feelings she needed to squelch.

She motioned to Regan. "Come on. Let's get to the gym. I need to kick something."

"We're way too early," Regan argued.

"Don't leave yet," Alec said. "I want to show you something."

Aiden walked behind the desk and stood next to Alec, looking at the computer screen.

"I know what you're doing," Cordie said. "You're looking for Simone Taylor, aren't you? I wouldn't bother. That name is probably a lie, too, just like Natalie Smith. I spent hours and hours looking for Natalie on the Internet. Is that what you're doing, Alec?"

"Uh-huh," he answered as he typed on the keyboard.

"You're wasting your time."

Alec sat back. He was staring at the screen as he said, "I wouldn't be too sure."

Aiden glanced at Cordie, then back at the screen. "Wow," he whispered.

"Wow, what?" Cordie asked.

"Come see."

She rounded the desk, stepped in front of Aiden, and looked at what had captured their attention. There was a photo, and for a second Cordie thought it was of her. Same eyes, same dark hair . . . same smile . . .

Alec tilted the screen up so she could get a better look and said, "Meet Simone Taylor."

NINE

"Simone was seventeen when this photo was taken. She had just won some beauty pageant," Alec explained.

"Was it difficult finding her?" Cordie asked. She couldn't stop staring at her double on the screen. The resemblance was freaking her out.

"Not difficult at all," Alec said.

Regan leaned over her husband's shoulder. "Because you had her real name." She looked up at Regan and added, "Hillary Black was telling the truth."

Alec had found other information as well. "Simone's mother isn't alive, but her father, Julian Taylor, is. He's about to retire and his son-in-law is set to take over the family business."

"What is the family business?" Cordie asked.

"Merrick Enterprises," Alec answered.

"Merrick Enterprises?" Aiden responded with surprise.

"You know them?" Cordie asked.

"They're probably the biggest real estate developers in Australia, not to mention the other businesses they own. I don't recall meeting the Taylor family, but I've attended so many events in Sydney and Melbourne, there's a good chance I've run into them."

Pointing to the computer screen, Regan said, "This photo is more than twenty years old. Can you find one that's more current?"

Alec turned back to the computer. "Not yet, but I just started searching."

Aiden's phone rang. He checked to see who was calling and clenched his jaw.

"Aren't you going to answer that?" Regan asked. "It could be important."

"No, it isn't important. Lester Chambers is calling again. He's trying to get me to change my mind about buying his property. He called a few minutes ago, and I did something I'm not proud of," he confessed.

"Then why are you smiling?" Regan wondered.

"What'd you do?" Alec asked at the same time.

"I dumped it all on Spencer." His phone rang again. Muttering something under his breath, he walked toward the doorway before he answered.

"Do you think Simone has tried to find photos of you, Cordie?" Regan asked.

Cordie stopped watching Aiden and turned to her friend. "I doubt it. She erased me, remember?"

Regan nodded. Aiden was obviously a master at multitasking, because he was still on the phone when he asked Cordie for clarification. "How did she erase you?"

"She decided she didn't get married and she didn't have me."

"That doesn't make any sense," Aiden said before going back to his phone conversation.

Why was he lingering? Cordie wondered. He was usually in such a hurry. If she asked him why he was hanging around, the question would come out as rude. He could go anywhere he wanted;

it was his hotel. It was next to impossible not to look at him. He was wearing a deep-navy suit and a white shirt that accentuated his tanned complexion. He'd obviously been playing a lot of rugby. He had the muscles to prove it . . . and the bruises. There was a new one on his forehead, small but still noticeable. Rugby could be a brutal game, which was apparently why he liked it so much. No holds barred, no diplomacy, just brute force and strategy. Alec had caught the fever and was now a player on Aiden's team. They were, of course, undefeated and loved to boast about it.

"Don't you have a game today?" she asked when he joined them again.

"That's tomorrow," Aiden answered. "Regan mentioned you were thinking about going to Australia. Is that true?"

"I don't know what I want to do anymore," she admitted. "When I found out my mother didn't die, that she just walked out, I had no desire to find her. Then I read the letter she left for my father, and I changed my mind. I didn't want to speak to her. I just needed to see for myself if she got what she wanted. But now, knowing about the fake ID she used to marry my father and all the lies she told him . . . if I do go, I'll probably get arrested."

Alec's head came up. "Arrested for what?"

"Assault."

Alec laughed. Cordie was one of the gentlest women he had ever known. She could never knowingly cause any other person pain. "You're thinking about punching Simone?"

She shrugged, then said, "I don't know what I'll do if I ever come face-to-face with her."

"Cordie, you couldn't deliberately hurt anyone, no matter how horrible or sleazy he or she may be," Regan said.

"Here we go," Alec said, nodding toward the screen. "Simone

Taylor Rayburn. Craig Rayburn is Simone's husband. She was twenty-one and he was thirty-four when they married. They have two sons, and they live in Sydney. Want me to go on?" he asked.

"Is there a family photo?" Regan asked.

"Yes." Alec pulled up a magazine website and scrolled through the pages to find the one he wanted. He leaned back so Cordie could get a closer look.

Cordie stared at the happy family smiling back at her from the computer screen and began to shake with anger. She kept thinking about her father and the anguish Simone had put him through. Her reaction to the photo was intense, and—God help her—she really did want to punch the woman.

She didn't realize she was leaning into Aiden's side until he put his arm around her. She knew he could feel her trembling and was thankful he didn't comment on it. Forcing herself to move away from him, she grabbed her purse and said, "I've heard enough for now. Come on, Regan. We should go."

"Hold on a minute," Alec said. "I went ahead and e-mailed my friend Liam. Let me know when you're going to Australia, and he'll meet you."

"I don't need a babysitter," Cordie protested.

"Liam knows his way around Sydney, and he has a lot of contacts. If you were to get into trouble—"

She folded her arms defiantly. "Why would I get into trouble?"

Alec shrugged. "I'm just saying. You won't know anyone there. He can show you around. He'll be happy to help. Like I said, he owes me."

"Aiden, are you and Spencer going to Sydney or Melbourne anytime soon?" Regan asked. "If so, Cordie could go on the company jet with you."

"No, that's not necessary," Cordie said. "Really, I don't think—"

"It would be fun," Regan said. "And so much nicer than flying commercial. It's a long trip. You might as well enjoy it, right?"

"You'll have a good time with Liam, too," Alec said. He stood and stretched. "Just be careful. Women tend to fall under his spell. At least that's what I've been told."

"Fall under his spell? What does that mean?" Aiden asked suspiciously.

"Liam likes women, and they like him. He's gonna love Cordie," Alec predicted. "Come on, Aiden. Open your eyes and look at her. Really look at her. She'll be a dream come true for Liam."

"Cordelia has enough to deal with. She doesn't need some sexually frustrated man hanging all over her."

Alec hid his smile. Aiden was so easy to read. Maybe he was finally waking up. Alec just hoped it wasn't too late. Since her father's death Cordie had been different, and she was making big changes. Moving to Boston was one. She wanted a new life, and she was leaving Aiden behind.

"I'm going to the gym, Regan. Are you coming or not?" Cordie asked.

"I'm right behind you," she stammered. She kissed Alec, grabbed her gym bag, and followed.

They had just reached the French doors when Aiden stopped them. "Cordelia?"

"Yes, Aiden?"

"Is your passport up to date?"

Frowning now, she turned to him. "Yes, but I haven't decided—"

Aiden wasn't looking at her. He had pulled out his cell phone and was checking appointments on his calendar. "We'll leave tomorrow. Be ready."

———

Arrogance wasn't Aiden's greatest sin. Bossiness was. Did he think she was one of his employees he could order about, expecting her to hop to? And why did he believe it was okay for him to get in the middle of her personal problems?

There was a bigger and even more confusing question to be answered. Why was she meekly going along? Maybe not so meekly, she corrected. In fact, she'd thrown a fit. While Regan held the elevator, Cordie had chased Aiden down the hall and around the corner to his office. She told him she wasn't ready to go anywhere, and while she appreciated his concern, he really needed to stop worrying about her. She said all this and more to his back, because he didn't bother to turn around. He just kept walking.

She'd been emphatic. She'd even poked him in his shoulder while she once again explained she wasn't going anywhere with him. She might have even raised her voice, which was so unlike her, but she stopped arguing when she followed him into his office and found two strangers waiting for him. Aiden gave her his undivided attention then. He dismissed her.

"I'll see you tomorrow," he said as he put his hands on her shoulders, backed her into the hallway, and shut the door in her face.

One day. That was all the time Aiden had given her. Since Cordie wasn't one to make a scene in front of others, she planned to call Aiden later and calmly but strongly decline his invitation to fly to Australia with him. She could be tough on the phone, and she wouldn't give him time to argue with her. But first she had to come up with a viable reason, because he would ask for an explanation. She was still trying to come up with that good reason when his driver knocked on her door, carried her luggage to the town car, and drove her to the private airport.

Her stomach was in knots. Getting to fly to Australia in a private jet instead of flying commercial sounded wonderful and a little decadent. The problem was Aiden. If he weren't going, she could relax and enjoy the experience. She was so tense around him these days, and anxious. She remembered how she used to follow him, so enamored was she, but now she was trying to run away from him. She just wasn't having much success. Once she was settled in her new home in Boston, everything would change, especially her outlook on life. That was the hope, anyway. Out of sight, out of mind. Oh, how she hoped that could be true.

She took a deep breath and told herself to enjoy flying in luxury. It was a once-in-a-lifetime experience. Besides, it was all going to work out. She could handle Aiden.

Her five minutes of bravado were quickly spent. Handle Aiden? Who was she kidding? She had a feeling those words were going to come back to bite her.

The Hamilton jet was magnificent. She felt as though she was entering a fantasy. It was all so elegant. There were plush leather seats that magically turned into beds with heavenly down comforters, a sofa with a dining area, and behind the spacious bathroom was a private office that connected to a bedroom with a gorgeous custom-built bed to accommodate Aiden's height.

Aiden hadn't arrived yet. Cordie took her seat and pulled out her laptop. Maybe she could find out something about Simone and Craig Rayburn. With less than a day to get ready, she hadn't had time to do any research. She didn't even know why she was going. Would she confront Simone? She kept going back and forth. One minute she wanted to, and the next minute she didn't. If she had to explain why she was going to all this trouble, she couldn't, unless "Beats me" was a suitable reply.

She hated being vulnerable. She used to have it all together—at least she thought she did—and now she felt as though her life was spiraling out of control. She'd never thought she would be afraid of change, but right this minute she was feeling like a coward, afraid to go forward and afraid to go back. Tears gathered in her eyes. Oh God, she really missed her father.

A young man wearing a light gray shirt with navy pants asked her if she would like something to drink before takeoff. His name was Tom and he explained he would be serving dinner later.

Looking out the window, she saw another black town car driving across the tarmac. Aiden had arrived. She wondered if one of his new blond companions was going to accompany him. She hoped not. She wasn't jealous, she told herself. She just remembered how obnoxious his last two girlfriends were, and she didn't want to be stuck trying to be polite for twenty hours.

Aiden did have strange taste in women, she decided, and she once again reminded herself that she was very lucky she had come to her senses and gotten over her ridiculous infatuation.

After coming on board, Aiden stood just outside the cockpit talking to the pilots for several minutes and then removed his suit jacket and handed it to the male attendant. Loosening his tie, he walked down the aisle and took the seat next to her. He could have sat in any other seat in the cabin, but apparently he would rather crowd her. Was this just one more of his intimidating tactics to get her to do what he wanted? When he turned toward her, she could see the flecks of gray in his eyes.

"Are you ready for this?" he asked.

"The flight? Or Australia?"

"Both."

"No, I'm not ready."

She closed her laptop in preparation for takeoff. Aiden took it from her and slipped it into the leather pouch attached to his seat.

"Australia is a beautiful country," she said. "I've read so much about it. I want to take the time to see as much as I can. How long will you be staying?"

"Depends," he said. "But when I go home, you're going with me."

"I'm what?" She was sure she hadn't heard him correctly.

"I think you should go home with me. I don't want to leave you there."

"Why?"

"Because I'm responsible for you."

She could feel her face heating up. "No, you're not."

Aiden knew he'd pushed the wrong buttons. He decided to try another tack. "I know Sydney. I'll show you around."

"I can show myself around," she said. She was more bewildered than angry. What was going on inside his head? "And if I do need any kind of assistance, I can always call Liam Scott. Alec already talked to him, and he's . . . Why are you shaking your head at me?"

"I don't think you should call Scott."

The set of his jaw told her he was digging in on this issue. She couldn't for the life of her understand why he was acting so . . . territorial. She was determined to get to the bottom of his problem, whether he was stubborn or not. Something was bugging him, but what?

"Have you ever met Liam?" she asked.

"No."

"So you have no reason to distrust him."

"Of course not. I don't know him."

"Then why . . ."

She didn't finish her sentence. The jet was gathering a tremendous amount of speed for takeoff. Without thinking what she was doing, she grabbed hold of Aiden's hand. She was a nervous flyer. Takeoffs and landings scared her, but once the plane was in the air or on the ground she could relax. Being the gentleman he was,

Aiden didn't mention that she was gripping his hand with all her might.

Aiden watched the color drain from her face and did his best to distract her.

"I promised Alec and Regan that I would look out for you, and that's what I'm going to do." Before she could protest, he continued, "Have you read the background on the Taylor family? Alec did a lot of research."

"I haven't seen it."

"He must not have e-mailed it to you. I'll send you a copy."

"If your goal is to change the subject, it isn't working. I'm not helpless, Aiden. I'm perfectly capable of seeing the sights on my own."

He ignored her protest. "Simone's father, Julian Taylor, has enormous wealth and power. He doesn't just control the business. He controls the family."

"What does that mean?"

"They have to behave themselves. From what I've read, Julian is a stickler for his rules. It sounds as though he's wound tight," he added. "He nearly disowned Simone when he found out she entered a beauty pageant. According to Alec's notes, Julian thought her behavior was crass."

"She's back in his good graces now, I take it."

"Yes," he answered. "Unless or until there's a scandal."

"And I'm the scandal."

"You could be if you decide to ruffle some feathers."

She closed her eyes, leaned back against the headrest, and thought about a plan of action once she landed in Sydney. Indecision was making her crazy. She was on her way to Australia—she was in the air, for Pete's sake—and she still hadn't made up her mind if or when she would confront Simone. This was so unlike her, and she began to wonder if others thought of her as weak or wishy-washy. Did Aiden think of her as a weakling? Was that why he was insisting he stay with her while she was in Australia? Did he think she couldn't make her way across the street without his help? If that was how he really felt, she decided she needed to set him straight.

Aiden interrupted her thoughts. "Cordelia—"

"I'm a strong, independent woman, Aiden."

"Uh-huh."

"I can take care of myself."

"Uh-huh."

"You believe me, don't you?"

"Sure I do," he said. "But . . ."

Cordie turned to him, ready for an argument. "But what?"

"I was wondering if you'll be needing to hold my hand for the entire flight or if I could get some work done."

TEN

So much for being independent.

As soon as Cordie let go of his hand, Aiden disappeared into the bedroom, and when she next saw him he was wearing a light gray T-shirt and sweatpants. The clothes had seen better days and should have been put in the rag pile, yet he looked amazing. Only Aiden could be sexy in sweats, she thought.

After making sure she had everything she needed, he went into his office to work, but he kept coming into the main cabin to check on her. It was as though he was making certain she was still there. What did he expect? That she might step outside for some fresh air?

A couple of hours into the flight, when he next looked in on her, she was reading a biochemistry book. It was the latest edition by Frederick Full-of-Himself Fulmer. The author's massive ego came through in nearly every chapter. He took credit for discovering everything but air. Had she been at home, she would have tossed it into the recycle bin.

"Are you enjoying your book?" Aiden asked.

She decided to tone down her opinion. "It's a bit pedantic." Her hand covered the title of the book, but all he had to do was look over her shoulder and read a sentence or two—which he did—to know what the subject matter was.

"Pedantic, huh?" Smiling, he went back into his office.

The next time he checked on her she had moved to the sofa with her iPad and was finishing a drawing. He sat beside her, leaned into her, and asked, "What's that supposed to be?"

"A schematic."

"A schematic of what?"

She was embarrassed to tell him. She felt foolish. "I was trying to design a more efficient fuel-injection system." She erased the drawing and added, "It didn't work."

He was sitting so close she didn't dare look up at him. She would lose her train of thought if she did, and he would know why. She wished to God she had never kissed him, and the second that thought popped into her head she knew it was a lie. She wanted him to kiss her again. God, he smelled heavenly.

No, it was all wrong. A relationship with Aiden, no matter how brief, could never go anywhere. They were ill suited to each other. While Mr. Sophisticated was buying land and building beautiful five-star hotels, she was immersed in biochemistry and cars. How much more nerdy could she get?

He wasn't perfect by any means. He had more than a few irritating flaws. It was just that he was so incredibly handsome, people—women in particular—tended to overlook them. She didn't have blinders, though. Aiden could be such an arrogant know-it-all, and he was far more stubborn than she was.

She knew he regretted touching her, but she doubted he would ever admit it. In that moment when his mouth covered hers and he began to caress her, everything had changed between them. There was a tension now that hadn't been there before, and it was all her fault. She'd practically attacked him. It was mortifying to acknowledge that she had been the aggressor, and she was amazed she could even look him in the eye now.

Thank goodness she was over her infatuation with him. Yes, right. Over him. That lie was as thin as Saran Wrap. Her move to Boston couldn't come soon enough.

When he remained next to her, she thought he wanted something. She waited for him to tell her what it was, but then they started their descent into Los Angeles, and she guessed what he was doing. She'd grabbed him during takeoff, letting him know she was freaked, and he must have assumed she didn't like landings either. He was right, for she grabbed his arm and held on until the wheels hit the runway and glided to a stop.

It was terribly sweet that he didn't comment or tease her, which was totally out of character for him. Aiden had many positive attributes, but being sweet wasn't one of them.

Refueling didn't take any time at all, and within thirty minutes they were back in the air and on their way to Sydney. Aiden stayed beside her reading and pretty much ignoring her until they leveled out at thirty thousand feet and she was able to let go of him. Then he went back into his office to finish a report. At least that's what he told her. She thought he might be staying at his desk to avoid having to entertain her. As if that were necessary.

She wished they could go back to the way things used to be, when he barely noticed she existed. She'd certainly ruined any chances of that happening. Just fifteen more hours until touchdown, she thought. Then she would go her way and he would go his.

It had been a long day. She was tired and stressed, but she didn't think she would be able to sleep. She washed her face, brushed her teeth, and changed into a pink T-shirt and black yoga pants. Maybe watching a movie would help her relax. Aiden was still at his desk working on his laptop. The door to the bedroom behind him was open, and the sheets on the bed had been turned down. She didn't want to interrupt him, and so she simply stood in the doorway and waited for him to notice her.

Aiden knew she was there, of course. He closed out the file he was working on, leaned back in his swivel chair, and looked at her. His pulse skipped a beat and then began to race. God, she was beautiful. And the most sensual woman he'd ever seen. Her hair wasn't pulled back into a ponytail now but fell in soft waves past her shoulders. Her face was flushed with color, and even though the T-shirt wasn't fitted, he could tell she'd removed her bra. He remembered how soft her full breasts had felt, how perfect. She was so soft everywhere, so damn feminine, and right this minute all he could think about was taking her into his arms. He wanted to finish what they had started, but he knew that was impossible and crazy. This was Cordelia, not one of the women he took out to dinner and then home to his bed. He had known her most of her life, and they had become good friends. She was sweet, smart, funny Cordelia. He had never let himself see her any other way.

How could he go back to being oblivious? He supposed he'd always thought she was a little sexy—he'd have to be dead not to notice—but he'd never allowed himself to do more than notice. Ignoring her had been easy . . . until he'd taken her into his arms and kissed her. Her mouth was so erotic, her lips so soft . . .

His voice was gruff when he finally spoke. "What do you need?"

She wasn't put off by his brisk tone. "I'd like to watch a movie. Are the DVDs in here?"

"No," he answered. "All you have to do is turn the television on and pull up the menu. Come with me. I'll show you."

She followed him into the bedroom. The remote was on a side table next to the bed. He turned on the television, called up the menu, and handed the remote to her.

"You can watch it in here. Picture's better."

"I don't want to take your bed. You should get some sleep. It's a long flight."

"I'll sleep later."

"Are you going back to work?"

"No," he answered. "I'm going to pull up a list of events in Sydney, important fund-raisers, charity balls, and the like, that Simone Rayburn and her husband will most likely attend." Shrugging, he added, "I can get a list of those invited."

He disappeared into his office but came back a minute later with his laptop. "Sydney's a very cosmopolitan city. There's always something going on. I've got a couple of sources in Sydney looking for me."

He sat on the bed, leaned back against the upholstered leather headboard, opened his laptop, and began to type. Cordie wasn't sure what she should do. She wanted to be casual about it all, to convince herself that there wasn't anything wrong with being in bed with the man she desperately wanted to get away from.

Oh, he looked good. His hair was messed, a lock falling down onto his forehead. He impatiently brushed it back and continued to read the message he'd pulled up. He was very relaxed. His long legs stretched out, one ankle over the other. He definitely was comfortable in his own skin. Did he know how handsome he was? His appearance probably wasn't even relevant to him. She doubted he ever felt self-conscious or insecure. She, on the other hand, was a jumble of nerves. Okay, she decided, she could be casual about this. All she had to do was go back to thinking that Aiden was just her friend's brother. Nothing more. She would forget all about the way he'd held her and kissed her.

Giving herself a lobotomy would be easier.

"Here are a couple of events."

She crawled up the bed to sit next to him. He put his arm around her and pulled her closer, then angled the laptop toward her so she could look over the guest list.

"The Rayburns are scheduled to attend the Gallery Ball on the twentieth and a university fund-raiser on the twenty-seventh. They're both formal events. You choose. Unless . . ."

"Unless what?" she asked. She looked up into his eyes and promptly lost her train of thought. She could stare at him the rest of the night. With his strong jawline and his lean, hard body, he could have been a model. She forced herself to look at the screen.

"Unless you decide to walk up to their door and introduce yourself," Aiden said.

A shiver of dread went through her. "That's not going to happen."

"What are you hoping to accomplish?"

"I just want to make sense of it, to understand how she could have done it. How she could have discarded her life with my father. She threw us away." She closed her eyes for a moment and then said, "I want Simone to know she hasn't gotten away with her deception, that there are people who know who she was and what she did, that she can't run away and erase the past. But most of all I want her to know . . ." She paused, finding it difficult to say the words.

"What's that?" Aiden asked.

"She can't erase me." She dropped her head back against the headboard and sighed. "I'm still not sure how I'll let her know. The idea of talking to her makes me nauseous."

"Then don't talk to her. There will be around three hundred people at the Gallery Ball. You could see her there without her knowing."

She nodded. "I could blend in."

"No, you could never blend in," Aiden said, a smile in his voice. He didn't tell her that every eye would be on her. She could attend wearing jeans and a T-shirt, and she would be the most beautiful woman there. Oh hell, he had it bad tonight. He hadn't slept in more than twenty-four hours, and that was probably why he was having so much trouble controlling his reaction to her. That and the fact that every time he looked at her he remembered how she'd responded when he'd kissed her, how her scent had aroused him, how she'd tasted, and how she'd felt in his arms. She sure as certain had rattled him.

There had been a mound of work to get done before he left Chicago. Sydney wasn't on his schedule for another month, and yet on the spur of the moment he had made the decision to take Cordelia there. He didn't like the idea of her going by herself. Yes, she was a capable adult and usually levelheaded, but she'd lost her father and had found out some damning information about the woman who had given birth to her. Besides, she would be walking into a hornet's nest. Simone and Craig Rayburn and Simone's father, Julian Taylor, were considered upper crust in Sydney society, and Julian abhorred scandal. In all the photos taken of them at various events, he was standing with Simone and Craig, but he was never smiling. He appeared to be a real prick. Aiden realized he was jumping to conclusions, but where Cordelia was concerned, he wasn't taking any chances. If and when she met the family, he would be by her side. He probably should tell her what he had decided, knowing full well she would argue fiercely, but it wouldn't matter. He would get his way.

Alec had enlisted Liam Scott to look out for Cordelia while she was in Sydney. Aiden had done a little research on him, too, and he didn't like what he'd read. There was very little actual information, but there were photos, and in every one of them Liam had a pretty woman on his arm. He was obviously a player, and that was the last thing Cordelia needed now, someone trying to get her in his bed. Aiden knew he was being extremely territorial. She didn't have to answer to him. It didn't matter, though. As long as she was in Australia, she sure as hell did belong to him.

"How about the Gallery Ball on the twentieth? I'll be invited, and you'll be my guest. What do you think?" he asked her.

She didn't answer him. Her head was on his shoulder. He nudged her chin up and then smiled. She was sound asleep. Yawning, he asked softly, "Was I that boring?"

He put the laptop on the table and eased her down on the bed so that her head could rest on the pillow. He started to pull away, then changed his mind. Reaching up, he turned the light off and pulled her into his side with the top of her head nestled under his chin. He rubbed his jaw against her silky hair. The wonderful fragrance of peach shampoo mingling with her own feminine scent aroused him. It was odd to feel strangely content when he was with her. Too tired to try to figure it out, he wrapped his arms around her and went to sleep.

ELEVEN

Cordie knew she would like Sydney, but as it turned out, it was love at first sight. She had done quite a lot of reading about the beautiful city and the friendly people who lived there, and she'd seen countless photos of the special attractions. The Sydney Opera House, a performing arts center and one of Australia's proudest icons, was featured in many of the photos Cordie had seen, and she'd thought it was pretty, especially with the lights at night bringing it to life, but the photos really didn't do it justice. Seeing it in person, Cordie was in awe. It was magnificent. And so was the Harbour Bridge.

It was closing in on midnight when they circled the city and landed. A car was waiting to take them to the new Hamilton, which overlooked the harbor. Even though she was determined to avoid Aiden whenever possible, she felt it would be disloyal to stay at any other hotel.

She had made her reservation for a single room, but when they arrived at the hotel, she wasn't given a choice. She was about to check in at the desk when Aiden grabbed her hand and pulled her in the opposite direction. As they passed through the lobby, every member of the staff smiled, looking genuinely happy to see their boss, and, from the bell captain to the front-desk clerk to the concierge, Aiden greeted each of them by name. Cordie tried to pull away, but he merely tightened his hold and continued on toward the bank of elevators. Unwilling to make a scene, she decided to wait until they were alone to give him a piece of her mind.

Yes, Aiden owned the hotel, and yes, he was used to getting his way; however, it didn't make it right for him to be so high-handed with her. He didn't ask where she wanted to stay. He pushed the button for the top floor and simply told her she would be sharing the two-bedroom penthouse suite with him.

"What is it with you and top floors?"

He flashed a smile. "I like being on top."

Her mind immediately went to sex, and even though she tried, she couldn't block the image of Aiden naked and sweaty on top of her. She could feel her cheeks warming and bowed her head so he wouldn't notice.

The elevator doors opened, and they walked into a wide foyer. The suite was gorgeous. Ahead was a large living room decorated with plush sofas and chairs and fresh flowers on nearly every table. To the side was a spacious dining area with a rectangular table of marble and mahogany and a fully stocked bar behind it. The colors in the suite were rich earth tones: creams and browns and bronzes, with accents of black. It was contemporary and masculine yet refined and elegant. But the real attention-getter was the view. One entire wall was glass from floor to twelve-foot-high ceiling, and beyond was the spectacular Harbour Bridge. Cordie was a bit overwhelmed by it all.

The bellman carried in her two bags and deposited them in the bedroom on the left. Aiden had only a small carry-on and his briefcase. He went into the bedroom on the right and opened a door that revealed a walk-in closet filled with clothes. He set his bag on a chest of drawers and came out to a desk in his bedroom, where he placed his briefcase.

Cordie stood outside his door watching him arrange his laptop and some files on the desk. "You don't ever let guests stay here? Just you?"

"Regan and Alec can stay here, and Spencer, of course."

"What about Walker?" she asked.

His jaw tightened. "No," he said curtly.

He obviously hadn't worked out his issues with his youngest brother. Regan had told her about their troublesome sibling, and Cordie was fairly certain it was all the lawsuits Walker had caused with his careless lifestyle that were weighing on Aiden's mind. He usually attacked problems head-on. It wasn't like him to ignore or bury whatever was bothering him, but this was a family matter, and that made it different and more difficult.

"Do you have your schedule for tomorrow?" He asked the question without looking up as he opened his computer and powered it on.

"My schedule?" She almost laughed. Rigid schedules and Aiden were one and the same. "I thought I'd rent a car, get a map from the concierge, and see some of the city."

"You have a car and driver." Leaving the computer screen open, he passed her on his way through the living room to the bar. He got a bottle of water out of the built-in refrigerator, handed it to her, and reached for another. "Tell the truth, Cordelia. You've got the Rayburns' address, and you want to drive by, see their house, right?"

She shrugged. "Maybe."

"They live in a gated community. You'll have to scale the wall in order to see their house." He grinned, picturing it.

"That isn't going to happen," she said. "And how do you know where they live?"

"I had one of my assistants look them up," he explained.

"I do want to see them without their knowing."

"The Gallery Ball will be the perfect time, then," he said. "Remember, I told you the Rayburns will be attending the ball. It's a benefit for the arts. They have one every year."

"And you're invited every year?"

"Yes."

"Have you ever gone?"

"No," he answered. "But I'm a benefactor."

"Meaning you give them money."

"Yes."

"And you're sure they'll be there?"

"Louis sent me the guest list I showed you. The Rayburns were on it. So was Simone's father, Julian Taylor."

"Who is Louis?"

"One of my managers. He pretty much runs this hotel."

"Okay, then," she said. "I'd like to go to the ball with you if that's all right."

"Of course."

Aiden returned to his bedroom, went straight to his computer, and pulled up his e-mails, his plan to get some work done. He could operate at full capacity on three hours of sleep a night, and he had almost eighty messages to get through.

"Cordelia?" he called. He looked through the open door and could see she hadn't moved from her spot in the living room.

"Yes?"

"What's the matter? You're standing there looking frozen," Aiden remarked. Concerned, he added, "You don't have to do anything you don't want to do."

"I know. I was just wondering if I'm going to cringe when I see her."

"You'll be fine," he predicted. "Now, get some sleep."

Walking toward her bedroom she asked over her shoulder, "When is the ball?"

"Saturday."

"That soon? That's only three days away." She was ready to protest but stopped herself. "I can do it," she said, deciding she could shop for a ball gown tomorrow, beg for quick alterations—nothing ever fit off the rack—and be ready by Saturday night.

"Two days, Cordelia. It's Thursday now."

"No, it's . . ."

"Time difference," he reminded her. "Sydney is a day ahead of us."

She'd forgotten the time change, and she was completely rattled. Only two days to get mentally ready to come face-to-face with Simone. "I'll have to shop to find something suitable . . . I don't usually pack a ball gown when I travel."

"Louis knows who to call. He'll help you tomorrow. Now, get some rest."

She didn't argue. She was tired and out of sorts, but sleep eluded her. Aiden was the reason. She couldn't stop thinking about him. Boston was going to be her salvation, she remembered. All she had to do was get through this trip. Once she was away from him, she wouldn't have to see his blond beauty queens hanging on his arm, wouldn't have to put up with any of that nonsense, and wouldn't have to constantly pretend it didn't bother her that he completely ignored her. She would be alone, and that was what she wanted. Right?

When she finally crashed, she slept hard and didn't wake until after nine the next morning. Her eyes slowly opened and squinted against the bright sun shining through her window. It took her a few seconds to get her bearings, and then she threw back the thick duvet and sat on the side of the bed, watching a tall ship glide its way into the harbor. She detected the aroma of fresh-brewed coffee coming from the next room, but she wasn't a coffee drinker. She preferred an icy-cold Diet Coke to wake her up. After she showered and dressed in a short pale-pink dress and nude flats, she put her hair in a ponytail and went in search of caffeine. She walked into the living room and came to a quick stop. Aiden was standing by the window with two other men in suits. They all turned when she entered the room. In his black suit and crisp white shirt, Aiden looked refreshed and completely put together. Nothing new about that, she thought grudgingly.

"Good morning," she said softly. "I didn't mean to interrupt. I'll just get a Diet Coke and be out of your way."

"Cordelia, I'd like you to meet Louis. He'll set your schedule for today."

A young man with sandy hair and handsome hazel eyes came forward to shake her hand.

Aiden nodded toward the other man. "And this is Cavanaugh. He'll be your driver while we're here."

Cavanaugh was either a fitness trainer or a bodyguard, and she was betting on her second guess. He was tall and as solid as a hundred-year-old oak and had the neck to prove it. He, too, came forward to shake her hand. Then he gave her his card with his phone number.

"Keep this with you, please. I'll be in the lobby," he explained. "Whenever you're ready, call or text me and I'll bring the car around."

She didn't feel it was appropriate to argue because Cavanaugh was following orders, but she did not need a driver. It seemed a waste of his time to wait around for her.

"Aiden, may I have a word?"

He was flipping through some papers but paused to look at her. "What do you need?" he asked impatiently.

She turned back to Louis. "Did he say you'll set my schedule?" she asked, wondering what exactly that meant.

Louis handed her a sheet of stationery with times and locations listed. "I took the liberty of making an appointment for you at Chasnoff's dress shop first. It's quite exclusive and isn't open to the public," he explained. "It's by appointment only, and you're scheduled for eleven o'clock this morning. The owner has been given approximate specifications and should have a good selection of ball gowns for you to try on."

"By 'approximate specifications' you mean measurements?"

"Yes, that's right."

"Who came up with my measurements?"

"I did," Aiden said, grinning. "I guessed."

She didn't know what to say, but the bell saved her from the awkward conversation. Louis opened the door for a waiter who pushed in a cart filled with food. He went to the dining table, set two places, and proceeded to lay out a spread worthy of a king. Besides the usual breakfast fare of eggs, bacon, scones, yogurt, and granola, there was a huge bowl of every kind of fruit imaginable.

Louis handed Cordie a card with his cell phone number, and then he and Cavanaugh left. She immediately headed to the refrigerator to get her Diet Coke. She put ice in a glass and carried the bottle over to the table and sat. She didn't realize how hungry she was until she took a bite of the buttery scone.

Aiden joined her. "I've got meetings all day," he said as he poured himself a cup of coffee from the silver carafe. "But I wanted to talk to you before I left."

"Okay. What would you like to talk about?" she asked as she popped a plump, ripe strawberry into her mouth.

"The Rayburns," he said. "They're a prominent family here in Sydney, and their status comes primarily from Simone's family owning Merrick Enterprises. Craig and Simone are a power couple. Craig Rayburn works for Merrick, and he's become quite wealthy because of it. From the lifestyle he lives, he certainly knows how to spend money."

"Which is probably why Simone married him. Money is important to her. It certainly wasn't because of his looks. Though it's cruel of me to say, he reminds me of a bulldog."

Aiden laughed. "I think the photo of the family that Alec found was fairly recent . . . and now that you mention it, he did look a little like a bulldog."

Serious once again, Aiden continued. "Craig and Simone have become pillars of the community. They're major benefactors to half a dozen institutions, everything from hospitals to universities. They're often seen together at various functions. By all accounts, the Rayburns are a model family, and the sons treat their mother like a queen."

Cordie pushed her plate away. The thought of Simone surrounded by an adoring family made her suddenly lose her appetite.

Aiden continued. "You're about to drop a grenade into their lives. We need to anticipate their reaction."

He'd included himself in the plan, and she thought that was terribly nice of him. Aiden could actually be very considerate and kind when he wanted to be. In fact, on numerous occasions she'd seen him come to the rescue of someone who needed help. Yes, he was domineering and bossy, but when he let his guard down, there was definitely a softer side to him. Maybe it was jet lag, but right now all she could think about was kissing him. She suddenly realized she was staring at his mouth, so she closed her eyes and took a breath. Get a little control, she told herself.

"Are you falling asleep on me?" Aiden asked, shaking her from her fantasy.

She laughed. "Just jet leg."

"Did you hear what I said?"

"About the grenade? Yes, I did."

"I don't like going in without a plan, so you've got until tomorrow night to decide exactly what you want to do. Agreed?"

"Agreed."

She watched him pick up his cell phone and keys, slip them into his pocket. He opened his briefcase and deposited the papers he'd been reading earlier. "If you need anything, just ask Louis." He snapped the case closed and walked out the door.

Cordie checked her watch. It was almost eleven, so she went to her room and called for the car. Cavanaugh was waiting just inside the lobby doors. It was a beautiful day, a bit on the chilly side, in the high fifties, and she was glad she'd carried along a lightweight coat. Cavanaugh reminded her that it was winter now in Sydney, which made her smile. Compared to winter in Chicago and Boston, Sydney was Utopia. Traffic was just as congested, though. It took a long while to get to the dress shop. There wasn't a name on the door, and there wasn't a front window with pretty dresses on display. It was almost as though Chasnoff's was hiding the fact that it was in business.

Miss Marie, an older woman with a no-nonsense attitude, met her at the door and introduced herself. She took Cordie by the arm and led her into the back of the shop, where a seamstress waited along with two salesladies eager to assist. The room Cordie was ushered into didn't have any windows, but the white walls and white carpet made it seem quite large. There were three wingback chairs in a semicircle, and directly ahead was a carpet-covered circular platform that faced three huge mirrors guaranteed to show every flaw.

Miss Marie was thrilled with Cordie's figure. "It's about time I dressed someone who isn't built like a stick. And those eyes. Your fabulous eyes. You must wear a sapphire-blue gown. I insist. You really are stunning, you know."

No, she didn't know, and she wasn't sure how to respond to the exaggerated compliments. Stunning? Miss Marie was obviously nearsighted.

"We'll take care of everything," she continued. "Your undergarments, makeup, gowns, and dresses, and of course wraps. Shall we get started?"

"I just need one ball gown," Cordie explained.

"Those weren't my instructions from Mr. Madison," she replied.

Cordie tried to argue, but Miss Marie wasn't paying her any attention. For the next three and a half hours Cordie tried on beautiful gowns and dresses and skirts and wonderful silk blouses. Miss Marie and her staff treated her like a mannequin, tugging and pulling and pretty much ignoring any of her opinions, but once Miss Marie was finished, Cordie had a new name for her . . . Miracle Worker.

Cavanaugh was waiting for her when she walked out of the shop. He drove her back to the hotel by way of a scenic route. She had wanted to experience some of the city, but jet lag wasn't through with her. All she wanted now was a hot bath and a bed.

She didn't see Aiden that night or the next morning. He had already left for yet another round of meetings by the time she awoke, so she called down to Cavanaugh, who took her on a sightseeing tour. They rode the ferry around the harbor. It was drizzling, but Cordie didn't mind. In her estimation the afternoon was perfect. Seeing the spectacular city from this vantage point only made her want to see more.

Miss Marie and two assistants arrived at the penthouse at promptly six o'clock. They came in with a rack filled with clothes hidden by garment bags. Cordie was rendered speechless when she was told all of the clothes were for her. Since most of the items had been altered, she couldn't send them back.

Once again she was treated like a mannequin. They tugged and pulled, spackled, sprayed, and curled, and by seven thirty the transformation was complete. Her hair was brushed back and fashioned into curls with loose tendrils floating down to the base of her neck. In the past, Cordie had always applied makeup sparingly. She never used eyeliner or shadow. Occasionally she would brush on a little mascara, but that was rare. Miss Marie, however, had her own ideas and went to town with her makeup kit, all the while chastising Cordie for ignoring her incredible features. Never in her career, she said, had she seen such a flawless complexion, such beautiful eyes, such full lips. When she finally let Cordie look in the mirror, she barely recognized herself. Her eyes, her face, her body, had been transformed. Miss Marie really was a miracle worker.

The gown, in a color that matched her eyes exactly, was exquisite. It had a plunging scoop neckline, and the bodice fit so perfectly it looked as though it was molded to her body. The floor-length skirt was straight with a slit that reached the top of her knee. Cordie had never worn anything so magnificent and didn't think it could possibly be improved on, and then Miss Marie handed her a hooded cape. It was black velvet with a lining the same sapphire blue as the dress. Miss Marie even provided a small beaded clutch. Cordie couldn't believe the vision that stared back at her in the mirror and decided she didn't want to know how much it was all going to cost her. One huge splurge in her life was all right. Besides, she was going to a ball with Aiden.

She felt like a princess in a fairy tale. Too bad Aiden wasn't acting like Prince Charming. He had knocked on her door several times and reminded her they were going to be late if she didn't hurry up. From the frown he gave her when she finally joined him in the living room, she concluded he was more of an ogre than a prince. He obviously was irritated at her for making him wait, and his only comment when he saw her was negative.

"That top doesn't cover much."

"Thank you," she said sweetly. "You look nice, too." She smiled as she gave the jab.

It was an understatement. Aiden in a tuxedo was perfection . . . even with a frown on his face.

"You're beautiful, Cordelia. That color suits you," he said, seeming a bit contrite.

"I *should* look beautiful. It took a team of women to make this," she said, putting her arms out as she did a slow turn.

"A team, huh?"

"I'm serious."

He laughed. "I know. Are you ready?"

As he was helping her with her cape, he bent down close to her ear and whispered, "I like your perfume."

His warm breath on her neck made her shiver. She wanted to lean into him but took a step forward instead. "Shall we go?" she asked.

He pushed the elevator button. "Have you decided what you're going to do?"

"Yes. I've given it a lot of thought. I still don't want to talk to her, but I have a letter for her. I'll ask a waiter to give it to her."

"You wrote a letter?" He waited for her to answer. She was biting her lip and staring down at the bag clutched in her hands as though still weighing her decision. She didn't answer his question.

"I want to see the look in her eyes when I give her the shock of her life. If that makes me petty, so be it."

Cavanaugh was waiting for them. He did a double take when he saw Cordie, but Aiden's frown stopped him from making a comment.

The Gallery Ball was being held at the Hoffman-Sitz Center, which was located just a few miles south of the hotel. Town cars and limos lined the drive to the front doors in a slow procession. Cordie's stomach was in knots. She was too nervous to talk, and Aiden must have noticed her unease, because he took hold of her hand.

"I can feel you trembling."

"I'm a bit anxious," she admitted. "I'm afraid I might do something to humiliate you."

He was astounded by her worry. He looked into her eyes and smiled. "Nothing you could do would ever humiliate me."

Wanna bet? she thought. It was a terribly kind thing for him to say to her, but also totally untrue. "So if I lose it completely and go for Simone's throat, you won't be bothered?"

"Not at all," he said with a straight face. "Do you plan to go for her throat?"

The laughter in his voice made her smile. "I might."

They came to a stop in front of the steps leading up to the doors. A valet came forward, an open umbrella at the ready.

"I'll be around the corner waiting for your call to collect you," Cavanaugh said.

It was beginning to drizzle, so Cordie pulled the hood of the cape over her head. She took Aiden's arm and went up the steps, lifting the hem of her gown as she moved along.

Aiden wanted to find a spot where Cordelia could watch the crowd. He suspected every eye would be on her as soon as she removed her cape, and he was right. He even heard several gasps. In case they needed to make a hasty exit, he didn't check her cape. He draped it over his arm, took hold of her hand, and led her into the gathering.

The main ballroom was like a huge and beautiful inverted fishbowl, circular with a leaded-glass dome overhead. Guests entered on the first level, which wrapped around the room, and a ring of steps led down to a round dance floor. Huge pillars soared to the ceiling, and between these were small round tables that sat no more than four people, perfect spots for the guests to observe the orchestra stage at the far end of the room and the dancers below. The colors were muted, which made the colorful gowns the women wore all the more vibrant.

They had walked halfway around the circle before Aiden stopped. From where they stood, they could easily see the entrance and all of the dance floor. He draped her cape over one of the chairs and turned to the entrance, satisfied that the pillar next to them would conceal Cordelia from the crowd but still allow a wide view.

"It's chilly in here," she remarked.

It wasn't, but he decided to agree. He put his arm around her and drew her closer. "Better?"

"Yes," she answered, grateful for his warmth and his reassuring hug.

Aiden knew quite a few of the guests, and as the ballroom began to fill, several couples stopped to say hello. While Aiden was politely shaking hands, Cordie noticed a very good-looking man making his way toward them. He was in his thirties, with brown hair streaked blond by the sun and a smile that would make most women weak in the knees. His hair covered his collar, longer than what was considered fashionable, and she made the deduction that he was a nonconformist. She couldn't stop staring at him. He looked almost as good as Aiden in his tuxedo. He was every bit as tall, though not as lean. His clear green eyes seemed to sparkle with mischief.

Aiden had been talking to a young man who was trying very hard to sell his company's services to the Hamilton Hotels, but out of the corner of his eye Aiden was watching the approaching man. He knew who he was. He dismissed the enthusiastic young man by saying, "I'm not in the habit of discussing business at these affairs. If you'll call my office and make an appointment, we'll talk." He didn't take his eyes off the man coming their way.

The man stopped just a foot away from Cordie, and his smile widened. She couldn't help but notice the adorable dimple in his cheek.

"Cordie."

"Yes?"

"I'm Liam Scott."

He took her hand, pulling her to him. Aiden still had his arm around her shoulders and wasn't letting go. A tug-of-war ensued until Cordie stopped it by extracting her hand from Liam's and shrugging Aiden's arm away. Liam's greeting was not over. He bent down and kissed her on both cheeks. He finally turned to Aiden and shook his hand.

"Aiden," he said briskly.

"Liam," Aiden responded curtly.

Aiden didn't have to be reminded of Alec's warning that Liam was a womanizer. The way the man was looking at Cordelia was all the evidence he needed, and Aiden didn't like it one bit. He was downright rude when he asked, "What are you doing here?"

"I wouldn't miss it," he said, keeping his gaze locked on Cordelia. "I'm a patron of the arts."

Cordie didn't know what Aiden's problem was. There was absolutely no reason to be so antagonistic. "Then you attend these Gallery Balls each year?" she asked.

"No, this is my first." He added as he tugged on his collar, "And hopefully my last."

Aiden wasn't amused. "Again, why are you here?" he asked, and before Liam could answer, Aiden guessed, "Alec sent you, didn't he?"

Liam nodded. "He wanted me to meet Cordie."

"And you chose the Gallery Ball to introduce yourself?"

Liam shrugged. "From what Alec told me about Cordie, I was curious to meet her as soon as I could."

"What did he tell you about her?" Aiden folded his arms across his chest so he wouldn't give in to the urge to shove Liam down the steps. He had taken an instant dislike to him and wasn't in the mood to play games.

"He said she was drop-dead gorgeous." Turning to Cordie, he said, "He was right."

She could feel herself blushing and wanted to turn the discussion away from herself. "Alec mentioned you used to work for Interpol?"

Liam gave her a quizzical look and then began to laugh. "He said that, did he?"

"You didn't work for Interpol?" she asked, confused.

Evidently he thought her question hilarious, because his laughter grew louder until she could almost see tears in his eyes. "Alec does have a sense of humor. I didn't work for them. I was wanted by Interpol. It was all a misunderstanding," he said offhandedly. "A painting was there, and then it wasn't, but then it was again. See? Just a misunderstanding."

Cordie couldn't tell if he was joking or not, but she wasn't given the chance to pursue the subject because Liam grew serious when he turned the conversation to another matter.

"Now it's my turn to ask questions," he said. "What are you going to do when Simone and Craig Rayburn arrive? I've already checked. You don't have a gun, so I know you aren't going to shoot them. What's the plan?"

Aiden answered for her. "Cordelia wants to give Simone the shock of her life, but she doesn't want to talk to her."

"Then how is she going to shock her?" He turned to Cordie. "Did you bring a Taser? That would shock the hell out of her."

"No, I—" Cordie began.

"Because if you didn't," he continued, "I've got one in the car you can borrow." He looked around at the gathering crowd. "Are you hiding behind this pillar?"

"No, of course not," she said, knowing full well it was a lie. "I'm waiting for the Rayburns to arrive."

He grinned. "So you can shock them."

Liam was having a bit too much fun for her liking. Before she could tell him so, he changed the subject again by asking her how she liked Sydney and then launching into a litany of the attractions she should see. As he spoke, he took her hand and pulled out a chair at the table for her. He sat down next to her and leaned in, focusing on her as though she were the only person in the room. She could tell that Aiden was trying his best to remain composed and polite, but he was not happy about Liam's intrusion. He looked as though he was about to say something when a man came up and greeted him. From that point on he was distracted by a steady stream of men and women who recognized him. Each man wanted to talk about various projects he just knew Aiden would want to invest in, and each woman simply wanted Aiden. Cordie couldn't blame the women. Aiden was what she'd heard one of them call a real catch, and from the way they were eyeing Liam, he was just as attractive to females on the prowl. Cordie wasn't immune to Liam's good looks and charm, but in her estimation he paled in comparison to Aiden. She thought that was a pity. She desperately wanted to be attracted to another man.

A waiter appeared with glasses of champagne on a silver tray. Cordie was so nervous she had to force herself not to guzzle the drink. There was a short welcoming speech by the president of something or other—she wasn't paying attention—and then the orchestra began to play.

Aiden extricated himself from his growing entourage and walked over to Liam. "I'd like a word with you, Scott," he said, his tone downright belligerent.

Liam looked up. "Sure, go ahead."

"I don't believe you've answered my question yet. Why are you here?"

Liam pushed the chair back and stood. "Alec thought there might be trouble, and I owe him a favor, so here I am. He's worried about Cordie."

"I can take care of Cordelia." Aiden's voice radiated anger.

Liam wasn't fazed by the heated response. "And I can take care of Rayburn and his sons . . . if there's trouble."

Cordie rolled her eyes. She wasn't impressed by the testosterone throwdown. She stood between the two men and sweetly said, "How about I take care of myself?"

"Heads up," Liam said, looking over Cordie's shoulder.

Cordie and Aiden turned toward the entrance.

"The Rayburns are here," Aiden said.

TWELVE

Simone and Craig Rayburn seemed to be the in couple.

They stopped just inside the entrance, apparently oblivious to the fact that they were clogging the pathway for other guests behind them as they greeted friends and business associates. Craig removed Simone's wrap and handed it to a hovering coat-check lady, then took Simone's elbow and guided her through the crowd. They slowly made their way to the opposite side of the ballroom, pausing again and again to chat with people vying for their attention. Cordie couldn't get a good look at Simone because other guests obstructed her view. She saw Craig clearly, though, and the bulldog comparison was even more accurate than she'd imagined. His jutting lower jaw was rather impressive, and his bottom teeth showed when he spoke. He wasn't an attractive man by anyone's standards, but from the way people were reacting to him, he obviously had achieved a certain level of stature among the wealthy elite. Shaking hands and kissing cheeks, he worked the room with great finesse. Each person he greeted seemed happy, even thrilled, at his attention, and there was no doubt he relished all the adulation. His smile seemed genuine enough, but there was a hint of arrogance behind it.

The couple reached their reserved table and took their seats. After a few minutes, their friends gradually drifted away to their own tables, and Cordie saw Simone clearly for the first time. She wore a shimmering silver strapless gown. In person, Cordie didn't think they looked all that much alike. Simone's hair was just as dark as hers and she seemed to be the same height, but their body shapes were different. Simone was extremely thin. She didn't have any curves or an ounce of fat, though judging by her skinny sculpted arms, she worked out daily. Simone turned toward the dance floor. Cordie couldn't see the color of her eyes, though she guessed they were blue. In the photo Alec had shown her, Cordie saw the resemblance, but now she was having trouble finding the similarities. Some would consider Simone a beautiful woman, but compared to the picture, the angles of her face were sharper and more defined. She was in her forties now, so the lines were probably because of age and stress. No, that wasn't true. Simone wasn't affected by stress—she caused it. Others might think they looked alike, but Cordie didn't want there to be any resemblance at all.

Aiden put a supportive arm around her shoulders. He leaned down and whispered, "Are you okay?"

"I don't want to look like her," Cordie said.

"I know."

Cordie couldn't take her eyes off the couple. They were having a fine old time. Craig said something Simone thought was quite funny. She put her hand on his chest, laughed, and shook her head.

Alec had filled Liam in on Cordie's situation, and Liam hadn't really had an opinion until this moment, but watching Simone laughing and carrying on with her husband and her friends, as though she was a queen holding court, he felt a jolt of anger for Cordie. Simone had accomplished the impossible. She had successfully rewritten history.

Craig suddenly spotted someone in the crowd. He stood and waved to draw their attention. Cordie turned in that direction and saw the Rayburns' two sons, Glen and Knox, enter the ballroom.

"The sons look like their father," Liam remarked. "That's a real shame."

The brothers were not handsome, but they were impeccably dressed in their designer tuxedos, and they exuded unusual confidence for such young men. Cordie guessed the older brother, Glen, was around eighteen. They headed straight for their parents, and Simone greeted them with a broad smile as they approached. When each son embraced his mother warmly, Cordie felt a blow, like a fist to the stomach. She was outraged, and the longer she watched the outwardly touching scene of family affection, the angrier she became. This was the woman her father had loved, the one he had ached to see again. She had lied to him and caused him so much pain. All those years were wasted as he pined for Natalie Smith, a woman who didn't exist.

Cordie reached for her beaded bag and took out the letter she'd sealed in a hotel envelope. Stopping a passing waiter, she handed the letter to him and pointed across the room to Simone as she gave him instructions.

Liam watched with growing curiosity. "I know it isn't my business, but may I ask what's in the envelope? Is Simone going to go postal when she sees it?"

Aiden was just as curious, but he had intended to wait until they were back in the car to find out. "If you don't want to tell us what you wrote—" he began.

"I didn't write a letter," she said quietly, her eyes still on Simone.

"Then what's in the envelope?" Aiden asked.

"A copy of the letter she left for my father. I thought she might want to read it again. Years have passed since she wrote it, and she might have forgotten some of the cruel things she said. I wanted to remind her and to let her know . . ." Her voice drifted off as her attention remained fixed on Simone and her family.

Neither Liam nor Aiden asked any more questions. They kept their eyes on the waiter, watching him weave in and out of the crowd to get to Simone.

Craig Rayburn had left his wife's side and was sitting at a table with friends. A couple came up the stairs from the dance floor and stopped to talk to Simone just as the waiter reached her. Smiling, Simone took the envelope and walked a few feet away from her friends before she opened it.

Cordie watched her pull the letter out and unfold it. Simone didn't have to read much to know what it was. She stiffened, and there was such a look of panic on her face it was almost as though she had seen something grotesque. She frantically looked to her left, then to her right, as she folded the letter and refolded it. Mindless of where she was, she stuffed the letter down the bodice of her gown. Out of sight, out of mind? Was that her mantra? For a brief second or two she looked terrified. Glancing around one last time to see if anyone was watching, she again plastered a serene expression on her face and rejoined her friends.

Cordie wasn't through taking the woman down memory lane. She wanted one more jab to make certain Simone understood that she hadn't gotten away with her little scam, that the daughter she'd tried to erase knew what she had done. She didn't intend to cause a scene or confront Simone. She just wanted some vindication for her father, to make Simone realize her deceptions had not evaporated into thin air. They existed. Once she saw that recognition in Simone's eyes, Cordie would let go of the anger, never say Simone's name again, and get on with her own life.

Cordie walked around the table and took a spot in front of a pillar. Standing on the top step, she simply stared at Simone and waited.

Aiden wasn't sure what Cordelia planned to do, but he wasn't going to let her do it alone. Liam followed him. They stood on either side of her.

Across the room Simone was smiling and nodding, but her eyes were not on the people in front of her. She seemed to be distracted, impatiently looking around as though waiting for someone to jump out at her.

"Here comes good old dad," Liam said.

Julian Taylor, a tall, thin man who walked with an air of authority, was making his way toward his daughter, stopping to shake a few hands, and deigning to give a rigid smile to only a few people.

When Simone saw her father, her expression changed. Like someone who was looking for an escape, she glanced around the room in desperation. And that was when she saw Cordie. Her face turned white in an instant. She shook her head as though trying to change what she was seeing. Taking a step in retreat, she looked again at her father, and then stiffly turned back to Cordie, no doubt making sure she was still there. Cordie could detect a hint of anger now, and that surprised her.

She could almost see Simone's mind racing. How could she keep her father from seeing what she was seeing? She turned in his direction and her hand went to her throat. Letting out a soft cry, she slowly and dramatically fell to the floor. It was the most graceful and phony faint Cordie had ever seen. She wasn't the only one who noticed.

"Should we clap?" Aiden asked.

"You wanted to shock her," Liam reminded.

Cordie nodded. "Shall we go?"

Aiden draped her cape around her shoulders and took her hand. "You're sure you're finished here?"

"Oh yes," she said, smiling. "I'm finished." She looked across the ballroom one last time. A crowd had gathered around Simone, who was still pretending to be in a dead faint. Her husband had her in his arms and was talking to his sons as he nodded toward the entrance.

Liam walked to the doors with Cordie and Aiden, who had already texted Cavanaugh to tell him to bring the car around. He was suddenly anxious to get Cordelia away.

"You could tear that family apart just by telling them who you are," Liam remarked.

She shook her head. "I don't want to destroy her family. Like I said, I just wanted her to know. Now I'm finished. I don't ever want to hear her name again."

Seeing one of the Rayburns' sons pushing his way through the crowd and heading to the entrance, Aiden increased the pace.

Cavanaugh pulled up just as they exited the building.

"It was a pleasure meeting you both," Liam said. He shook Aiden's hand and then turned to Cordie, taking her hand in both of his. "I'll call you tomorrow."

Aiden thought the good-bye was lasting longer than necessary, so he took Cordelia by the arm and ushered her into the backseat.

Cordie was quiet on the way back to the hotel. She was thankful Aiden wasn't asking her questions, because she wasn't ready to talk about the Rayburns. The only good thing she could say about them was that they lived on a different continent and she would never have to worry about running into them. She stared out the window. Her hands were shaking and she was spent. Taking deep breaths, she tried to slow her racing heart. She had been so nervous the entire time she was at the Gallery Ball, but now it was over, and she could relax and get rid of her anxiety. She just wasn't sure how to go about it. Yoga would help. At least that's what Regan often told her.

Yoga was good for stress, she'd said. She had even bought Cordie a yoga mat. Whatever had she done with it? she wondered. She'd have to search for it when she got home.

Aiden finished listening to his messages and reading his texts, then turned to Cordelia and said, "Have you calmed down?"

"I've always been calm. Why would you think I wasn't?"

"You were hyperventilating, and your face was red. It isn't now, so you must be feeling a bit calmer." He added, "But you're still frowning."

"I'm fine."

"No, you're not."

"I'm just trying to remember where I put my yoga mat."

He wasn't buying her obvious attempt to look relaxed. "You do yoga?"

"No."

"But you have a mat."

"Yes, Regan gave it to me. Yoga helps with stress."

He put his hand on top of hers. She was still shaking. "Would you like to go out to eat, or do you want to go back to the hotel and do yoga?"

She didn't acknowledge his wisecrack. "Back to the hotel."

"Then that's what we'll do."

"You could go out. You could drop me off if you want."

He laughed. "I could? Thanks."

Cordie really did relax then. For a while there, Aiden had been a sympathetic, almost loving, man, but now he was back to being his arrogant and impertinent self, and she felt a sense of normalcy again.

Several minutes passed in silence, and then Cordie said, "I'm going to have to wear this beautiful gown somewhere else so I won't associate it with them."

"'Them' being the Rayburns?"

"Yes. It probably cost a fortune," she said. Her fingers gently brushed the fabric of her skirt. "Miss Marie's bill for all the outfits will be astronomical. Oh, I know what you're thinking. I can afford it, right? My father left me a fortune. That's true; however, I'm going to be sensible about it. I'm not used to spending that kind of money on clothes, and designer labels are lost on me. My father was a generous man, but I've always survived on my own. I taught in a Catholic high school, for Pete's sake. Do you know what the teachers make? Zip. They make zip."

She continued her running monologue until they pulled up in front of the hotel. Aiden helped her out of the car, waited while she thanked Cavanaugh, and then said, "The bill will be zip."

"What does that mean?" she asked.

As they crossed the lobby, Aiden twice stopped to answer questions from the staff. He inserted his card in the elevator slot, and the doors opened.

"The bill was taken care of," he said as they entered and the doors closed.

"By whom? Oh no, Aiden. I'm paying for my clothes, not you."

He was ignoring her while he read a text. She poked him in his chest. "I said—"

"I heard you."

"All right, then."

She assumed he had agreed with her. Mollified, she said, "I appreciate the offer. I don't want you to think I'm not grateful . . . Oh my God, you're so rude," she declared, raising her voice. "You shouldn't text while someone is talking to you."

Her indignation was short-lived. His smile could melt the hardest of hearts. He put his phone back in his pocket just as the elevator doors opened to their foyer.

"What do you want to eat? You haven't had dinner," he said.

"I'm not hungry." She hurried across the living room to get to her bedroom. "Maybe just a hamburger. That would be nice . . . and French fries. I really shouldn't have fries . . . and a milk shake. Chocolate, please. I deserve it after the night I've had."

He stood in the middle of the foyer watching her disappear into her room.

"And no cheese," she called out. "Oh, and pickles, please. Lots of pickles." As she was closing her door, she said, "That's a lot to remember. Just wait until I change, and I'll order."

Aiden looked around the living room and shook his head. Her scarf was on the back of the sofa. Her purse, which was the size of a suitcase, was on the floor, and her shoes were under a chair. What looked like a tube of lipstick was on the coffee table next to a pair of reading glasses and a leather-bound book he was sure had something to do with chemistry. On the wingback chair was a packet of tissues. Why in God's name would she leave tissues on a chair? It looked as though a whirlwind had gone through, but it was just clutter, he told himself. And he hated clutter. Yet her clutter didn't bother him. What was that about?

THIRTEEN

On her way to the bedroom Cordie pulled the pins out of her hair and ran her fingers through the thick strands. She should have taken off the gown before she washed her face, but she couldn't wait another second. The Spackle Miss Marie called makeup was making her skin itch like mad. She was careful not to get a single drop of water on the gown, and once she had patted her face dry and applied a little moisturizer, she felt so much better. Cinderella was gone, and plain old Cordie was back, which she much preferred. Dressing like a princess took way too much time and work, though she had to admit that walking into the Gallery Ball on Aiden's arm had been a little bit magical.

Carefully she removed the gown, hung it on the special hanger Miss Marie had provided, then zipped it in the garment bag and put it in the closet. It was chilly in her bedroom, so she slipped into a navy-blue silk nightgown. She didn't think her clingy silk robe would be appropriate, so she put on one of the thick terry-cloth robes the hotel provided.

Aiden knocked on the door. "Food's here."

He wasn't supposed to have ordered it, but she was glad he had because her stomach was grumbling. She hurried out into the living room. He had changed into a white undershirt and a pair of old jeans. They rode low on his hips, making him look all the more sexy.

Aiden, phone to his ear, pulled the chair from the table for her and handed her a napkin. She didn't know whom he was talking to, but from his tone of voice she could tell he wasn't happy with what he was hearing.

"Which leg?" she heard him ask. A few seconds later he said, "Yeah, I'll tell her hello."

He disconnected the call, dropped the phone on the table, and sat down across from her. "Spencer says hello."

"Did he have bad news?" she asked. "You sounded angry."

"Walker was in another crash."

"Was anyone hurt?" she asked.

"Just Walker," he answered. "He broke his right leg and destroyed a two-hundred-thousand-dollar Lamborghini."

Aiden's jaw clenched, and she knew the real reason he was so angry. "You don't care about the car. Walker could have killed himself. That's why you're so upset," she said.

He shrugged. "I'm too angry to be worried. He's not going to stop until he kills himself or someone else. It's going to be a disaster. I see it coming, but I can't . . ."

"Control him."

He nodded; then he abruptly changed the subject. "What did Liam mean when he said he would see you tomorrow?"

Cordie cut her hamburger in half and said, "This thing is huge. Would you like some?"

"No."

"You're just going to eat sushi? That's not very filling."

He reached across the table and took half of her hamburger. "Answer my question."

"While Liam and I were sitting at the table tonight, he asked me if I would like to climb to the top of the Harbour Bridge. It's a thing here," she added.

Smiling, he said, "Yes, I know."

"But you need to go before dawn."

He nodded again. "I know. I've done it. It's impressive, watching the sun come up over the water."

"It sounded exciting, but I declined."

"Why?"

"Climbing to the top of anything doesn't appeal to me."

"Are you afraid of heights?"

"Not unreasonably so."

"If you declined his invitation, why is he calling you tomorrow?"

"To do some sightseeing," she said. "I didn't know if I would be available or not."

"You won't be," he said firmly.

"I won't. Why not?"

"You'll be going with me."

His phone rang. He saw who was calling and said, "Sorry, I've got to take this." He stood and crossed the room to the window. Cordie ate half the hamburger and a couple of fries, but she didn't touch the milk shake. Her stomach hadn't calmed down as much as she had thought. She drank a bottle of water instead. When she was finished, she went back into her bathroom and brushed her teeth. Her mind was on Walker. He was so different from his brothers, Aiden and Spencer, and his sister. They were all hardworking and responsible. Walker wasn't. He never had been. He was the ultimate playboy, and she worried he didn't have any sense of right and wrong. She thought about that while she brushed her hair. How could that have happened with such moral siblings? Regan, especially, was such a kindhearted woman, always thinking about the needs of others. Walker seemed to have room to think only about himself. He had never had to work for anything. And maybe that was the problem. Aiden had always felt a certain responsibility for Walker and, as he did in his dealings with almost everyone, he needed to take charge, to make things right. Maybe it was time for Aiden to step back and take a long, hard look at his relationship with his brother. He needed to see that he couldn't change Walker . . . or save him from himself. She hated to watch the anxiety cross Aiden's face whenever his brother made another bad decision, but she wanted him to know she understood.

She went in search of Aiden. His phone was on the coffee table, but he was nowhere in sight. The table with their dinner had already been removed, though she hadn't heard anyone come in or leave. His bedroom door was open. She knocked and called his name.

"What do you need?" he asked. He was around the corner by the window plugging in his laptop.

She leaned against the doorframe. "Why do you always ask me that? I don't need anything. I think I'll start asking you that question every time you say hello. Then you'll see how irritating it is."

"Cordelia . . ." He said her name in what she thought was a warning voice.

"You left your phone in the living room."

"That's your phone. Mine's being charged."

"Oh." She was about to tell him what she had concluded about Walker, but she was unable to collect her thoughts or speak. He had the most intense look on his face.

Aiden couldn't stop staring. Was she aware of how provocative she looked? Her robe was open, and she was wearing a sexy low-cut nightgown that didn't reach her knees. God, she had a good body. No, he thought, it was a great body. He'd been fighting the battle to stay away from her all evening, and damn, it was difficult. If he was being totally honest, the battle had begun on the night he'd kissed her. From that moment on, no matter how hard he tried to forget her and block her from his mind, she kept wandering into his thoughts. Whether he was in a meeting, on a business call, or going about his daily routine, she was there in his head, playing with his concentration. Tonight, when she'd walked out in her ball gown, she'd looked like a gorgeous movie star, and he knew every man would fantasize about her. But now, seeing her stand there with her hair down and wearing no makeup, he was certain he'd never seen a more beautiful or more seductive woman in his life.

He began to walk toward her. She was like a magnet drawing him to her, and the closer he got, the more he wanted her. Her scent aroused him. And her mouth . . . He couldn't look at her sweet, full lips without thinking about all the ways she could please him.

As Aiden approached, Cordie's legs went weak. The smoldering lust in his eyes sent shivers down to her toes. He wanted her. The realization nearly overwhelmed her.

"Cordelia?" His voice was rough with his desire.

In a bare whisper she asked him the same question he always asked her. "What do you need, Aiden?"

He was just inches away from her now. "You. I need you."

"You do?" she whispered. She barely had enough breath to get the words out.

"I do," he said as he grabbed the lapels of her robe and pulled her toward him. Wrapping his arms around her, he held her tight against him as his mouth came down on hers. He made love to her with his mouth and his tongue, rubbing against hers, desperate for the taste of her again. Touching her had become addictive for him. Her lips were so soft, so sweet, and she was so giving and so damned sexy. All she had to do was look at him and he got hard.

Cordie wasn't passive. She threaded her fingers through his hair and kissed him just as passionately. She was as ravenous for him as he was for her. She couldn't get close enough, fast enough. In his arms all the anxiety and fear she'd felt at the ball were wiped away. Aiden made her forget everything but him. All that mattered was his touch.

By the time he ended the kiss, she was shaking with desire. He stepped back and stared into her eyes. He was panting as though he had run a long way. An endless minute passed in silence as tension crackled between them.

"Let me be clear." His voice shook.

She let out a long, raspy breath. She didn't know what to say, and so she simply nodded.

"I want you writhing under me, Cordelia. I want you to tell me what you like so I can drive you out of your mind. Am I clear?"

She nodded again. She was so flustered she couldn't speak. She could barely think.

"I want you clinging to me. I want your nails digging into my shoulders, and I want you screaming my name when you come."

She felt as though her heart was about to leap out of her chest. She was amazed she was still standing. His voice was so passionate, and the way he was looking at her made her hot . . . very hot.

He pulled his T-shirt over his head and tossed it on the bed. He reached for her robe next. She didn't resist as he removed it and dropped it on a chair.

"Take your nightgown off." It wasn't a request but a command.

She could barely catch her breath. She wanted him to take her into his arms again. The bedroom was cast in shadows, and she was thankful the lights weren't on, because once she removed her nightgown, she would be vulnerable. Her body wasn't perfect, and she knew Aiden was used to perfection with his women. She didn't want him to be disappointed.

"Cordelia, take off your nightgown."

With unsteady hands she reached for the straps and slowly pulled them down over her arms. She stopped when the material skimmed her breasts.

"Are you sure, Aiden?" She didn't want him to regret this night. It would kill her if he did.

Had he not been so aroused, he would have laughed. "Yes, I'm sure."

She took a deep breath and let the nightgown drop to the floor.

His gaze slowly moved down her body. "My God, you're beautiful."

Anxious now to hold her, Aiden stripped out of the rest of his clothes and reached for her. He lifted her into his arms and carried her to the bed. The sheets were pulled back. He gently placed her on the bed, then came down on top of her with a loud, satisfied growl.

Cordie was reeling from the contact of his hot muscular body on top of hers. He was all male, hard and hot, and oh, he smelled divine. Her senses were overwhelmed by him. He settled between her thighs, and she rubbed her toes against his legs while she stroked his shoulders. She wanted to touch him everywhere. His skin was so warm, but the muscles rolling beneath were hard.

Aiden was savoring the sensation of her pressed against him. He could feel her heart pounding under his. He lifted up, shifting his weight on his arms so he wouldn't crush her. Looking into her beautiful eyes, he saw the passion, and he took her mouth in a wild, wet kiss that held nothing back. He continued to kiss her again and again while his hands caressed her. When she moved restlessly beneath him, he slowly moved down her body, kissing her full breasts. He took one nipple in his mouth. She arched up and moaned. She was so responsive to his touch. He slid the palm of his hand between her thighs. His fingers teased and tormented until she was begging for release.

"Please. Aiden, please," she panted.

He slid lower, kissing her silky thighs, then moved between them. He knew the second she came apart. She arched up, clinging to his shoulders and crying his name.

The tremors of her release took Cordie by surprise. Squeezing her eyes shut, she let the waves of pleasure pour over her.

"I like the way you taste." He had only gotten started driving her out of her mind. Twice more she climaxed before his control shattered. "I need to be inside you."

"Not yet," she whispered, her voice shaking with emotion.

She pushed him onto his back and began to drive him wild. She bit his earlobe, smiling when he grunted in reaction. She kissed every inch of his chest, and when she moved down to take him into her mouth, he moaned. He couldn't wait any longer to be inside her. He grabbed a condom from a drawer, and when he was ready, he rolled her onto her back and once again covered her. He wasn't gentle with her, but she didn't want him to be. He slid his arms under her thighs and thrust deep inside. He exhaled a satisfied moan and wanted to slam into her again and again but forced himself to stay still.

"Are you okay?" he asked as he kissed a path down the side of her neck.

Her nails dug into his shoulders. "Oh yes," she said as she lifted her legs and squeezed him.

The sensation was so intense he almost climaxed then and there.

He began to move slowly at first and then faster, thrusting deep each time. He could feel her tightening around him.

Surges of ecstasy ripped through Cordie. She couldn't stop the orgasm. Clinging to him, she felt a rush she had never felt before, and it seemed to go on and on in waves.

Her climax triggered his. It was unlike anything Aiden had ever experienced, and it was incredible. He sank deeper and let out a consuming sigh.

He couldn't move for long minutes. They were both panting. His body was covered with the gleam of perspiration. Making love to Cordelia had taken all he had to give. And then some. He didn't have to wonder how long it would take for him to want her again. He was already thinking about it.

Aiden didn't give her any lovey-dovey words of praise, but Cordie didn't expect that he would. He leaned up on his elbows, kissed her long and thoroughly, then rolled out of bed and went into his bathroom. Aiden was just being Aiden, she reminded herself. Abrupt and in control. She wasn't sure what to do. He wouldn't tell her to leave his bed, but he might not expect her to sleep with him either.

She didn't want it to be awkward. She got out of bed, grabbed her robe, and went back to her bedroom. Her heart was racing. Having sex with Aiden might just kill her if she kept it up. The idea of it made her smile. What a way to go.

After getting ready for bed, she slipped under the sheets, flipped the light off, and closed her eyes, but sleep eluded her. After several minutes of tossing and turning, she heard a phone ring. Another call for Aiden, she guessed.

It took a while, but she finally relaxed. She was just about to drift off when she heard a sound beside her bed. She opened her eyes and saw Aiden in the dim light. He dropped something on the bedside table, pulled the covers back, and lay down next to her. He reached for her and kissed the side of her neck. Cordie glanced over his shoulder to see a package of condoms lying on the table.

"Should I be afraid?" she asked, laughing. He responded by pushing her onto her back and rolling on top of her. "What are you doing?"

She could hear a smile in his voice as he replied. "I told you I like to be on top."

FOURTEEN

C ordie woke up alone. She opened one eye to look at the clock. It was already ten. She wasn't used to sleeping this late, but then she wasn't used to having mind-blowing sex most of the night with an insatiable man. Admittedly, she wasn't used to having sex all night with any man, and she had the sore muscles to prove it.

She groaned getting out of bed. She needed to work out more, she decided. Yeah, right. Who was she kidding? She needed to *start* working out so she could get in better shape. How did one get physically fit for sex?

She glanced down at the indentation on Aiden's pillow. It must have been almost dawn when she had fallen asleep in his arms, and she hadn't heard him get up. She listened for any sound coming from the suite but heard nothing. The memory of their night together played out in her mind, and her face grew warm just thinking about it. Never in her life had she been so uninhibited. Never had she felt such passion, such total ecstasy. Aiden was an amazing lover, gentle and giving, yet demanding. She smiled for just a second remembering, but her smile quickly disappeared as reality set in.

Oh God, what had she done? In one night her entire plan for

getting away from Aiden had gone up in smoke. Granted, it was an incredible and euphoric night, but it changed everything. Or did it? What was last night? She sat on the edge of the bed and pondered her situation. Was it a one-night stand? Two people giving in to their desires? Maybe. They were both adults, after all, and it was totally natural under the circumstances for them to be drawn to each other.

Or was it something more? Aiden had been very tender and affectionate, but there were no words of endearment, no mention of love. Why would there be? He probably had taken dozens of women to his bed in the past; why would she be different? Her heart ached just a little, but she wouldn't let herself dwell on the negative. Last night had been fantastic. She would file it away as a wonderful memory and move on.

A hot shower revitalized her . . . sort of, anyway. Aiden had mentioned that he expected her to go somewhere with him today, but he hadn't told her where. Knowing Aiden, jeans wouldn't be appropriate wherever he was taking her. She decided to wear one of the lovely dresses Miss Marie had insisted she add to her wardrobe. It was a deep purple dress with a jewel neck, long sleeves, and a flared skirt. She slipped into her favorite nude heels. She didn't want to mess with her hair, so she pulled it up in a ponytail, applied her perfume, and was ready to go.

Breakfast was waiting for her. The table was set for one, and on the place mat were a bottle of Diet Coke and a silver bowl of ice with a container of blueberry yogurt. There was also a basket of croissants and pastries and another basket filled with fruit. She didn't eat much, just a little of her yogurt, because Aiden had left her a note telling her he was taking her to lunch at the Empire and to be ready at noon.

While she sipped her Diet Coke she answered e-mails. There

were more than thirty of them, several from students begging her to return to school. They were having trouble with their chemistry class and blamed the teachers. Apparently the first teacher Sister Delores had hired for the summer school session had lasted one week before he had had enough and quit. According to one student's e-mail they were going through teachers faster than they could scarf down a bag of Doritos. The impassioned pleas tugged at Cordie's heartstrings. The boys could be difficult, but they weren't impossible to handle. All it took was a firm hand, patience, and a sense of humor. She was surprised by how much she already missed them.

She saved the longest e-mail she had to write for last. She knew Sophie and Regan were waiting to hear how it was going, and it took a while for her to put her tumultuous thoughts into words. She told them a little about the ball and seeing Simone with her doting family. She also mentioned Simone's ridiculous fainting spell and promised to give them more details when she got back to Chicago. Cordie was sorry she hadn't tried to sneak a couple of photos with her smartphone to send, but she hadn't thought about it until she was on her way back to the hotel. Yes, it was a missed opportunity, and she doubted she would get another chance, because Aiden had informed her they would be returning to Chicago tomorrow after a meeting he had scheduled in the morning. She was ready to go home. She had accomplished what she had set out to do, and now she wanted to get as far away from the Rayburns as possible.

It was only after she had sent the e-mail that she realized she hadn't said much about Aiden. Would her friends think that was odd? Even though Sophie and Regan were her closest friends, she didn't want them to know she'd slept with him. Besides, she had convinced herself that what had happened with Aiden was a fluke, and it would never happen again.

The last e-mail she sent was to Alec telling him she had met his friend Liam Scott and how charismatic she thought the man was. She had just one question: Which side of the law was he on?

At eleven thirty she texted Aiden and told him she wanted to stop in the gift shop and she would meet him in the lobby by the atrium at noon. She tossed her sunglasses and phone into her purse, applied lip gloss, and was heading to the elevator when the hotel phone rang. On the chance it might be Aiden she was quick to answer.

She didn't recognize the man's voice, but it was pleasant.

"Is Andrew Kane there? I'd like to talk to him."

That question got her attention. "Who is calling?" she asked.

"A friend."

"Your name?" she pressed politely.

"A friend," he said again, but this time his voice wasn't quite so pleasant.

All right, then . . . if that was how he wanted to play it. "Mr. Andrew Kane is not available."

"When will he be back?"

"I couldn't say."

"What about the daughter? Is she available?"

"No," she answered.

Before she could demand an explanation, he responded with, "Thank you. I'll try again later," and hung up.

She replaced the phone and fell back against the credenza. What was that all about? A burst of anger seized her. Simone had to be behind the call. Who else could it be? And evidently she thought Cordie's father was still alive. The way she had reacted to seeing Cordie at the ball made it perfectly clear she wasn't going to spread the word anytime soon that she had an illegitimate daughter she had abandoned. If word got out, it would ruin her standing in the community. Women who threw their babies away didn't win Mother of the Year. The caller was either related to Simone or worked for her, right? That was the only thing that made sense. But what did Simone want?

Cordie's hands were shaking. The call had rattled her, but now that she thought about it, she shouldn't be surprised. She certainly had made it easy for Simone to find her. Not only had she put the letter in a Hamilton Hotel envelope, but she had also been at Aiden's side, and practically everyone in Sydney society knew who he was. There might as well have been a neon arrow over the hotel pointing to her whereabouts.

Now what? Cordie couldn't squelch her anger long enough to think like a logical person. She didn't know what she should do—if anything. She decided to put it aside for now, until she could think clearly and calmly. The gift shop. She suddenly remembered she was heading downstairs to buy a bottle of the hotel's special body lotion. Maybe by the time she met Aiden for lunch she could be reasonable again.

The lobby was crowded with guests checking in and out. She skirted her way around a large group of businessmen and headed to the corridor that led to the gift shop. Adjacent to the hallway was a beautiful floor-to-ceiling crackled mirror and in front of it was a mahogany table with a huge vase of fresh-cut flowers. The colors were spectacular, and Cordie stopped to admire the arrangement. As she was leaning over to take in the wonderful fragrance of the hyacinths, she glanced into the mirror and froze. Over her right shoulder she saw the reflection of Simone Rayburn walking toward the front desk. There were two men behind her, and Cordie couldn't tell if they were with Simone or not. Wearing dark suits with solid conservative ties, they reminded her of CIA agents she'd seen in movies: stiff and unapproachable. One of them was of medium height with a stocky build and thick, wavy hair. His bushy eyebrows shaded dark eyes with deep lines around them, and his mouth seemed to be dragged down by the Fu Manchu mustache that ended at his jowl line. The other man with him was tall. His head was bald, most likely shaved to give a strong, manly appearance, but his attempt to be macho was contradicted by the round wire-rimmed glasses that made him look like a midlife-crisis Harry Potter. The two men followed at a discreet distance, and when Simone stopped at the desk, they paused, too. They were definitely with her. They were looking around the lobby, and Cordie knew they would eventually spot her once the crowd thinned out.

"Cordelia?" Louis, the general manager of the hotel, was walking toward her from the hallway.

She flinched at the sound of her name but quickly recovered and smiled. She didn't waste time on pleasantries. "I have a favor to ask. Would you please stay in the lobby? The woman in the blue suit talking to the concierge, and the two men she brought along want to talk to me. It isn't going to be . . . amiable. Will you stay close by?"

"Of course. Would you like me to sit in on the meeting with you?"

"No, thank you," she said.

He nodded, then said, "Here she comes. I believe I'll post two guards at the front door."

"Hopefully this will be quick," Cordie said. She braced herself and turned around.

Simone had recognized her and was waiting for Cordie to come to her. They met in the center of the lobby.

Cordie's greeting wasn't cordial. "What do you want?"

Simone didn't seem fazed by Cordie's anger. "I thought we could go somewhere private to talk. There's so much to say." She motioned to the men behind her.

Cordie watched them walk past Simone and come toward her. Oh hell no. "I'm not going anywhere with you. Why would you think I would?"

The man with the Harry Potter glasses grabbed Cordie's upper arm with a tight grip. She was astonished. Did Simone think she could drag Cordie out of the hotel?

"I don't wish to be seen with you," Simone whispered. "We look so much alike. I know a lot of people, and they'll talk."

Cordie looked down at the hand squeezing her as the thug forcefully pulled her away. She tried to yank her arm from his grasp as she screamed at the top of her voice, "Let go of me!"

Every person in the lobby turned toward her. Several men started forward to offer assistance, including Louis, who was all but running to her.

Simone gasped. "Bloody . . . Charles, let go of her. Arnold, step back."

They quickly obeyed. When they moved to stand behind Simone again, Cordie put her hand up so Louis and the others would know she was okay.

"You have a choice, Simone. Or should I call you Natalie just for fun?"

Simone's face became a mask. She wasn't giving anything away.

Cordie pointed to the other side of the lobby. "You can either sit over there at one of the tables by the bar and talk, or you can leave. Which is it? I'm rooting for the second."

Without a word, Simone walked to the tables. She chose one cast in shadows and sat with her back to the lobby. The men who came with her stayed where they were. Cordie took her time following. When she finally sat down at the table across from Simone, she stared at the woman and waited. Simone couldn't quite meet her gaze. She nervously crossed her legs and brushed imaginary lint off her skirt, stalling while she gathered her thoughts and chose the perfect words to say.

Impatient, Cordie repeated the first words she'd said to her. "What do you want?"

Simone finally looked at Cordie. "That is the very question I have for you. Do you want money to keep silent? How much will it take?"

"I don't want money."

She didn't think Simone believed her, and that guess was confirmed when Simone said, "Your father is a mechanic. Of course you want money."

Cordie laughed. "No, I really don't."

"Then what?" Simone demanded, her frustration rising to the surface. She drummed her perfectly manicured fingernails on the tabletop. "Do you want an apology? Does Andrew? An explanation? I was young, very young. I didn't even know I was pregnant until it was too late to do anything about it."

Lovely, Cordie thought. "Should I feel sorry for you because you couldn't abort me?"

Simone shook her head. "No, of course not. This isn't going the way I thought it would. You're a very . . . hostile young lady."

Cordie wasn't going to argue. She *was* hostile.

"How is your father?" Simone asked. Her voice was softer now. "Tell him I'm sorry if I caused him pain." In the blink of an eye her voice hardened. "Did he send you?"

"No."

"Revenge, then?"

"I'm sorry?"

"Did you come here seeking revenge because I left you?"

"No," she answered. "I had a wonderful childhood."

"Then why did you come here?" Simone asked with actual bewilderment.

If Simone weren't sitting there looking at her so disdainfully, Cordie might have had just the slightest speck of sympathy for her, but the woman was so caught up in her self-absorbed world she didn't have a clue. There wasn't an ounce of regret or contrition for what she had done. Her grand deception was a thing of the past, a fluke. If it didn't impact her life, it wasn't important.

The scene Cordie had witnessed at the ball came back to her. Simone was surrounded by her friends and devoted family. By all appearances, her two sons were affectionate, even solicitous, toward their mother. Her husband seemed to genuinely care for her, and her father, the patriarch of the family, obviously had a strong bond with his daughter, because she clearly did not want to upset or disappoint him. She was loved and admired, and she lived in a world that never knew Natalie Smith.

"I don't expect you to understand," Cordie answered, "but it's important to me that you know there's someone out there who sees you for who you really are."

Simone leaned forward with a look as cold as ice. "You asked me what I want . . . ," she began.

"Yes?"

"Go home and keep quiet."

"Even if I give you my word, how will you know I'll keep it?"

Simone paled, but the steely tone in her voice did not change. "I won't know. I can't trust you."

"No, you can't."

Cordie saw Aiden walk into the hotel and head in the direction of the atrium. He was in a hurry, and since they were supposed to meet at noon, she thought he would be looking for her. Time to wrap up this twisted reunion, she decided.

She stood to leave, but before she walked away, she got the final word. "I'm going home tomorrow, and it is my sincere hope that I never have to speak to you again. You deceived a good and honorable man, and you abandoned your child. Do you honestly think I would tell anyone about you? You're an embarrassment."

FIFTEEN

Aiden was livid. Louis had texted him to let him know about Simone and the two enforcers she'd brought along to the hotel, and when he heard that they had tried to take Cordelia, he went ballistic.

He all but shouted at her. "The second that son of a bitch put his hand on you he should have been thrown out of the hotel. What was Louis thinking? Why didn't he—"

"He came running. You can't be angry with him."

Aiden and Cordie were standing together in the security room. She thought she had entered NORAD when she'd first walked in. There were monitors everywhere. The room was the size of their suite—maybe bigger—and one of the technicians was pulling up the footage of what Cordie called the incident. Aiden's words were a little more descriptive: "I'm going to smash that bastard's face in." Cordie had never seen him so furious.

She had been nervous at first when she'd caught up with him in the lobby. She didn't know how he would react to her after their passionate night together, and she was feeling self-conscious and a bit unsure of herself. Would things be awkward between them now? She had her answer within seconds. All her concerns were eliminated when Aiden heard about her unexpected visitors. He immediately took charge and began to bark out orders. He was the old Aiden again, confident and in control, and his attitude toward her was no different than it had been. He was still as bossy as ever.

"Here it is," the technician said. "Do you want audio, sir?"

"You can listen to conversations in the lobby?" Cordie didn't know if she should be appalled or impressed. "You shouldn't listen to other people's private conversations."

"No, we shouldn't," Aiden agreed. Then to the technician he said, "Isolate the audio and play it."

"Aiden, that can't be legal," Cordie complained.

He didn't agree or disagree. His hands shoved into his pockets, he stood behind the technician and watched the monitor. Neither he nor Cordie said another word while they listened to a replay of the horrible conversation she'd had with Simone. She was amazed that the technician could remove background noise just by adjusting some knobs. She kept glancing up at Aiden to gauge his reaction, but there wasn't any, until Simone whispered that she didn't want to be seen with Cordie, followed by Cordelia's scream. He smiled then. Cordie had to admit the look on Simone's face was priceless. She looked as though she'd just noticed she wasn't wearing any clothes.

"Freeze the frames and get two good photos of those men, and send them to this number," Aiden ordered as he handed a card to the tech. "Send them to me as well."

"Yes, sir."

"Thanks," he said, taking Cordie's hand. "Good work, Harold." He opened the door for her. "Maybe we should cancel lunch. We can eat here in the hotel."

"Why? Did we miss our reservation?"

He shook his head. "I thought you might want to stay in after your encounter."

"Not at all," she answered decisively. "Let's go. I've got until three thirty."

Cavanaugh was waiting in the car. It wasn't until they were on their way that Aiden asked her what she was doing at three thirty.

"Are you going to the spa?" he wondered.

"No," she replied. She looked out the window and sighed. It was a clear, sunny day. The harbor was stunning, with shards of light piercing the sparkling water.

"This is a beautiful city," she remarked.

"Yes, it is," he agreed. "What are you doing at three thirty?"

"I have an appointment at the Garvan Institute of Medical Research."

"I should have guessed that's where you'd want to go."

"My academic advisor back home has arranged for me to meet a couple of the researchers working on genome sequencing. It's exciting work," she said enthusiastically, adding, "and I'm dying to see the DNA-inspired staircase. It's a spiral. I've seen photos, of course, but I want to see it up close."

"I had hoped you would stay inside the hotel until we fly home tomorrow."

"I can't miss Garvan." She was appalled by the possibility. "What has you worried?"

"What has me worried?" His tone was curt. "I just watched your meeting with Simone. Did you look at those two men with her? They're dangerous."

"Yes, but Simone had her say, and I made it clear I wouldn't make trouble."

Aiden was annoyed by her naive interpretation of the conversation. "They were going to drag you out of the hotel. What makes you think they won't try again? And don't tell me you trust that woman to leave you alone."

She hadn't realized how upset he was until she noticed his clenched jaw.

"I don't want you to go anywhere without me," he commanded.

"I'm betting you'll love the Garvan."

"In other words, I'm going with *you*?"

She nodded, then changed the subject. "Who did you send those photos to? You handed the tech a business card . . ."

"Liam," he answered. "I figure we might need his help. Besides, he might know those men. He'll check them out."

"I thought you didn't like him."

"I don't like him around you," Aiden admitted. "But I trust Alec's judgment, and he says Liam's good at what he does."

"Have you figured out what that is?"

Aiden laughed. "Not really. I just know we want him on our side."

The conversation ended when Cavanaugh pulled up in front of the Empire building. The restaurant was on the top floor, and all the windows overlooked the water. They were shown into a large private room. As it turned out, it was a working lunch for Aiden. There was a group of sixteen men and women waiting for him, and the talk centered on permits and expansion. Cordie was impressed with Aiden's negotiating skills. He was fair yet got everything he wanted and then some. The women ogled him, but she couldn't be angry. The man was gorgeous. There had been a time she had ogled him, too.

The food at the Empire was delicious. She ate every bit of her fish. How could she not? It was so fresh it wiggled on her plate. At the end of the lunch most of the guests lingered, and she was able to meet and talk to some of them. They were an eclectic group of politicians, community leaders, contractors, and business owners, and she was impressed by how cordial and welcoming they were toward her. After a couple of conversations, though, she realized several of the men thought she worked for Aiden. One asked her if she would like to go to dinner; another asked if he could show her some of the city that tourists didn't know about; and yet another just wanted to "hang out" with her. She graciously declined all the invitations.

Once they were back in the car, Aiden asked, "How bored were you?"

"Oh no, I wasn't bored. They're interesting people."

"How many men hit on you?"

"They were just being friendly."

"How many?" He was frowning now.

"Three."

He didn't like hearing that. "They knew you were with me."

"They thought I worked for you."

"I'd never get anything done if you worked for me."

"Is that a complaint or flattery?"

"A complaint, of course. You distract me." He didn't seem at all bothered by it.

"And you're rude," she said sweetly. Before he could comment, she leaned forward in her seat and said, "Cavanaugh, is the Garvan far from here? I don't want to be late."

"We'll be there in ten minutes," the driver promised. "You'll be a little early."

Aiden glanced up from answering a text on his phone. "You're looking forward to the Garvan, aren't you?"

"Oh yes," she said. She could barely contain her enthusiasm. "I can't wait to see their new genome-sequencing machine and talk to some of the researchers. They're doing such wonderful work. I think you'll be impressed with the facility, too."

As it turned out, he was impressed, so much so he promised to make a donation. He didn't seem to be in any hurry, and they stayed longer than they probably should have, taking up valuable work time, but everyone was so gracious, and Cordie had at least fifty questions. When they were leaving, one of the directors suggested she send him her résumé.

On the way back to the hotel Aiden asked her if she would ever consider working at the Garvan.

"I think Sydney would be a wonderful place to live, and the people here—most people—are very friendly and kindhearted, but as long as the Rayburns are living here, no. I want to be as far away from them as possible."

"I want you far away from them, too."

They returned to the hotel and went directly to their suite. She noticed there were two security guards posted in front of the private elevator. She knew Aiden was responsible but didn't ask if it was necessary because she knew he'd get huffy about it. One couldn't be too careful. He'd say that or something similar.

It seemed to Cordie that Aiden never stopped working. He took his suit jacket off and loosened his tie, which, for him, was casual attire during the week. Then he sat down at his desk, opened his laptop, and for the next couple of hours didn't move. At dinnertime they ordered room service, and Aiden didn't waste time on chitchat. After eating, he put on his suit jacket, adjusted his tie, and went downstairs to meet some associates in the bar. He would have dragged her along if she hadn't promised again and again that she wouldn't leave the suite.

She was happy to be rid of him for a little while. She thought the way he worried about her was very considerate, but he was a little overzealous about it. A man had grabbed her arm, yes. And yes, it had been his intention to take her out of the hotel against her wishes. Still, he hadn't threatened her or hurt her. He was only following Simone's orders, and all she'd wanted was privacy for their talk.

After Cordie packed for the trip home, she took a shower and put on a black silk camisole and matching boxer shorts. More than anything she wanted to talk to Regan and Sophie and tell them more about meeting Simone, but she didn't want to e-mail or talk over the phone. This needed to be an in-person conversation. She put on the terry-cloth robe, grabbed her lip balm and tube of hand lotion, and went into the living room. Restless, she curled up on the sofa and turned on the television with the remote. There was a special program on about great white sharks, and by the time it ended, she swore she would never go into the ocean again. Channel surfing, she found an old Sherlock Holmes mystery on the BBC. She settled in and tried to pay attention, but her mind wouldn't cooperate. She couldn't believe how tired she was, and it wasn't even ten o'clock yet. Stress, she decided, was the culprit. She was anxious to get back home.

She couldn't stop thinking about Simone. She'd never met such a cold, self-involved woman. How could Cordie's father have loved her? Was it possible that Simone was different back then, when she was pretending to be Natalie Smith? Cordie doubted it. Maybe she was also pretending to be a decent, loving person. Maybe she'd been pretending all her life, never letting people see what was truly in her heart. Cordie's encounter with Simone had been tense and upsetting, but it was behind her now. As she seemed to be doing over and over again, she vowed to let go of the past and move on.

Aiden came back to the suite much sooner than she expected. He looked tired, too. He barely said hello before he disappeared into his bedroom. Twenty minutes later he came back out. He had showered and was wearing sweats and a T-shirt. He moved her feet out of his way and sat next to her. His chest was still damp from the shower, and the T-shirt was molded to him. She tried not to stare, but God, he was ripped. His body was amazing.

"Are you watching this?" he asked, pointing to the television.

"Not really. You can change it."

"The news should be coming on." He looked around at the tables and down at the floor. "Where's the remote?"

It took a while to locate it. He found her tube of hand lotion wedged between the cushions and her lip balm under the sofa. The remote was caught up in her robe. She stood and untied her belt, and the remote dropped to the floor.

The instant Aiden saw what she was wearing, all reason went out the window. Their eyes met, and no words were necessary. He gently pulled her down onto his lap. His eyes delved deep into hers as he slowly removed her robe and tossed it on the floor. Her camisole was next. Then he pulled off his shirt, and his gaze moved down to her beautiful breasts.

Cordie knew with one word she could stop him, but she didn't want to. After the awful confrontation with Simone, she needed to lose herself in him. She didn't care that all he felt for her was lust, that she was a convenience, nothing more. No, tonight she didn't care.

She slid her arms around his neck and traced his lower lip with the tip of her tongue. When his hands roughly cupped her breasts and his thumbs brushed across her nipples, she sucked in a breath and held it.

"I've been thinking about this all day," he whispered. One hand moved to the back of her neck. "How many times do you want to come tonight?"

She couldn't speak. It was all she could do to breathe. He didn't wait for an answer. His mouth covered hers in a long, intense kiss. His tongue slid inside, coaxing her to respond. For long minutes he kissed and caressed her until they were both desperate for more. He swept her up in his arms and carried her into his bedroom and laid her on his bed. Her silk shorts tore in his impatience to remove them. Kicking off his sweats, he covered her body with his. He wouldn't let her move, pinning her to the bed as he slowly moved down her body to kiss every part of her. He didn't have to ask her if she was ready for him. Her need was so intense, her nails dug into his skin. When he entered her, the pleasure shattered her into a million pieces, and she cried out.

"You're so tight." He sighed. "So perfect."

He began to move, harder, deeper, and faster until Cordie couldn't hold back. She tightened all around him and clung to him, letting out a shout as she climaxed. The sensations coursing through her seemed to go on and on. It was both glorious and frightening. She was spiraling down, letting herself fall into the all-consuming rapture, and she never wanted to come back up. Aiden accommodated her. His endurance was incredible. She had two more orgasms before he finally found his own release.

It took much longer for Aiden to recover this time, longer, too, to let go of her. He was panting when he lifted up and looked into her eyes. He could see the passion was still there, which pleased him considerably. She was so responsive to his touch, so honest and giving. He kissed her again, long and hard; then, as before, he got out of bed without a word and went into the bathroom.

Cordie watched him disappear behind the closed door. She dropped back onto the pillow and laughed. No pillow talk, no cuddling, not even a high five. Her legs trembled and she felt weak as she got out of bed and walked into the living room. Dehydration, she decided, was the cause. That . . . and lots of sex. She found her robe, slipped it on, and got a bottle of water from the bar refrigerator, guzzling it down like a teenager at a keg party.

The phone rang. Normally she would have thought whoever was calling wasn't very considerate, since it was after eleven, but Aiden got calls from all over the world, night and day.

"That's probably Liam," Aiden called out.

Cordie answered the phone expecting to hear Liam's distinct British accent. It wasn't Liam, but she recognized the voice. It was the same man who had called earlier asking for her father.

Now he was asking again. "Is Andrew Kane there?"

"No."

"Will he be back soon?"

"Not likely."

"Are you his daughter?"

Should she let him know her father had died? No, she wasn't going tell him or Simone anything. "Yes, I am," she replied.

His voice turned sinister. "Are you waiting for a payout?"

A payout? Apparently Cordie hadn't convinced Simone she wasn't here to blackmail her. Of course Simone would think she wanted money. That was all she cared about. Cordie's answer was emphatic. "No."

"You came here to make trouble, didn't you? To stir it all up. We can't let you do that."

"We?"

"I've got a message for you."

"Who is the message from?" she asked, wondering if he would tell her.

"You don't know what you're getting into."

"What's the message?"

"Keep your mouth shut. If you tell anyone, if you even suggest . . ."

"Yes . . . ?" She deliberately drew out the word to irritate him.

"I'll feed you to the crocodiles. I'll put a bullet in the back of your head."

"Which is it?" she asked. "Feed me to the crocodiles or put a bullet in my head? Make up your mind." She slammed the phone down. When she turned around, she was shocked to see Aiden standing behind her. "What are you? A ninja? How long have you been standing there?"

He didn't think the question needed an answer. "Who was on the phone? Who the—" He stopped himself before he said a foul word. "Who was threatening you?"

"I—"

The phone rang again. "Don't answer it. I'll get it." He frowned at Cordie while he listened to the caller. "No, we're both awake. Come on up."

Come on up? The second he ended the call she demanded to know who was visiting at this hour.

"Liam."

"Oh God. I'm naked, Aiden."

"No, you're wearing a robe," he replied. "But yeah, you should probably put on some clothes." He was talking to air. Cordie had disappeared into her bedroom and shut the door.

"Who was on the damn phone?" he shouted through the door as he put on his T-shirt.

The bell sounded for the elevator. The door opened and Liam walked into the foyer.

Aiden greeted him with a question. "Did you go into the security room and look at the footage?"

"Yes," he answered. "I listened to the audio, too." He added, shaking his head, "They really thought they could drag her from the hotel."

Cordie rushed out to join them. She'd put on jeans and a white blouse. She hadn't taken the time to tuck it in, and she hadn't bothered with shoes either. A quick brush through her hair had taken out the tangles. Aiden tried not to react. Every time he looked at her, she became more beautiful. Her face was flushed, and he thought he could see some slight scratches on her neck from his day's growth of whiskers. For some inexplicable reason, he liked that.

"Hello, Liam," Cordie said. She felt the color warming her cheeks and wondered if Liam could see what she was thinking or could tell what she and Aiden had been doing just minutes before. She was relieved when he didn't seem to detect her embarrassment. He greeted her with a wide grin and a big hug.

Aiden felt a surge of possessiveness and thought it might be fun to throw Liam down the elevator shaft. It was crazy, his reaction. What was wrong with him? Fortunately, he was a master at keeping his emotions hidden. He'd done it most of his life.

"You've said hello. Now let go of her."

"Would you like something to drink?" Cordie offered, stepping back.

"I could use a beer. I'll get it," Liam said, and headed to the bar.

Cordie was about to sit on the sofa when she noticed her black camisole. Mortified, she grabbed it and stuffed it behind the cushion a second before Liam sat down across from her.

Aiden stood over Cordie as he explained to Liam, "Someone called and threatened to kill her."

"Not the first call," she corrected.

"What?" Aiden was incredulous. "He's called more than once?"

She nodded. "I recognized the voice. He called earlier today and asked to speak to my father."

"Your father's dead," Aiden said.

Exasperated, she replied. "I know. I was at the funeral."

"I meant to ask if you told him your father was dead," Aiden clarified.

"No, I just told him he wasn't here, and he said he would call back later."

"And the second phone call?"

"He asked to speak to my father again, and then he threatened me. He said if I didn't keep quiet he would feed me to the crocodiles and put a bullet in my head. He was making me mad, but I probably shouldn't have taunted him."

"How?" Liam asked.

"I asked him to make up his mind."

Liam smiled. "Aren't you going back to Chicago tomorrow? The last time I checked there weren't any crocodiles in Lake Michigan."

"Right," she agreed. "So I guess it's a bullet."

"Don't be flippant about this," Aiden snapped.

"Will you settle someplace, please, and stop hovering over me?"

He dropped down beside her. "What did you find out about the men with Simone?" he asked Liam.

"They work as bodyguards, and both have squeaky-clean records. Never had a single complaint lodged against them, yet they tried to drag a woman out of a hotel lobby packed with people. Pretty damned gutsy for squeaky-clean bodyguards, wouldn't you say?"

Aiden nodded. "Keep looking."

"They had to have been hired by Simone. She couldn't very well have asked her husband or her father," Cordie said.

Liam put his beer on the table. "Let me tell you about the Taylor/Rayburn family and their little empire." He leaned forward and braced his arms on his knees. "They're pretty guarded about their personal lives and their business dealings, so it took some digging to get any information on them. Their wealth and power come from Merrick Enterprises, a company that was built by Simone's grandfather, Howard Merrick. Some would say he was a ruthless businessman, but you don't take over in business like he did without getting rid of your competition. He started out investing in real estate and branched out into other areas of construction and manufacturing from there. Estimates say the company's worth hundreds of millions today.

"When Merrick died, the estate, including his business, went to his firstborn, Alice, who by then had married Julian Taylor. Alice had no interest in business and, by all accounts, was a rather weak, sickly woman. This left the door open for her husband, Julian, to take over. To this day, Julian runs the company. Merrick Enterprises was successful when he took charge, but he's increased its value many times over. He controls everything and everyone with an iron fist. Simone seems to be intimidated by him. My guess is that she's become so accustomed to her cushy life, she's afraid of anything that will disrupt it.

"Simone's husband, Craig Rayburn, is second-in-command at the company. Now, there's an interesting guy. He grew up in a small town in Western Australia and came to Sydney right out of school. His first job at Merrick Enterprises was as an assistant to a regional manager, but he was ambitious. Most would say he was obsessed. Within a few years he had worked his way up to being head of one of Merrick's real estate companies, and that's when Julian took a personal interest. If there's anything that turns Julian on, it's ambition—that and the ability to take orders, and in Craig's case, do what your father-in-law demands. Julian began to turn more and more responsibility over to Craig, and it became apparent to everyone that he was the chosen one. Marriage to Julian's daughter cinched the deal. Craig's landed in a pot of gold and he's loving every minute of it. He has all the trappings: big mansion, yacht, vacation home on his own island. You name it. He's become quite the mogul and is destined to take over when Julian steps down, though it's a pretty good guess, as long as Julian's alive, Craig will be his puppet.

"And that brings us to the two sons, Glen and Knox. Grandpa Julian has been grooming them since they were born. Talk about chips off the old block. They go to the best schools and even now are being molded in Julian's image. I haven't found the details of their inheritance yet, but they're most likely going to take over when the time comes. There's no doubt they'll be taking orders from Julian and Craig for years to come.

"Simone, despite her misspent youth, has reinvented herself. While the men are off making all that money, she has become one of the grand dames of society. The role really suits her. She lends her name to a couple of charity boards, and the good people of Sydney have all but canonized her. She was even named Woman of the Year by some philanthropic organization a couple of years ago.

"Julian puts his family on display as though they're God's gift to Australia. Every month or so there will be an article in the news about some charity event the family's involved in. Ask anyone in Sydney. They'll tell you Julian Taylor and the Rayburn family are just swell, not a black sheep among them. They're a little too Stepford if you ask me, but they're definitely a Julian Taylor creation."

Cordie listened to Liam's report on the family with rapt attention. When he was finished, she sat back and mulled over what he had discovered. "Simone has a lot to lose if her secret gets out," she said. "If anyone found out she abandoned her husband and child, her standing in the community would be gone, and her entire family would suffer. The disgrace and humiliation would destroy her."

Liam nodded. "So the question is: How far would she go to keep her secret safe?"

SIXTEEN

Aiden wasn't quite so hostile toward Liam now. They continued to talk about Julian Taylor and his brood, and the more Cordie heard, the happier she was that she was going home and wouldn't have to worry about seeing any of them again.

She left the men to their discussion, said good night, and went to bed. She could hear the low voices in the other room talking about Simone and the members of her family. She didn't want to think about that vile woman anymore. How long would it take to get Simone out of her head? Regan and Sophie were right. She never should have come here, never should have started this, never should have let her anger control her. It was so unlike her not to be logical. Yet, since she found out the truth about Simone, she had been too enraged to be rational. She hadn't been thinking at all. As appalling as it was to admit, she had let her emotions control her.

And then there was Aiden. She knew what was going to happen once they were back in Chicago. He would return to his skinny, flat-chested blondes, and she would finish getting her house ready to sell and move to Boston. Dear God, how depressing.

Tomorrow she would remember why she was moving on. To-night she needed him. She wanted to sleep in his arms because with him she felt safe and protected. She thought she heard the elevator bell and was pretty certain Liam had just left. Still, she wasn't going to walk into the living room without a stitch of clothing. She slipped her robe on, took a deep breath, and opened the door.

Aiden was taking off his T-shirt again. He noticed her watching him and stilled. "Liam just left."

She untied her belt. "I thought I heard the bell."

Aiden waited to see what she would do. She was blushing, which he thought was sweet. She was acting shy, but he knew what she was like in bed. She was just as wild as he was, just as crazed.

Cordie removed her robe and let it drop to the floor. She walked toward him, and the way he looked at her made her feel like the sexiest woman in the world. When she reached him, she put her arms around his neck, stretched up on her tiptoes, and nibbled on his earlobe. "I want to sleep with you."

He lifted her into his arms. "You can sleep on the plane."

It was hot and humid in Chicago. Cordie hadn't gotten much sleep on the way home, and she was feeling jet-lagged and sleep deprived. She didn't even know what day it was, but she blamed that on the time change.

Aiden rode with her from the airport. He carried in her luggage, kissed her good-bye, and he was gone. She was too tired to care if and when she would see him again. She knew he wasn't going to be getting much sleep with all the problems waiting for him. Just before they left Sydney, he'd received a text from his brother Spencer letting him know that Walker, accompanied by medical personnel, had flown back to Chicago and was now recuperating at the Hamilton. He had been scheduled to enter a rehab facility where he would receive physical therapy daily but at the last minute had changed his mind. Spencer ended his message with a warning to Aiden that Walker was being a real pain.

There was also an issue with the expansion of the Miami Hamilton, and Aiden had mentioned he would be flying out in the next day or two. He didn't seem to need much sleep, and she worried that one day it would catch up with him. She, on the other hand, needed six hours every night.

Feeling like a zombie, she crawled into bed and slept for a solid eight hours. She still dragged all the next day. She drove to the supermarket to get milk and bread and a few other necessities and by the time she was finished shopping and on her way back home, she was wiped out.

Dark clouds were gathering overhead, and she felt the first drops of rain as she hurried up the steps to her door. Shifting the heavy bags to one arm, she fumbled through her purse for her house key and inserted it into the lock, but the door opened before she could turn the key. That was odd, she thought. It was unlike her to forget to lock her door, especially after the lecture Aiden had given her when he'd found it unlocked. She'd learned to be very safety conscious since then. She couldn't believe she'd been so careless, but then, her head was still fuzzy from the trip home. Balancing the bags in both arms again, she went inside and kicked the door closed behind her. Only a few steps in, she tripped over something in her way. One bag of groceries went flying, and she juggled to control the other as she grabbed the banister to keep from banging her head. Her shin throbbed in pain. When she looked down to see what had caused the spill, she found one of her moving boxes sitting precariously in her pathway. After limping into the kitchen and depositing her bag on the kitchen table, she returned to the front hall to pick up the scattered groceries.

Puzzled, she stood and stared at the errant box for a few seconds. She could have sworn she had the boxes stacked three high against the wall. How did this one end up on the floor? It was too heavy to topple off the stack by itself, and she certainly didn't recall taking it down. As she dropped the loose groceries back into the bag and took it to the kitchen, she tried to make sense of what had just happened. True, she'd been in a bit of a fog the last day or so, but she'd never been this careless before.

Maybe Aiden was responsible. He was messing with her head. She couldn't stop thinking about him. Where was he now? What was he doing? She had to move on, she told herself. It wasn't quite so easy, though, especially after the sex-filled nights she'd spent with him. She couldn't think about that without feeling the heat.

The remodel in Boston was moving at a snail's pace. The rooms still hadn't been painted, and the floors hadn't been refinished. Nick left a message for her that there was an issue with the roof and he was going to pay for a new one. Unfortunately, the roofers couldn't start for another two weeks.

Boston was key to her plan for moving on, but for now she was stuck in Chicago. She vowed to stay away from the Hamilton Hotel so she wouldn't see him. She didn't expect him to call her . . . but would he? Was he thinking about her at all? Oh God, she was acting like a teenager.

Regan and Sophie were anxious to see Cordie but were letting her get some rest. They gave her a couple of days to recover, and then Regan invited her to dinner. She and Alec were renting a tiny house on the edge of Cordie's neighborhood and were trying to make time to look for a house to buy. Since Cordie lived on the way to the Buchanans' house, Jack and Sophie picked her up. Fortunately, Jack was behind the wheel, which meant Cordie didn't have to grip her seat and frantically pray that Sophie wouldn't get them killed.

Dinner was ready when they walked in, and after a quick greeting, they squeezed around a table meant for three. Regan was turning into a great cook. She served lasagna and a salad, and tiramisu for dessert. During dinner they talked about Sydney and how much Cordie loved it. She went into great detail about the Garvan and meeting some of the brilliant researchers.

"I thought you wanted to explore a little bit of Australia," Jack said. "You mentioned wanting to see Melbourne and Perth. What happened?"

"I met Simone," Cordie answered.

"Okay, she brought it up," Sophie pointed out. "Now we can talk about what happened with those people." Turning to Cordie she explained, "Regan made us promise not to grill you until dinner was over."

"What was she like?" Regan asked.

"Vile."

"Start at the beginning," Jack suggested. Alec nodded in agreement, but other than that he seemed content to sit back and observe and listen.

Without mentioning what had happened between Aiden and her, she told them everything. It took a long while because they all kept interrupting to ask more questions. Alec laughed when Cordie told them about Liam and how charming he was.

"Is he with the police over there?" Sophie asked.

"I don't know. I don't think he knows either," she said.

The only time she mentioned Aiden was when she told them

how furious he'd been when he'd learned about the two men who'd accompanied Simone to the hotel.

"One of them grabbed you?" Sophie was astounded. "In the lobby? That takes nerve."

"You can understand why I wanted to come home." She went on to tell them about the anonymous phone calls.

"Do you think it was one of the men with Simone who called you?" Sophie asked.

"That's my guess."

"He threatened to kill you if you told anyone Simone was your mother?" Regan shook her head. "That's pretty extreme, isn't it?"

"Of course it's extreme," Cordie replied. "I think they're all crazy. Liam said the family's reputation is on the line. He thinks they'll do anything to keep it pristine."

"'They'?" Jack asked.

"Simone; her husband, Craig; and Simone's father, Julian. He runs that family with a tight fist."

"It's a big enough scandal to ruin them, I suppose," Regan said.

"Maybe," Cordie replied. "They're pillars of society right now. You should have seen the way they were fawned over at the ball. It was nauseating."

"And getting that kind of attention and adulation can become addictive for some people," Jack remarked. "Alec and I have seen it."

"People have killed for less," Alec interjected.

"I can't imagine killing to keep a secret," Cordie said.

"That's because you don't think like Simone. Your values are different. The fact is, you're a threat to the family's little dynasty."

"I'll bet she didn't believe you when you said you didn't want money," Sophie said.

"Aren't you worried?" Regan asked. "You're so calm about it all. Why aren't you freaking out?"

"Of the three of us, Cordie's always been the calm one," Sophie commented.

"The man was just trying to scare me," she said. "As long as I don't put it out there and ruin Simone's perfect lie of a life, I'll be okay. Besides, you're forgetting, I don't want anyone to know I'm related to those freaks. I wouldn't put it out there no matter what. I thought I made that clear to Simone, but apparently not, if she was asking, 'How can I trust you?'"

"And what did you say?" Alec asked.

"I told her she shouldn't."

"That might be the reason he called to threaten you," Jack surmised.

Sophie carried her plate to the sink, then turned around and said, "Cordie, do you realize you just told two FBI agents that someone threatened you? They'll probably want to investigate."

Jack laughed. "Probably?"

"Liam will run it," Alec said.

"Run what?" Cordie asked.

"The investigation."

"What investigation? There is no investigation," Cordie said.

Ignoring her protest, Alec took out his phone and began to text. "There is now."

Cordie closed her eyes and rubbed her temples. "Could we please talk about something else? I've thought enough about Simone and her family in the last week to fill a lifetime." She turned to Regan. "How's Walker doing?"

"Settling in," Regan answered. "He told Spencer he's going to start getting involved in the company business. Aiden won't like hearing that. He's in Miami now."

"I don't know how he does it. I'm still jet-lagged."

"How was Aiden in Sydney?" Alec asked.

Cordie wasn't sure what to say. Alec was so good at reading her. "Busy. He was busy."

"He's always busy," Regan said. "I wish he would slow down and enjoy life."

Cordie couldn't understand why she was suddenly feeling so nervous. "He went with me to the Garvan," she blurted. "He asked me to send my résumé."

They all looked confused.

"Why would Aiden want you to send him your résumé?" Sophie asked.

Cordie could feel her face turning red. "Not Aiden. One of the directors asked me to send my résumé."

"Would you work there?"

"Not as long as the Borgias live there," she said with a shudder. She got up to clear the dishes and bumped her hip on the edge of the counter. Cordie thought living in such a tiny space—even if it was temporary—must be driving Regan and Alec crazy. Her kitchen was at least five times the size of theirs.

Sophie, Jack, and Regan went in the living room, and Alec stayed behind to help.

"How's the hunt for a house going?" she asked.

"I found one I really like," Alec said. "Regan loves it, but she doesn't want to buy it."

Cordie put the Parmesan in the refrigerator. "That doesn't make sense. Why doesn't she want to buy it?"

"Because she doesn't want you to move."

Her eyes widened and then she laughed. "You want to buy my house?"

"Yes," he answered. He straddled a chair and motioned for her to sit. "It's perfect for us."

"This is crazy. I bought your brother's house, and now you're buying mine."

They talked about the house for several more minutes, and then Alec asked, "Are you absolutely certain you want to move to Boston?"

"I'd better be," she said. "I own your brother's town house."

Frowning now, he reminded her, "You love your house here, and you love this city."

"I also love the house I just purchased, and I love Boston."

"Didn't you like teaching at St. Matthew's?"

"Yes, I did, but I'm ready for a change."

"Maybe you should take some more time to think about it."

She wanted Alec to stop pressing. Did he know the real reason she was leaving? She thought maybe he did. Regan and Sophie believed Cordie had gotten over her silly infatuation with Aiden a long time ago, but Alec was far more observant and not so easily fooled. She told herself it didn't matter. If he did know the truth, he would never tell anyone. Her secrets were safe with him.

"If you're serious about buying my brownstone, it's yours."

And the question of her moving was finally put to rest. Alec started talking about the changes he would make, and he became ridiculously enthusiastic when he described, in detail, how he would finish the basement and put in a wall-to-wall flat-screen 3-D television. He also had grand plans for the large backyard, quadrupling the size of the patio, for starters, to accommodate his new grill and smoker. Typical man, she thought. It was all about the barbecue. Hopefully, Regan would rein him in.

Reconnecting with her friends was comforting, and spilling her guts—as Sophie would say—about Simone was cathartic. She didn't get home until midnight, and, because she'd been so absentminded these days, twice she checked to make sure her doors were locked before she went to bed.

The home appraisal and inspection were put on the schedule the next day, and aside from measuring for new drapes and choosing different paint colors for the walls, Regan and Alec weren't in any hurry to close on the house, which saved Cordie from having to put her things in storage. The house in Boston wasn't going to be ready for at least three weeks, maybe as many as four.

Since she didn't have to stage her house to sell it, she decided to do what her father had done when he sold his home and get rid of some of her furniture. The pretty but uncomfortable chairs were the first to go. Watching them being hauled off gave her a new sense of freedom. She got a little carried away then and donated everything but her books, her bed, a small table, and a couple of chairs. The only painting she kept was an abstract Alec's sister-in-law, Laurant, had painted for her. It was bold and empowering, and she loved it.

The following week was filled with meetings with bankers and attorneys to work out the financial details of her father's estate and other less important appointments and errands she needed to get done before she left for Boston. Every day was a whirlwind of activity. She couldn't pinpoint exactly when she started getting a weird feeling that someone was watching her, but the feeling was there, and it was growing stronger.

The first time she acknowledged her suspicion was after her dentist appointment. As she was walking toward her car in the parking garage, she heard footsteps behind her, keeping pace with her; but when she turned around, there wasn't anyone there. She didn't hear the sound again as she ran to her car. Had she just imagined it?

The next incident happened at the art gallery. She had gone there to say good-bye to all her favorite paintings and was alone in a large area she called the blue room. All of a sudden she felt a chill on the back of her neck, an intuitive sense that someone was standing behind her, but when she turned around, all she saw was a shadow crossing the doorway to the next exhibit. Was it just her overactive imagination again?

She got the strongest feeling the day she made a visit to her father's grave. When she drove into the cemetery, she noticed a dark sedan with tinted windows pull in behind her. It stayed several hundred feet away, and when she stopped her car and climbed the hill to the grave site, the car stopped, too. While she arranged the fresh flowers she'd brought, she glanced over her shoulder several times. No one emerged from the sedan, but she had an intense sensation that she was being watched. She quickly gathered up her things and rushed back to her car. As she drove away, she checked in her rearview mirror. The black car was still sitting there.

She had no idea if her fears were valid, and without any kind of proof, she wasn't about to bother Alec or Jack. They were busy with their work, and she didn't want to become a nuisance. She decided to do a little detective work on her own. Walking down Michigan Avenue she stopped to window-shop and watch people coming and going in the reflection of the glass. That didn't get her anywhere, so she tried another trick. She pulled out her compact and applied blush to her cheeks, all the while looking in the mirror at the people behind her. She swiveled in a couple of directions to get a panoramic view. No one suspicious was ever there. After employing that method four or five times on her stroll, her cheeks were so red she was beginning to look like a clown.

On her way home, she decided she had been overreacting . . . or she was becoming paranoid. She couldn't blame her craziness on jet lag now. At least she wasn't obsessing about Aiden. That happened only at night when she was in bed and the memories of the way he had kissed her and caressed her made her melancholy. It was an awful way to go to sleep, but a ritual she kept repeating. The only bright thought she could muster was that everything would be better as soon as she was settled in her new home in Boston. Her imagination would stop running rampant, her instincts would get back to normal, and she could start a new life with a new house, new furniture, new everything.

SEVENTEEN

The phone calls between Sydney and Chicago were short and to the point.

He followed strict instructions. He was to call Sydney at precisely eleven o'clock in the evening, Sydney time, which translated to eight o'clock in the morning in Chicago. Unless of course there was an emergency. Then he was to call at any time, day or night.

He stood by the window of his hotel room, his cell phone gripped in his hand. He'd already entered the phone number but waited until exactly eight o'clock to make the call.

There was no greeting. "What have you found out?"

"She's meeting with bankers and attorneys." He heard the in-drawn breath, then a blasphemy, and he rushed on. "I followed her to the cemetery the other day. She went to her father's grave."

"Andrew Kane is dead?"

"Yes."

"When did he die?" There was no emotion behind the question.

"Not long ago. There isn't a headstone yet. I'll find out."

"What about the attorneys?"

"They're estate lawyers. Her father left her money, a lot of money."

"How much?"

"Millions."

"That's not possible. He was a mechanic."

"Do you want me—"

"I'll look into her financials. I should have done that already. I had hoped to control her with money. Perhaps I still can."

"She doesn't need money."

"It's not a matter of need. No one can have enough. You know that. Is she talking to anyone about me, about the family? I want to get ahead of this. I need to know what she's planning. It's making me very . . . anxious. There's a lot to lose here."

He didn't agree, but he didn't dare argue. It wasn't his place to express an opinion. "You don't think she will let it go and move on?"

"No, of course she won't. She's planning now. I'm sure of it. That's what I would do. I'd carefully plan. Is there anything else to report?"

"She has two close women friends."

"Yes, you mentioned them last phone call."

"I'm sure they know."

"She could destroy this family, destroy me."

"There's something more I've discovered," he said. He'd been holding this information, waiting for the right moment.

"The two women friends . . ."

"What about them?"

"They're married to FBI agents."

A long minute of silence followed. Then a hiss. "Something has to be done before she ruins me. I don't want to worry that one day I'll turn on the television and see her giving an interview . . . telling everyone who she is."

"Yes, I know."

"Do you understand what I'm saying?"

"Yes. I understand."

EIGHTEEN

She'd had little time for her friends, and she was glad to hear from Regan, who called on Friday morning just to chat. She told Cordie that Sophie and Jack were going up north to a friend's lake house for the weekend. They would be back late Sunday. She also told her that there was a sale at Neiman Marcus. They talked for quite a while, and Regan happened to mention that Aiden was on his way home from the airport—he should be landing any time now—and she expected fireworks when he confronted Walker, who had made a deal with some congressman to build a new hotel. Regan continued with her news, but all Cordie heard was that Aiden was back in Chicago, and her heart skipped a beat. She didn't want to run into him, didn't want to chance seeing him with another woman. As long as she stayed away from the hotel, she figured, she would be okay.

After she ended the call with Regan, she was determined to avoid thinking about Aiden. Focusing on a few chores around her house wasn't working, so she decided to do some shopping. The weather was hot but bearable. She changed into a pale blue cotton sundress. The humidity was climbing, and her hair was reacting with its usual curl, so she went with her go-to hairstyle and pulled it back into a ponytail. By the time she reached the shops on Michigan Avenue, she was wilting and wondering why in God's name she'd thought it was a good idea to wear heels. She stood at the curb with a crowd of men and women around her waiting for the light to change. Cars were zooming past. She spotted two former students, Sean Corrigan and Jayden Martin, across the street waiting for the light. She hadn't seen them since the funeral, when Jayden surprised everyone by giving his rather ambiguous testament to her father's kindness in the matter of a stolen car. Both were decent boys who struggled with authority. Jayden, especially, had big trust issues. Sean saw her and waved. Jayden gave her an abrupt nod, which made her smile. He still liked to act the tough guy, she thought.

What happened next defied logic. She had just glanced up at the light. One second she was watching for the signal to turn, and the next she was standing in front of a car barreling toward her. In a crazy attempt to ward off the inevitable, she put her hand out to try to stop it from happening and jumped back. The driver hit the brakes, but it was too late, and the vehicle, brakes screeching, slammed into her.

The impact threw her into the air. The left side of her body was struck first, and she was tossed onto the hood. Her shoulder and head hit the windshield, and as the car skidded to a stop, she was thrown again and ended up on the ground. She had never experienced such horrific pain. The world began to swirl above her, and she heard people screaming as everything faded to black. She was barely conscious, but she could make out the sounds of worried voices and blaring sirens before she drifted into oblivion.

The emergency room physician and three specialists all told her how lucky she was to be alive. She didn't feel lucky. She felt as though she had just been hit by a car.

Her injuries weren't all that severe . . . considering. Her left arm was broken, the wrist was fractured, and she was bruised everywhere. She hadn't suffered a concussion or broken any other bones, which really was miraculous, she supposed. As soon as she was given something for the pain, she became coherent and was able to give the hospital staff the information they needed to fill out the paperwork. A nurse told her that her purse hadn't made it to the hospital with her. Either it had been left at the accident scene or someone had taken it. Her cell phone was missing, too.

A few minutes later she was given a shot that knocked her out, and the next time she opened her eyes, she was sporting a cast from her fingers to her elbow. And Aiden was standing at the foot of her bed. How was that possible? She closed her eyes, opened them again, and he was still there.

"What are you doing here?" she asked. "How did you know? The accident just happened . . . didn't it?" Had she been asleep for hours . . . or days?

"Alec phoned the hotel looking for Regan. The staff couldn't locate her. Spencer and I had just walked into the office and heard the news. We turned around and came right over. You gave me quite a scare. Don't ever do that again." He was scolding her, but there was worry in his voice. He added, "Alec and Spencer are here. They're talking to the police right now."

"But how did Alec know?"

She was struggling to sit up, so Aiden walked to the side of the bed and pushed a button until she was upright.

"I'll let Alec explain," he said. "How are you feeling?" he asked.

Horrible, she wanted to say. Really horrible. Her entire body was aching. Her arm throbbed. "I'm okay," she said, and even she could hear how pathetic she sounded.

"You look like hell." He actually smiled while he insulted her.

"Let me run over you with my car a couple of times, and I'll bet you'll look like hell, too."

"You're going to have two black eyes." Spencer made the announcement as he pulled the curtain back. "Put on a cape and you'll look like Zorro."

Alec joined them. He winced when he saw her and said what he was thinking. "You look bad."

Spencer stood beside him at the foot of the bed and nodded in agreement.

"Don't you people know how to be sympathetic?" she snapped.

All three of them shook their heads. For some inexplicable reason, they made her feel a little better.

"You don't want us to lie to you, do you?" Spencer asked.

"Yes, I do. I really do." Turning to Alec she asked, "How did you find out I was in an accident?"

"I called you on your cell phone to ask you a house question, and some kid answered. He wouldn't tell me his name. He said that Miss Kane was hit by a car and was on her way to the hospital."

"Sounds like one of your students, calling you Miss Kane," Spencer said.

She suddenly remembered seeing Sean and Jayden at the stoplight. "Did he say anything else?"

Alec answered. "He took your purse and your phone. He said someone was trying to grab it, so he grabbed it first. I told him where to bring it."

"It was either Jayden or Sean, and they both know where I live."

Spencer started to say something, but Aiden shook his head and he stopped. What was that about?

Alec turned her attention. "The kid on the phone said it wasn't bad, that you only bounced a couple of times before you landed. Let's hope he doesn't go into the medical field."

A young policeman came around the corner and introduced himself as Officer Talbot. "Are you feeling up to answering a couple of questions, Miss Kane?" he asked.

When Cordie nodded, he proceeded to quiz her about the accident. Witnesses reported that there had been a loud bang from a delivery truck backfiring. They were so startled they looked in the direction of the noise, and they didn't turn back until they heard tires screeching and she was lying on the street. Did she remember the noise? No, she responded, but then everything was a blur from the time she was standing on the curb until she ended up on the pavement. Was it possible she jumped when she heard the explosion? She supposed it was possible, she told him, but she didn't think it was probable that she would jump so far as to end up in the street. Was there anything else she could report about the incident? She told him she saw her former students across the street, but she assured him she was very aware of the light and the traffic. Other than that, she couldn't recall what had happened. It was all so sudden.

After making a few notes, he thanked her and turned to leave. "You're a lucky lady, Miss Kane. You could have been killed."

The severity of what had happened to her was beginning to sink in, but she couldn't concentrate. The nurse had given her pain medicine that was fogging her brain. She lay back and closed her eyes. The urge to sleep was too strong to fight.

A nurse told the men to step outside while she helped Cordie get dressed. The doctor had just signed her discharge papers, and she was free to go, but she could not be alone. There was a long list of what she could and could not do and three prescriptions that needed to be filled.

"She'll want to go home," Spencer said.

"Too bad," Aiden responded. "She's going to the hotel. She can't handle steps. With all the meds she'll be taking, she could fall and break her neck. She's staying with me."

"Are you going to tell her, or should I?" Spencer asked.

"No one needs to tell her. She'll figure it out soon enough."

As Spencer was leaving to get his car, he said, "It's a good thing it wasn't her right hand. She'll still be able to write . . ."

"Cordelia is left-handed," Aiden told him.

Alec smiled at his comment and said, "What else have you noticed?"

Aiden ignored him.

By the time Cordie was dressed, she was as white as a sheet, according to the nurse helping her. The doctor had ordered medication for her that would help her sleep and also help control the pain.

"You'll be a little loopy," the nurse said, "but since you're not driving anywhere, that's all right. You need to rest. I'd suggest tonight you get down on your knees and thank God you're still alive, but you'd probably topple over, so say your prayers in bed."

Cordie knew the woman was talking to her, but she couldn't clear her head enough to make out what she was saying. She felt as though she was at the bottom of a lake, and it was going to take far too much effort to swim to the top. All she could do was give in and sink down into the murky darkness. She was dozing off when she suddenly felt Aiden's strong arms around her. The way he lifted her was so effortless, he made her feel as light as air. He liked to carry her to his bed, she thought, as she put her head down on his shoulder and went to sleep.

Once they were at the hotel, Aiden helped her get to his suite. Like the hotel suite in Sydney, there were two bedrooms, one on each side of the living room. He guided her to the guest room. Not wanting her to sleep in her clothes, he removed them and got one of his shirts to put on her, carefully slipping her cast through the sleeve.

He was pulling the covers up when Spencer came in with the prescriptions and set them on the table next to the bed.

"How's she doing?" he asked in a whisper.

"You should see her legs and hip. They're black-and-blue."

"We should get one of Walker's nurses in here," Spencer said. "You won't hear her if she wakes up and needs help."

"We'll figure it out tomorrow. I'll stay in here tonight."

"You're going to sleep with her?"

"Yes."

"That will freak her out if she wakes up."

"No, I don't think it will."

Cordie slept through their conversation. She woke up in the middle of the night, and, disoriented, she looked around and squinted into the dark. Soft light spilled under the door from the room beyond, but she couldn't figure out what that room was. A closet? A bathroom? She turned her head and saw Aiden sound asleep beside her. Were they still in Sydney? When she tried to lift her arm, she felt the weight of the cast. She looked around, and on the nightstand next to her she spotted a black-leather folder with the letter *H* embossed on the cover. Clarity came like a bolt out of the blue. The Hamilton. She was at the Chicago Hamilton with Aiden.

How in the world had that happened?

NINETEEN

Alec laughed when he read the sign Spencer had taped to Cordie's bedroom door: *Warning. Don't poke the bear.*

"I'm assuming Cordie's the bear," Alec said.

Spencer nodded. He was sitting at the dining table with his laptop in front of him, trying to get some work done.

"Why aren't you in your office?" Alec asked him.

"I'm babysitting," Spencer answered. "Aiden doesn't want Cordie to be alone." Smiling, he added, "Those two really got into it. It was something to see. He can't intimidate her, though God knows he tried."

"What was the argument about?"

"She wants to go home, and he won't let her."

"Regan will be here in a little bit," Alec said.

Spencer nodded. "The nurse just left. She helped her shower and get dressed. Cordie was very appreciative. She's only taking her wrath out on Aiden and me."

"Why you?"

"I won't take her home. I'm telling you, Alec, this floor is turning into a war zone. Walker's a hundred times worse than Cordie.

She only argues with Aiden. Walker argues with everyone, and now that he's decided to get involved in the business, it's a nightmare."

"Getting involved . . . isn't that a good thing?"

"God no."

Alec tapped on Cordie's door, then went inside. The drapes were open and sunlight streamed in. She was sitting in bed, her back against the headboard. Dressed in a T-shirt, sweatpants, and socks, she had her laptop open, but when she saw him, she closed it and put it aside.

"You're looking better." He told the lie without laughing.

Exasperated, she said, "I look like a raccoon."

He gave up on trying to be diplomatic and dragged a chair over to the bed. Noticing the tray of food on the table, he lifted the silver dome and said, "Aren't you going to eat your lunch?"

"No, not now."

He popped a French fry into his mouth and reached for half the club sandwich. "You should eat. It looks really good." He then proceeded to devour every morsel.

She handed him a bottle of water, wincing as she stretched her legs out. "Alec, I'm being held against my will. Get me out of here. I want to go home."

"I think you should stay here a couple more days. If you go home, you might trip and fall and get blood all over my hardwood floors."

"They're not your hardwoods yet."

"How are you really feeling?"

"My arm hurts, and I'm sore, but I'm not going to take any more pain pills. They make me too emotional."

"How so?"

She didn't explain that the medication made her vulnerable and she needed to be at her best around Aiden. She didn't want to let her guard down and unintentionally say something she would regret. Not once had Aiden mentioned any feelings for her. The sex in Australia had been incredible, but there were no loving words afterward. For him it had been purely physical. She'd figured that out early on. But for her it had been love. She was worried sick she would tell him how she felt, and that would ruin everything.

The nurse, a stunning brunette, returned to check on her. She beamed when she saw the empty tray. "Thank goodness. You're getting your appetite back."

Before Alec could contradict her, Cordie said, "Yes, I am."

"You'll be going home in no time at all."

"That's the plan."

After the nurse had carried the tray out, Cordie asked, "Are all the nurses looking after Walker pretty?"

"Knowing Walker, I'd have to guess yes," he said as he got up and returned the chair to the desk. He went back to the bed and leaned down to kiss her forehead, being careful to stay away from the bruises. "I'll check on you later."

"You don't need to."

He ignored her protest and was turning to leave just as Aiden, followed by two teenage boys, walked in. Jayden Martin noticed Alec's gun and holster and took a step back. Sean Corrigan didn't see the gun. He was staring at Cordie and cringing.

"Sean, Jayden, I'm so happy to see you." She swung her legs over the side of the bed and slowly stood. Her arm was in a sling, but she still tried to protect it by holding it against her chest with her other hand. "Let's go into the living room and talk."

She took a couple of unsteady steps before getting her balance, but Aiden had already walked over to stand beside her. She didn't want him to treat her like an invalid any longer. "If you pick me up, I'm going to punch you," she whispered.

He laughed. It wasn't the reaction she was hoping for.

Jayden was looking as though he wanted to bolt, and she quickly introduced both boys to Alec. "You've seen Regan Buchanan at school lots of times. She helped me with fund-raisers. This is her husband, Alec Buchanan." She deliberately didn't mention that he was an FBI agent.

"Oh yeah," Sean said. "I remember her. She was real pretty."

"She still is," Alec said.

"I saw you at Mr. Kane's funeral," Jayden remarked, casting a wary glance in Alec's direction. He was holding a plastic shopping bag. He dropped it on the bed. "Your purse is in there," he told Cordie, following her into the living room. "We didn't take any-thing."

"I didn't think you would," she replied.

"The forty-two dollars is still in your wallet," Sean volunteered.

She smiled. "Thank you for keeping it safe for me."

"Some guy tried to take it, but Jayden was faster."

"He went for your phone, too, but I got it first," Jayden said. "Miss Kane, you should change your lock code on your phone."

"It didn't take much to figure it out," Sean agreed.

"What is it?" Alec asked.

Jayden looked at Cordie for approval before he answered. "Zero, zero, zero, zero."

"Yeah, you need to change it," Alec told her.

The boys were so uncomfortable with Aiden and Alec towering over them, Cordie sat on the sofa and motioned for them to sit in the chairs across from her.

"Thanks, but we should probably go," Jayden said.

"Did you see it happen?" Aiden asked as he removed his suit jacket and draped it over the back of the sofa. Rolling up his sleeves, he loosened his tie and waited for one of the boys to answer. They glanced at each other and couldn't seem to make up their minds about who should reply.

Aiden's patience was wearing thin and he was about to ask the question again when Sean said, "You should tell it, Jayden."

"Don't you remember what happened, Miss Kane?" Jayden asked.

"I don't. I remember seeing you two, and that's it."

Aiden stood next to Cordie with his arms folded across his chest, frowning as he continued to wait for a response. Didn't he know how threatening he looked?

"Aiden, sit down," she ordered.

Aiden took the hint, but instead of sitting, he strolled over to the tall windows and looked down on the street with his hands behind his back.

Alec detected the apprehension in the boys. It appeared they knew something more about Cordie's accident, and he didn't want them to stop talking. He took a seat in one of the upholstered chairs and leaned back.

Jayden paused a moment, suspicious of Aiden's question, and then said, "Yeah, I saw it all." He proceeded to describe in painful detail how she had bounced off the hood of the car. "Everyone was shouting," he told Cordie. "When I got to you, I heard this guy say you jumped right in front of the car. I couldn't figure out why he'd say such a—"

"That's crazy," Cordie asserted vehemently. "I did not jump in front of that car."

"I know," Jayden agreed. "You were pushed."

Aiden spun around. "What did you say?"

Jayden didn't hesitate. "I said she was pushed."

"That's right," Sean asserted. He turned to Cordie. "There was this loud bang and everybody jumped a little, but all it was, was a truck. It didn't scare me none, and I was looking right at you when you kinda lunged into traffic. I didn't see who pushed you because it was such a big crowd, and everything went crazy when you got hit."

Aiden couldn't stand still. The possibility of someone deliberately hurting Cordelia enraged him. He paced in front of the windows while he listened to the conversation.

"Maybe the guy who shoved you was just scared by the loud boom." Sean offered the theory. "Or it could have been a woman behind you."

"She'd have to be pretty strong," Jayden said. "I mean, you were propelled. You know . . . right in front of that car. You should have seen the way you bounced."

"I experienced it, Jayden," Cordie said.

"Yeah, but you didn't see it," Sean pointed out.

"Maybe you could see it," Jayden said. Turning to Alec he asked, "Aren't there cameras at all the lights?"

"That's right. There are," Alec answered.

"Maybe you could call, and they'll let you see the accident. I'll bet they would."

Alec had already asked for the video, but Jayden was so proud of himself for coming up with the idea, he went along. "Good thinking," he said. "I'll check into it."

Jayden nodded. "If someone hurt Miss Kane on purpose, you know what you should do?"

"What's that?" Alec had a pretty good idea what the kid was going to suggest. Most teenagers he'd dealt with subscribed to an-eye-for-an-eye philosophy.

"You should throw him in front of a speeding car," Jayden said with conviction.

Aiden stopped pacing and nodded. "I like that plan."

"No, that's not what should be done," Cordie said. "We follow the laws here."

"Most of the time we do," Aiden said.

The boys weren't as skittish now, Alec thought, because they were no longer eyeing his gun. "I'd like to ask a couple of questions," he said.

"About what?" Sean looked worried.

"About the accident," he explained.

"What else would he want to talk about?" Jayden muttered to Sean before addressing Alec. "Go ahead and ask your questions."

Alec wanted to know what the boys had noticed before they spotted Cordie. How observant had they been about the people around them? What were they doing on that corner? A couple of questions turned into quite a few, and he kept circling around to the minutes before the accident.

"I just remembered," Jayden said. His voice became animated. "I saw Miss Kane before she reached the light. I didn't know it was her at first because she was far away, but I was watching her walk down the street."

"Why were you watching her?" Alec asked.

"Well . . . you know . . ."

"Go ahead and tell me."

The kid's face turned red. "She was wearing a dress, and I noticed . . . you know . . . her legs."

"Yeah," Sean said as though the light had just dawned. "I noticed them, too. And the guy walking behind her sure was noticing."

"Yeah, that's right," Jayden said. "I forgot him. He was looking down. He definitely was interested."

"This guy . . . did he follow Miss Kane to the corner?" Alec asked.

"I don't know," Jayden answered. "There was a crowd of people squeezing into that corner, and I didn't see Miss Kane again until she was waiting for the signal."

The kids had seen a lot more than they'd realized. "That's a big help," Alec told them.

"If you're finished with your questions . . . ," Cordie said. When Alec nodded, she turned to Jayden. "How is your mother doing?"

"She's much better since the surgery."

"Please tell her I said hello. Sean, what about your family?"

"Everyone's good. We should probably go now, Jayden. I've got to get home before Mom does." Turning to Cordie he explained, "I'm grounded."

Cordie struggled to stand so she could walk the boys to the elevator. Sean rushed forward to help, and immediately she thought, oh no. If he yanked her or pulled on her, she'd probably pass out. Fortunately, Aiden got to her first and helped her up. He must have seen the panic in her eyes.

"Thank you so much for keeping my purse safe. All my identification was inside."

"And forty-two dollars," Sean reminded her.

"I think I should treat you to dinner. I'll just get my—" she began, but Aiden stopped her.

"Let me," he offered.

"Oh, you don't have to . . . ," Jayden started to protest, but Sean elbowed him.

Aiden pulled out his wallet and gave them enough cash to eat for a week, suspecting that most of it would go for video games or something other than food.

"Do you miss your dad?" Jayden asked Cordie as he stuffed the bills in his pocket.

"Yes, I do," she answered.

"I miss him, too."

"So do I," Sean said.

"Could I ask you a favor?" Jayden asked, stepping closer.

"Yes, of course." She realized she was leaning into Aiden and tried to pull away, then decided it was just easier to stay where she was.

"I got a new car," he said. "It's not really new. Your dad would call it a clunker."

After glancing up at Aiden, she turned to Jayden and whispered, "How did you get the car?"

"I paid for it. Honest," he said. "I saved up, and your dad . . . he gave me a little money for my birthday."

Another nice thing her father had done and never told her about. "What's the favor?" she asked.

"I was wondering if you would go for a ride and tell me what you think, maybe next week, when . . . you know . . . you look better."

She smiled. His assessment of her appearance may have been a little harsh, but she couldn't fault the accuracy. She knew she looked as if she'd been in a fight with a wrecking ball. After agreeing to the ride, she said good-bye, and Aiden walked the boys to the elevator.

As soon as the doors were closed, he said, "You were worried he might have stolen the car, weren't you?"

"Maybe a little," she admitted.

"I'm out of here," Alec said as he stood to leave. "I want to see what that street camera got, check out the crowd around you."

"I should look at the crowd, too," she said. "I might recognize someone . . . if I was pushed," she qualified. As she began to take slow steps back to the bedroom, she looked over her shoulder at Aiden and asked, "Will you take me home this afternoon?"

"No," he answered.

She refused to let him irritate her. "Okay," she said. "When will you take me home?"

He couldn't resist. "Maybe next week when . . . you know . . . you look better."

By seven o'clock that evening Cordie was convinced she was never going to get out of there. No one was willing to drive her home, not even Regan. Apparently they all thought they knew what was best for her. Or they were following Aiden's instructions, which seemed more likely. She thought about asking the doorman to get her a cab, but in order to get to the door, she'd have to cross the lobby in her socks. The tennis shoes Regan had brought her from the house had mysteriously disappeared. She even threatened to call the police, which Aiden thought was hilarious. He had a good laugh while Spencer put the sign back on her door.

Around seven thirty she came to the realization that she was acting like a spoiled ten-year-old. She should be thankful she had such good friends who wanted to take care of her. And at the Hamilton she was pampered. Earlier Regan had sent up a member of the spa staff to wash and blow-dry her hair. After she'd taken a lovely bath, the nurse came in to help her change and fix the sling for her cast. She was feeling so much better thanks to all the support she was getting.

Aiden knocked on her door to announce that he had ordered dinner and asked her to come out to the table.

"I really can take care of myself," she told him as he pulled the chair out for her and put the napkin in her lap.

"Yes, you mentioned that a couple of times earlier today." He lifted the silver plate cover to reveal filet mignon, asparagus, and baby red potatoes.

She stared at the mouthwatering steak for several seconds, then said, "You did that on purpose."

"Did what?" he asked innocently.

He knew she couldn't cut the steak, and that was why he'd ordered it, to prove to her she wasn't self-reliant just yet. He took the steak knife and fork and cut the meat into bite-size pieces.

"Want me to feed you?" There was laughter in his voice.

"That's not necessary," she grumbled as she picked up the fork with her free hand.

He sat across from her and uncovered the same meal on his plate. She was surprised he was having dinner with her because she knew he usually went out every evening, sometimes for business, sometimes for pleasure.

"Shall we have an argument-free dinner?" he proposed.

"We don't argue. I simply express my opinion, and you ignore it."

"So that's a no," he said dryly.

"We won't argue," she promised. And to prove it she thanked him for dinner.

He took a bite of steak and said, "This is good."

She agreed. It was delicious. "Tell me about the congressman making you crazy."

"Not much to tell, and it's Walker making me crazy." He then explained what had happened with Rock Point. "Spencer had worked hard on the deal, and the resort would bring that community back to life, but the congressman got greedy and demanded more money."

"He agreed to one price, then changed his mind."

Aiden nodded. He wasn't used to talking about his frustrations with anyone, and it felt good to get it all out. "The guy's a jerk," he said. "Know what he said? Giving his word and shaking my hand didn't mean anything. He hadn't signed anything, so it wasn't a done deal."

"How did Walker get involved, and why did he negotiate with the congressman?"

Aiden shook his head. "I don't know. I haven't talked to him yet. I thought I'd get over my anger first, but that's not happening."

"When is Armageddon?"

The question made him laugh, and his mood was suddenly lightened. "Tomorrow."

He then talked about the Houston property and the difficulty getting permits for the expansion. She couldn't imagine how he kept everything straight in his head. She would have trouble remembering how many hotels there were. Not Aiden. He oversaw every phase, from breaking ground to the grand opening, and he could rattle off numbers faster than a computer.

"How do you stay so organized?" she asked.

"I've got a lot of good people I can rely on to get the job done, and Spencer does as much as I do. We split the work," he explained. "He's just more laid-back about it."

She thought about what he had just said and decided she might have unjustly judged Walker as a giant liability and a man who refused responsibility. His older brothers had taken over the running of the business, and he had very little to say about it. Maybe Walker had more to offer than they realized.

"The four of you have an equal vote," Cordie said. "Isn't that right? Even though Regan runs the charity foundation, she still has a vote on any new development."

"That's right."

"And so does Walker?"

"Of course."

"What happens if Walker and Regan vote against you and Spencer?"

He shrugged. "I figure out a way to get what I want."

She laughed. "You're arrogant."

"Yes."

No apology came with the acknowledgment, but then she didn't expect he would view arrogance as a flaw. Aiden Madison was the ultimate alpha, and she, supposedly a liberated female, shouldn't be attracted to him. Should she?

"I've got to get some work done tonight," he told her.

"Are you going down to your office?"

"No, I'll work on my laptop here."

She pushed her chair back and stood. "I won't bother you. I should answer my e-mails. That will take forever." She hoped that when her fingers weren't so swollen she would be able to type, but for now she had to use the one-finger technique. Thank goodness Regan had brought over some of her electronics. Cordie would be lost without her laptop and her cell phone charger.

She went into the bedroom for her computer, then returned to the living room to find her phone so she could charge it. After a futile search, she picked up the hotel phone and called her cell. Following the ring, she located the phone under a chair. How had it gotten there?

Aiden leaned against the bar watching her. The living room was beginning to look as though it had been ransacked. The cushions on the sofas were askew; the coffee table was cluttered with Cordie's laptop, iPad, earbuds, and chargers. One of her robes was draped over a chair, and her e-reader was on the seat. She hadn't even been in the suite all that long. What would the room look like in a week? She needed to get organized, he decided.

"Do you know how much time you waste looking for things you've misplaced?"

Cordie was untangling her charger cord from the laptop. She straightened and asked, "Excuse me?"

He repeated his question.

"No, Aiden, I don't know how much time I waste looking for things. At home I have a place for my things. Here, I don't."

He couldn't argue with her because his phone rang. "It's Alec," he told her.

She waited impatiently for Aiden to finish his conversation and tell her what Alec wanted.

"He's coming over with the video," he explained.

"Why didn't he just e-mail it to us?"

"He wants to talk to you."

"What else did he say?" She leaned against the arm of the sofa. She didn't want to sit, afraid she wouldn't be able to get up. With all the bumps and bruises, by the end of the day moving was exhausting.

"He said it's official now. Sean and Jayden were on the mark. Someone deliberately pushed you into the path of that car."

She was astounded and outraged. "So it's for real. Now there's proof. Oh my God. Someone actually tried to kill me. I could have died."

He was surprised by her reaction. "We already knew you were pushed. This is confirmation."

"You're awful relaxed about it."

"No, I'm not."

He still sounded too calm to her. "I can't believe it. I should have paid attention. I slacked off. All week I've been looking behind me every time I thought someone was following me, and the minute I let my guard down, boom. I almost get killed."

Jaw clenched, he said her name in a warning tone. "Cordelia, you thought someone was following you?"

"Yes, and apparently I let him sneak right up behind me. I can't believe it. Do you know who's behind this? Because I do."

Aiden wanted to shout at her for not telling him sooner. He decided to wait for Alec to get the entire story out of her. Then he would get to yell.

"It's Simone," she announced unequivocally. "She's trying to dispose of me just like she did with her marriage to my father. That freak of a family in Australia won't know what hit them when I . . ."

She stopped ranting as soon as Aiden took her into his arms. "You know what this means, Cordelia?"

"What?"

He kissed her forehead. "You're not going anywhere."

TWENTY

He decided to wait until the agreed-on time to call Sydney. He wanted to downplay the incident, and for that reason he didn't make an emergency call.

"Anything to report?"

"Yes," he said. "As instructed, I've continued to follow and observe the woman. I didn't find anything in her house that would connect you."

"Good."

"I've been looking for the best time to dispose of the problem."

"Those were your instructions."

He cleared his throat. "An opportunity presented itself on a crowded street, and I made the decision to go ahead."

"What did you do?"

"I pushed the woman into heavy traffic."

"With witnesses? You said a crowded street. People saw you?"

"No, no one saw what I did," he rushed.

"But something did go wrong. I hear it in your voice."

"The woman survived. She had injuries, but she will recover."

"You idiot! What made you think that would work? I sent you there to take care of this problem and you failed."

He stammered, "Yes . . . yes . . . I realize I should have found a better way by now. The police believe it was an accident. She should have died, but the car was slowing down . . . I just acted on the spur of the moment because I saw an opportunity . . ." He realized he was making excuses.

"This should have been done already."

"I know. I did fail, but it won't happen again."

"It better not. No more waiting. You finish it."

TWENTY-ONE

Cordie watched the video at the table with Aiden beside her. Alec had gone to the bar to get a beer before he took a chair across from them.

"I really did bounce." She winced.

"See what you did there?" Aiden replayed the seconds before impact. "It looks like you tried to jump up, like a pole-vaulter, onto the hood of the car. That was smart."

"Are you seriously trying to put a positive spin on this?"

He shrugged. "Maybe."

"I think it looks like I tried to stop the car with my left arm."

"The blinkers were on," Alec commented. "It's a good thing the car was slowing down, or you could have been in much worse shape."

Cordie knew they were trying to be reassuring, but their attempts to make her see the glass as half full were not working. She backed up the video and watched it again. She saw herself step up to the edge of the curb and the crowd gather around her. Everyone was facing forward, and suddenly their heads turned. Apparently this was the point at which the truck backfired. Within a fraction of a second, Cordie lurched into the path of the oncoming car.

When she played the video again, she concentrated on the people behind her. Everyone was crammed together so closely, it was impossible to see faces. She backed up the image once more and watched the pedestrians heading to the corner. There was only one suspicious-looking character. He wore a baseball cap down low over his brow, and he never looked up so the traffic cam could catch his face. He seemed to disappear in the throng. She let the video continue to play. After the crash, some people ran to help her; some stood watching in shock; and others who wondered what was happening walked into the camera's view. The commotion lasted a couple of minutes before a few onlookers began to drift away. She looked closely as they dispersed and saw the baseball cap disappearing among them.

Alec and Aiden played the video at least twenty times more, looking at individuals but concentrating on the man in the cap and finally concluding they saw nothing that would identify an assailant.

"That's enough," she said. "I can't watch this again. I don't recognize anyone."

"Why don't you tell Alec how you let him sneak up on you," Aiden suggested.

"What are you talking about?" Alec asked.

"All week long I've had this weird feeling that someone was following me."

Alec didn't say anything for a couple of seconds. He took a long swig of beer. "All week long, huh?"

She nodded. From the look in his eyes, she could tell he was about to get testy.

"Do you want to tell me why you think someone was following you? And then maybe you could explain why you didn't tell me about it."

"It was just a feeling," she said, trying to defend herself. "I didn't have any proof, and every time I got that feeling and tuned around or looked in a mirror, there was never anyone there."

Aiden felt like banging his head against the wall. "For God's sake, Cordelia, the whole point would be to avoid being seen if he was any good at his job, and apparently he was."

"You needn't snap at me. I was going to mention it."

"Start mentioning it now," Alec said. "When did you first suspect someone was watching you?"

She went through her week, telling him about the art gallery, the parking garage, and the cemetery. When she was finished, all he said was, "Okay. Is there anything else you want to mention?"

Cordie couldn't tell if Alec was irritated with her now or not. Turning to Aiden, she asked, "What time is it in Sydney?"

He didn't have to think before he answered. "It's after nine here, so it's after twelve noon there. Why?"

"I want to call Liam."

"I've been talking to him," Alec said. "He's looking into a couple of things and will call me back."

What couple of things? Before she could ask, he said, "I'll let you know. You have to be patient, Cordie."

That was easier said than done. She wanted to help, but she didn't know how. It was frustrating, and fatigue was taking a toll. At least she didn't have to worry about getting dark circles under her eyes. The bruises would hide them.

"I hate being helpless," she admitted.

Aiden actually looked sympathetic. "I know, but you have to let us handle this for now. You've suffered quite a trauma."

The aches and pains she was feeling at the moment told her he was right.

"Regan and I have a favor to ask," Alec said. His demeanor had changed. He was no longer the professional and serious FBI agent, but her friend.

"What is it?"

"The attorneys still haven't gotten the papers ready to sign on the house."

"Would you like me to call them?"

He shook his head. "No, they promised they'll get it done. But Regan and I were hoping you wouldn't mind if we moved some of our things into the house now."

"No, of course I don't mind. Didn't Regan want to change the paint color in most of the rooms before you moved?"

"Just two rooms, and the painters will be there tomorrow . . . if that's okay."

"Yes, it's okay. Go ahead and do whatever you want to do."

Alec left a few minutes later. Aiden walked him to the door, and the two of them stood there talking for several minutes in low tones. They both glanced at her a couple of times, and she knew they were talking about her. She also knew neither one of them would tell her what they were saying, though she was relatively sure it had something to do with keeping her in the hotel.

Alec had e-mailed the video to her before he left. She opened it on her laptop and watched it again. "This video is going to stay in my head for a long time," she told Aiden when he returned to her.

"Maybe if you stopped watching it . . ."

He had a point. "Okay."

"Try to think about something else."

"What a brilliant idea. I never would have thought to do that."

"Glad I could help," he replied, totally unfazed by her sarcasm.

He walked back to the table with his laptop and sat down to check a file. Several minutes passed in silence. He was so engrossed in his work, Cordie went into her bedroom and sat on the bed while she pondered what she could do to speed the investigation along. She walked back into the living room. "Aiden, I was wondering . . . ," she began sweetly.

"What?" Abrupt as always.

"When are you going back to Sydney?"

He stopped typing and looked at her. "Why?"

"I'd like to go with you."

He gave her what she could interpret only as the are-you-crazy look. "No."

"Wouldn't you like to hear why I want to go with you?"

"No."

"I'm telling you anyway."

He sat back. "I thought you might."

"I want to knock on Simone Rayburn's door, and I'm going to make her admit she sent someone to get rid of me. Then I think I just might do what Jayden suggested."

It was difficult for Aiden not to smile. Cordie was really getting worked up. "What's that?" he asked.

"Run her over. I might even take out the whole family."

"Cordelia, you're not going to Sydney."

She stopped arguing. It felt good to rant for a minute or two about Simone and get rid of some of her anger, but she realized in the end she did need to be patient. Liam was investigating, and maybe soon he would get the proof needed to arrest Simone and the man or men she sent to Chicago. There was absolutely no question in her mind that it could be anyone else.

"I'll be leaving for an appointment in a few minutes," Aiden announced. He closed his laptop and took it into his bedroom. When he returned, he was putting on his sport coat.

He didn't tell her where he was going or when he would be back, and she didn't ask. If he wanted her to know, he would have taken the time to explain—which would have been the polite thing to do. He would rather be rude, however. Should she mention that it was already after ten? No, of course she shouldn't. Teachers went to bed at ten on school nights—at least she did when she was teaching—but millionaire CEOs could stay out all night partying if they wanted. They didn't have to do things like control teenage boys with raging hormones the next morning.

Slipping his cell phone into his coat pocket, he said, "There's a security guard in the hall."

"I know. I saw him."

"You'll be safe. He won't let anyone in or out."

Or out? In other words, she wasn't going anywhere. She decided to mess with him. "I don't want to go anywhere. I love it here. I may never leave. Have a nice time tonight." Without another word she walked into her bedroom and quietly shut the door.

She hadn't lied. She was exhausted and wanted only to sleep. It was a luxury to be pampered, and right now that was what she needed. Forget about being self-reliant. She had to have help to get her strength back. Staying at the hotel just a little longer wouldn't be such a bad thing. She'd rest one more day, and then she'd go home.

She watched television for a couple of hours and relaxed. She fell asleep around midnight but woke up later screaming. Bolting upright, she frantically looked around the room trying to find the threat. She heard a crash, then a curse, and suddenly Aiden was at her side.

"What the . . . Are you all right?" he panted.

She pushed the hair out of her eyes and squinted up at him. "Did I wake you?"

"I heard a bloodcurdling scream."

"I heard it, too," she explained. "I screamed, and that's what woke me up. I don't know why I did that." She sounded bewildered.

"Bad dream?"

"Probably. I don't remember."

Wearing nothing but boxers, he stood there staring down at her, and as worn out as she felt, she still noticed how sexy his body was, while hers was . . . colorful. Black-and-blue.

"Do you want me to sleep with you?" he asked.

"No."

"Okay." He pulled the sheet back and got in bed with her. "Put your head on my shoulder."

"You're even telling me how to sleep now?"

"Good night, Cordelia."

TWENTY-TWO

Aiden left the suite around seven to work out and didn't return until after nine. He looked in on Cordelia to make certain she was all right. She was still sleeping soundly. After changing, he left again to get coffee and meet Spencer to discuss what to do about their brother, Walker.

When Cordie awoke, her room was still dark, but a sliver of sun shone through the gap where the draperies met. She rolled out of bed, opened the draperies wide, and looked out on a beautiful sunny day. She convinced herself she was feeling much better. Her aches and pains weren't nearly as bad, and once she started moving around, the stiffness in her legs eased. Her horribly bruised hip still burned like fire, but it wasn't unbearable. She could take care of herself now, and to prove it she would get dressed before the nurse showed up to help. She was sure she could manage the plastic sleeve over her cast so it wouldn't get wet. A new day, a new positive attitude, she told herself.

She was feeling pretty chipper until she saw herself in the mirror. She looked like the kraken. The swelling had gone down, but the bruised skin was more vivid, and her hair—dear God, her hair looked as though it had been styled in front of a jet engine. The expression *her hair stood on end* didn't do it justice. Maybe she needed a little help after all.

Patty, the fortysomething nurse who arrived later, was a talker. A little on the plump side, with kind eyes and a maternal disposition, she wasn't anything at all like the voluptuous nurse who had visited the day before. After she introduced herself, she told Cordie she was happy to have a break from taking care of Walker.

"He's being difficult?" Cordie asked. She couldn't hide her surprise. Walker was usually the real charmer in the family.

Because Patty was so soft-spoken, what she said made Cordie laugh. "He's a pain in the ass." She removed Cordie's sling and folded it. "Never a 'please' or 'thank you,' and he yells whenever we try to help. Moving him from the bed to the wheelchair is a trial."

"I had planned to go see him today," Cordie said. "Maybe I should wait until he's feeling better."

"Don't wait. He might sweeten up with a friend there. He sure wasn't happy to see his physical therapist."

Cordie hoped Patty was exaggerating. She couldn't imagine Walker being rude to anyone. Aiden, absolutely. Spencer, maybe sometimes. But Walker? No, never.

Once she was dressed, she headed across the hall to Walker's suite. The guard looked as though he thought she was trying to pull something, but he let her pass and, like a shadow, followed a foot behind her.

"I'll be right out here," he reminded her.

"And I'll be right in here," she replied, smiling, as she opened the door and slipped inside.

The suite was dark, and it took a second for her eyes to adjust. All the draperies were closed, and a single lamp on an end table was the only source of light. She took a few steps past the foyer and saw him. Poor Walker. He looked so pale . . . and angry. He was sitting in a wheelchair in the center of the living room next to the coffee table. His leg was straight out in front of him. The cast reached the top of his knee, and Cordie couldn't tell if he could bend his leg or not.

He managed a smile for her and said, "I hear you got hit by a car."

"I hear you crashed a car."

She thought she would give him a kiss on the cheek, but the closer she got to him, the stronger the foul odor became. She abruptly stopped. "You smell rank," she blurted.

"He won't let us bathe him," Patty said. She walked past Cordie with a stack of towels.

Walker's face became a mask of indifference. He glared at Patty until she disappeared into his bedroom and then said, "I wish everyone would leave me the hell alone."

"What's the matter with you?" Cordie demanded. He acted as though he hadn't heard her. She repeated the question in a much louder voice. She was so focused on Walker, she wasn't aware that Aiden and Spencer had just walked in. "After you have a bath and put on clean clothes, we'll all leave you alone, for a little while anyway."

"Do I have to go in the bedroom and lock the door to get some peace?" he growled. "In fact, I think I'm going to do just that." He started to back his wheelchair away from the coffee table so he could turn around.

Aiden was about to step in and give Walker a piece of his mind for acting like a child until Cordie laughed. The puzzling reaction made him hesitate. What did she think was so funny?

"You think I can't get you out of a locked room? It would take me five minutes, tops," she said.

Walker scoffed and stopped turning the wheels of his chair. "What would you do? Get someone to kick in the door?"

"Nothing so barbaric," she said sweetly. "I know a lot of ways to get you to come out. I could use tear gas, I suppose. That's quick and easy. Your eyes will burn for a week, but I guarantee you'll open the door. Or I could—"

He stopped her. "You're out of your mind. Where are you going to buy tear gas?"

Exasperated, she asked, "What did I do at St. Matthew's High School?"

"You were a teacher."

"And what did I teach?"

Before he could guess, she said, "Chemistry, Walker. I taught chemistry. I won't buy tear gas. I'll make it, and room service will bring me everything I need. Some vinegar, a little baking soda, a few hot spices . . . should I go on? Or would you like to hear what else I could put together to get you out of a locked room?"

She was bluffing, of course. Yes, she did know how to make tear gas, but she never would, and she didn't have the faintest idea what she would say if he asked her how she would get the tear gas into the room.

"You're a ghoul," he grumbled.

"Yes, I am," she agreed cheerfully. "Now, are you going to bathe, or do I call room service and start mixing up a few surprises to get you to cooperate?"

He put his hands up in reluctant surrender. "Okay, you win."

Before he could change his mind, Patty swooped in to roll him into the bedroom.

"Don't leave, Cordie," Walker called out. "This won't take long."

The way he smelled? She thought it would take the rest of the afternoon.

Aiden came up behind her and put his arm on her shoulder. "Tear gas, Cordelia?"

"You really know how to make that stuff, don't you?" Spencer sounded impressed.

"Yes, I do," she said as she turned around to face them.

It had been a long time since she'd seen all three Madison brothers in the same place, and she couldn't help but notice the similarities. There were distinct differences as well. Spencer and Aiden were both tall, and their muscular builds were a testament to the time they spent working out. Spencer was slightly bulkier in the shoulders than Aiden, but Aiden had the more chiseled body. Walker, on the other hand, didn't show the same signs of physical fitness. It appeared his lifestyle was beginning to catch up with him, because he was thinner than she remembered, and his skin had a sallow hue that suggested living in the fast lane had finally taken its toll. Despite their different physiques, all three brothers were handsome and could be models. Aiden would look right at home in *GQ*. Spencer would be more suited to *Sports Illustrated*. And Walker . . . he was different. While at one time he would have been a candidate for the cover of *Esquire*, he now looked like a subject for a medical journal.

Spencer patted her on the shoulder. "You look so much better today. I can barely see the bruises," he told her. "I don't think anyone would even notice. Doesn't she look good, Aiden?"

"Cordelia always looks good."

She was about to thank them for their lies when a knock sounded at the door, and a big, burly man dressed in white came in.

"Walker's cooperating, Edward," Aiden said.

"Edward's an RN," Spencer told her. "He was going to help us drag Walker into a shower."

Aiden introduced the nurse to Cordelia. When he took her hand, he frowned and examined her face. "You were in the car with Walker?"

Cordie turned to Spencer and gave him an accusatory scowl. "Barely noticeable bruises, huh?" she said with a laugh.

"She was hit by a car," Aiden explained.

She didn't stop Edward when he gently removed her arm from the sling. He checked her fingers and remarked, "Not too much swelling. That's good. When do you see the doctor?"

She didn't have the faintest idea. She didn't even know the name of the doctor who had put the cast on.

Aiden answered. "She has an appointment with a specialist day after tomorrow."

"I do? How do you know that?" she asked.

"I made the appointment for you."

"When?"

"At the hospital."

"When were you going to tell me?" she asked, surprised and perturbed that he was making plans for her without her knowledge.

"Day after tomorrow."

"He won't take the cast off that soon," she said.

"No. It's just a check to make sure you're healing properly. I'll take you."

"Aiden, I might not be here in a couple of days."

"Yes, you will."

Cordie wasn't about to get in an argument with him now. She would wait until they were alone. Then she'd have her say and make him listen.

"I'll go help with Walker," Edward said. He turned to Cordie before he left. "It was a pleasure meeting you. If you have any problems, you let me know."

There was a big problem standing in front of her, but she doubted Edward would be able to help her with Aiden.

"If you'll excuse me, I have some calls to make." She crossed the room and stopped. "Spencer, why don't you call housekeeping and ask them to send someone to clean all this up. It's a mess." She saw Aiden's expression and put her hand up. "Yes, I see the parallel."

His laughter followed her out the door. It wasn't at all the same, though. Aiden's definition of messy was completely different from that of normal people. Leaving a scarf on a table made the room a mess to him. Okay, maybe she left a few more things around the living room than just a scarf, but it wasn't enough to be considered messy.

The security guard walked her back to her door. "Mr. Madison was concerned when he couldn't find you. He calmed down as soon as I explained you were looking in on his brother."

Aiden was concerned? Did he think she'd left the hotel? And if so, how would she have accomplished it? She couldn't step out the door without a guard shadowing her, and if she ever dared to push the elevator button, she'd probably be tackled and dragged back to the suite. As long as Aiden was running things, she wasn't going anywhere.

She went into her bedroom to get her phone, walked past the closet, and came to a quick stop. The closet had been empty the night before. Now it was filled with clothes. She flipped the light on and walked in. They were her clothes, and not just a few. All the racks were full. On one shelf were three pairs of jeans, all nicely folded. On another shelf were T-shirts.

Had Aiden done this? And if so, why? Moving everything back or packing it all for the trip to Boston was going to be a real pain. She heard the door to the suite open. Regan was talking on her phone as she walked into the living room. She put her phone on the table along with her purse, then glanced up and saw Cordie.

"Alec has a box of your shoes. He'll be here with them in a few minutes. He ran into a friend in the lobby," she said.

Thoroughly perplexed, Cordie asked, "Why is he bringing my shoes?"

"Since you're going to be staying here for a while, I thought you'd want your clothes and your shoes." She dropped down on the sofa and patted the cushion next to her. "You should relax."

"I've done nothing but relax," Cordie said. "Why do you think I'll be staying here? I'm ready to go home."

"But I just brought some of your clothes over."

"Why?"

"What do you mean, 'why'? You need your things." Regan patted the cushion again. "Please sit."

Cordie gave in and plopped down beside her. "Regan, what's going on?"

"Alec thinks you should stay here awhile longer. You're safe here, and he thinks it's going to take some time to figure out who pushed you in front of that car."

"We may never know who did it, although I do have my suspicions. I can't stay here forever," she argued. "This is Aiden's place, not mine. I've intruded long enough."

"He's the one who insisted you stay with him, and he's got plenty of room. The bedrooms are far apart," Regan pointed out. "You won't be in his way because he's rarely here. And no one can get to you, Cordie. You couldn't be any safer."

"Yes, I know, but—"

"You also have help here, getting dressed."

"I can dress myself."

"Can you put on your skinny jeans with one hand? What about hooking your bra? Maybe when you can move your fingers on your left hand it will be easier, but now you're kind of stuck, aren't you? Walker has nurses who will help you."

"When I get home, I can hire someone if I need to."

"What about security?"

"I'll lock my doors."

"You know you should stay here."

Living in such luxury—and yet she felt trapped. If she were being completely honest, she would admit her resistance had little to do with her feelings of independence and more to do with her fear of being alone with Aiden. How could she move on and forget about him if she was living under his roof, seeing him every day, yearning for him to touch her? Cordie wished she could pour her heart out to Regan and tell her what had happened with Aiden in Sydney, but she couldn't. A couple of nights of insanity in Aiden's arms didn't make a relationship, and if Regan knew, she would worry about Cordie, and God only knew what she would say or do to her brother. It wouldn't matter that they were consenting adults. There was also the fact that Cordie had gone to great lengths to make sure Regan and Sophie believed her infatuation with Aiden was a thing of the past. Boston, she decided for the hundredth time, couldn't come soon enough.

"I'm not used to being pampered, but I have to admit it's been very nice. Room service is wonderful, and having my sheets changed is lovely. I don't have to lift a finger."

"Then you'll stay a little longer?"

"Yes, just a little longer," she promised.

"And you won't complain?"

Cordie laughed. "I won't complain. Now, enough about me. What's going on with you?"

"There's a little news," she said. "I took the check over to the horrid woman we rent the cracker-box house from, and she said Alec and I had to sign a year's lease. We've been going month to month while we've been looking for a house."

"What did you do?"

"I took my check back and told her we'd be out by next weekend."

Cordie knew what was coming. "And?"

Regan bit her lip and with an imploring look said, "Could we move into your house now?"

"Of course you can. You're buying the house. Just put my things in the guest room until the movers pick them up."

"You're sure?"

"Absolutely."

Cordie didn't feel displaced. Things were moving more quickly than she had anticipated, but she was happy her friends were the new owners. Hopefully, everything would work out and she'd be in Boston soon. They talked about the house and the great neighborhood for several more minutes, and then the subject turned to Cordie's situation.

Regan shook her head in disgust. "I've been thinking about that witch, Simone."

"What about her?"

"She threatened you, didn't she? I think we can only conclude that she was behind what happened to you. And by any definition, that was attempted murder."

"That's my conclusion," Cordie agreed.

"She has to be in a panic that her secret will come out, so I say beat her at her own game."

"What do you mean?"

"Put it out there. Let everyone in Sydney know what she did to your father and how she abandoned you. Rent a billboard if you have to."

Cordie laughed. "A billboard?"

"Do whatever it takes," she said. "Once the secret's out, she won't have any reason to come after you. Hopefully, she'll leave you alone."

"Or she'll become so enraged she'll hire ten men to kill me."

"That's a possibility," Regan allowed.

"I'm not okay with Simone getting away with attempted murder. And what about the man who pushed me?" Before Regan could answer, Cordie said, "If I only expose Simone, what happens to him? I'm not letting him get away with it. He should go to prison with Simone. I want to catch both of them."

"How are you going to do that?"

"I don't have the faintest idea. I thought I'd talk to Alec and Jack about it. They'll come up with something."

Regan was pleased. "You have a lot of faith in my husband and Jack."

"Of course I do. But I know what Alec will say."

"What will I say?" Alec walked in carrying a large box.

Regan told him to put the box on the floor in Cordie's closet. "I'll organize them later."

Cordie waited until Alec returned to the living room and then said, "You'll say I'm jumping to conclusions without sufficient information and I should look at the whole picture."

"You're right. That's exactly what I'll say." He walked over to Cordie and kissed her on her forehead. "How are you feeling, sweetheart?"

"Just fine," she replied.

"Regan and I love our new house," he told Cordie.

"We don't exactly own it yet," Regan reminded him.

"We will soon," he promised. "I heard from Liam, Cordie."

"Did he have any news?"

"He's been checking on those two bodyguards with Simone.

They've disappeared. He can't locate them anywhere in Sydney. They haven't used their passports, but they could be using other identities. If they were on a flight to the United States in the last week, Liam will find out."

"Do you think they followed me to Chicago?"

"It's a strong possibility."

"I think you should set a trap. Waiting is nerve-racking," Regan offered.

"Liam will have some information soon," Alec promised. "Be patient."

"I am being patient," Cordie protested.

Alec grinned. "I was talking to my wife."

Cordie left them to their discussion and went into her bedroom to fetch a couple of magazines she was going to offer Walker. When she returned to the living room, her friends were wrapped in each other's arms and kissing passionately. Being married for more than a year certainly hadn't dampened their enthusiasm; they didn't even notice her walk out the door. There was a different security guard standing in front of the elevator, but he was wearing the same suspicious frown. She nodded to him and continued on to Walker's suite. The guard rushed ahead to open the door for her.

Walker was alone, sitting on the sofa with his broken leg in its stiff white cast propped up on a round ottoman. He was wearing clean clothes, gray sweats and white shirt, and had his laptop out.

"Am I interrupting?" she asked.

He looked up and smiled. "Come sit with me. You can be my good-luck charm when Aiden and Spencer come back for round two."

Cordie was happy to see there were signs of the old Walker, the one she liked, returning. He moved a stack of papers from the sofa so she could sit.

"How's the arm?" he asked, nodding at the sling holding her left arm at a right angle in front of her.

"Fine."

"Tell the truth, Kane."

She smiled. Walker always called Sophie and her by their last names. "It hurts," she said. "I can't straighten it and I feel so . . . useless. How's your leg?"

"It hurts off and on," he admitted. "I don't like taking pain pills, though. I don't like the way they make me feel."

"I don't either."

"Beer helps," he said, grinning. "Want one?"

She laughed. "No, thanks."

Walker turned back to his laptop. "I just watched a press conference with Congressman Mitchell Ray Chambers. A reporter e-mailed it to me. The guy's a real blowhard. Want to watch it?"

"Okay."

"I bought some land from him and his cousin. Struck a good deal, too," he bragged. "But Aiden is fighting me on it."

Cordie didn't usually take an instant dislike to anyone, but the congressman turned out to be an exception. As soon as he smiled into the camera and started talking, she was disgusted. He went on and on about how he had negotiated the deal of the century with Madison and how he had been working on it for more than a year. He stressed that Mayor Green had tried to ruin the sale of Rock Point and then blame him. He wanted his constituents to know he hadn't allowed that to happen, and he was now thrilled to announce at long last the Hamilton Hotel and Resort was going to be built on Rock Point. It was all thanks to him.

As soon as the conference ended, Cordie asked, "Is any of what he said true?"

"Some of it," Walker answered. "The congressman did come to

me and we worked out a figure to buy the land. I thought it was too good to pass up. It was half the amount Aiden and Spencer had agreed to pay. Half," he stressed.

"Why do you suppose that is? Why would he take so much less?"

"He's up for reelection, and Mayor Green is challenging him in the primary. Her poll numbers are sky-high, and his are in the basement. He'll do anything to get reelected."

"You said the cousin owns the land with the congressman. He went along with taking less money?"

"Yes, he did," Walker said. "Maybe Chambers is giving him his half to make up the difference. I don't know."

"What does Spencer think about all this?"

"When he talks about the town adjacent to Rock Point, I can tell he wants the hotel. He said the town's drying up because there's no work, and a new hotel and resort would change lives, but he's with Aiden and doesn't want to do business with Chambers. Aiden damn well better get behind this."

Walker was digging in and ready for a fight. Cordie wasn't about to get in the middle, but she couldn't help pointing out the obvious. "I can understand why Aiden and Spencer might be cautious."

"You're taking their side?"

"That question is something one of my high school students would ask. No, I'm not taking sides. I'm merely pointing out that you have never, ever shown any interest in the hotel business. Isn't that true?"

"I'm an equal partner."

"Who always abstains when there's a vote." She nudged him in his side. "Admit it. Until now you've not been that interested, have you?"

"No, I haven't," he admitted with a sigh of resignation. He

leaned back against the cushions, closed his laptop, and dropped it on the seat next to him. "I've decided I want to be involved in the family business. They're not going to let me."

"You're wrong," she said. "I know they could use the help." When he appeared to be about to argue, she rushed on, "And everyone knows you're a born negotiator."

"Yeah?"

"You're the charmer in the family, Walker," she said. "But do you really want to be a permanent part of the business, or are you doing this until you can go back to racing?"

"I'm through with racing. It's time for me to retire."

He sounded as though he meant what he said. He'd been racing cars for so long she didn't think he'd ever stop, yet she hoped his declaration was sincere. At his core, Walker was a good man. He just needed to slow down long enough to see it . . . and to let others see it.

Cordie spent the rest of the day making calls to contractors in Boston, and by the time the nurse helped her shower and put on her blue silk nightgown, she was ready to curl up in front of a television and zone out. Aiden came in around eleven. He locked the door and, without saying a word to her, went into his bedroom. He was probably sick of having her around, she decided. Did he think he was stuck with her? She thought about asking him that very question, then decided he wouldn't tell her the truth. He was a gentleman. Even if he wanted to, he couldn't kick her out.

What was the matter with her tonight? She was feeling restless and out of sorts and having ridiculous thoughts. She knew what was wrong, but it took her a good five minutes to circle around to the truth. She wanted him. She hated being this close to him and being ignored. Cordie was desperate to get out of town. She hated feeling vulnerable and knew she should protect herself. The problem was she didn't know how.

A detective show was playing on television. She hadn't been paying enough attention to be interested and was reaching for the remote to turn it off when Aiden walked in. His hair was wet. He was bare chested and wore a pair of old sweats. He looked good enough to eat. She self-consciously pulled her hair forward, realized what she was doing, and stopped. If a few bruises repulsed him, it was his problem, not hers.

His expression wasn't giving anything away. She didn't have the faintest idea what he was thinking. No wonder he never lost at poker.

"Did you want something?" Why she'd whispered the question was beyond her.

"Yeah, I do." He came around the sofa and sat down. Then he gently lifted her onto his lap, nudging her legs apart so that she straddled him.

Frowning, she leaned up on her knees and asked, "What are you doing?"

He slowly lifted her nightgown up to her hips. His hands slid over her thighs, and he smiled when he realized she wasn't wearing underwear. He stared into her eyes and said, "I'm going to make you feel good." Pulling her toward him, he began to kiss the side of her neck, causing shivers up and down her spine. "You won't have to do a thing, Cordelia."

"Aiden . . ."

His mouth covered hers, and anything she wanted to say was lost in the moment. One kiss, and he made her burn for him. His mouth never left hers as he stoked the fire inside her. When at last they came together, he wouldn't let her set the pace. He was gentle yet demanding at the same time. Her orgasm was explosive. She cried out and squeezed him tight inside her, triggering his release. He whispered her name when he came; she shouted his.

He carried her to bed and slept next to her that night, but there weren't any words of love or praise. She didn't expect them, and what she found profoundly odd was that she didn't need them.

TWENTY-THREE

There were fireworks going off in Walker's suite, and not the fun kind. Cordie walked into the middle of a colossal argument. All three brothers were there. Aiden was silent, leaning against a credenza with his arms folded as he watched Spencer pace and yell at Walker. The youngest brother seemed oblivious to the uproar. She turned around and tried to leave before she was noticed, but Aiden grabbed her hand.

"I'm telling you I gave my word, and a Madison doesn't go back on his word," Walker calmly stated. "Isn't that right, Aiden?"

"You did not have the authority to make any deals, Walker," Spencer railed.

"Cordie, come sit with me," Walker said.

Aiden let go of her hand. She didn't want to sit with Walker; she wanted to leave. "No, I think I'll—"

"Go sit," Spencer said. "I'll stop yelling. I promise."

The promise lasted a full minute. "What in God's name were you thinking? You've never shown the least amount of interest in what we do, and now you're going to build a hotel? What the hell's wrong with you?" Spencer demanded.

Cordie noticed Walker's hands were fisted. She put her hand on top of his and patted him.

"What do you think, Cordie?" Walker asked.

"I think you're having quite a lively discussion."

"Lively discussion?" Aiden laughed. "Is that what you'd call this?"

"I should let you three have some privacy." She tried to get up, but Walker pulled her back.

"Tell us your opinion," he said. "Aiden and Spencer won't bend, and neither will I," he explained. "Maybe you can make them see what a great deal this is."

"No, really, I should leave . . ."

Walker didn't let go. She gave up and sat quietly next to him. If he needed an ally, she'd do what she could. She looked around at each of the brothers. "May I ask a few questions?"

"Go ahead," Spencer said.

"Has a contract been signed?"

"Not yet," Walker answered. "Congressman Chambers said he's busy with the campaign right now, but we've set a date a week after the primary to sign the contracts. We worked out the terms on the phone."

"He'll say he didn't call," Spencer said. "Trust me, the bastard will go back on his word. He won't sell that property for pennies on the dollar."

Aiden nodded. "The congressman is . . ." He caught himself before he said the word he was thinking and substituted, "corrupt and immoral. I don't want to work with him. He can't be trusted."

"You wouldn't be working with him," Walker pointed out. "As soon as he signs the contract, he's out of the picture. He won't have anything to do with the hotel and resort."

"Is the contract ready to sign?" Cordie asked.

Walker nodded. "It's basically Spencer's original contract, but with the lower figure. Congressman Chambers told me he's gone over every detail and agrees to the new terms. His cousin has also read the contract and is ready to sign."

Spencer dropped into a chair facing Walker. He braced his arms on his knees, leaned forward, and said, "How did this happen? How did you get involved in the first place?"

"I told you. Chambers contacted me. He said he was willing to bargain, but you had shut the door to any future negotiations. I pulled up the original contract you and Aiden had taken to him that he refused to sign—"

"After giving his word," Spencer interjected.

"Yes, after giving his word. He said after he thought about it, he realized selling Rock Point would be such an economic boon for the community, he couldn't stand in the way. He asked me what it would take. I gave him a figure and he agreed. We're getting Rock Point for half the original price. That's a hell of a deal."

Aiden was trying to hold on to his temper. "He's not going to sign the contract," he said. "It's all a con to beat Mayor Green in the primary. Fallsborough is a one-party town, and whoever wins the primary will win in November."

Spencer nodded. "Green was way ahead until Congressman Chambers held a press conference to boast that he sold Rock Point to us. I'm betting he'll hold another press conference before the primary to remind voters he saved the day by bringing the Hamilton Hotel to town."

"He'll sign it," Walker insisted.

"No, he won't," Aiden argued, impatient at his brother's persistence. "He's never going to sign it for that amount of money. He's greedy and he's manipulative. You can't trust anything he says. The very fact that he's scheduled to sign the contract after the primary should have been a warning sign. He'll wait until he's won the election and then he'll back out of the deal. He still thinks he can get more out of Rock Point. He'll tell the press we changed our minds or he'll come up with an even better story."

Walker wasn't giving in. He was defiant when he said, "You think I let him manipulate me."

"Yes," Spencer said, and the argument escalated until Spencer was shouting and Aiden was once again stone-faced. After ten minutes of useless back-and-forth, Cordie raised her hand. The brothers stopped talking.

"We're not in a classroom, Cordelia. Did you want to say something?" Aiden asked.

"There are two different issues at play here. First is the congressman." Turning to Walker, she said, "I think agreeing to buy Rock Point for half the original price was brilliant. Now all you have to do is wait for Aiden to force the congressman and his cousin to sign the contract."

"How can he do that?" Spencer wanted to know.

"He's going to surprise him."

"I am?" A hint of a smile softened Aiden's expression.

She slowly nodded. "You know what to do." She didn't think she needed to spell it out for him. Aiden's mind was every bit as devious as hers.

"I have to go," she said, and stood to leave. "Sophie's coming over soon, and that's going to turn into a whole . . . thing."

Walker stopped her. "You said there were two issues."

"Yes, I did. The other issue is you, Walker. Spencer and Aiden are having difficulty dealing with the fact that you want to be part of the team. I suggest you three sit down and figure it all out."

Walker was nodding his agreement as she walked toward the door.

"I'll be right back," Aiden said to his brothers as he rushed around Cordie to open the door for her. Once they were in the hall, he smiled at her. "You're very shrewd, Dr. Kane."

"Thank you, Mr. Madison," she replied, somewhat surprised by his praise. Aiden didn't hand out compliments readily.

There was a different security guard in front of the elevator. He wasn't wearing a name tag, but Aiden knew him.

"How's your brother doing, Josh?" Aiden asked.

"Real good," the young man answered. "He's going to run track in the fall. He's pretty sure he'll make the team."

"That's good to hear," Aiden replied.

How did he keep everyone straight? Cordie wondered. He had hundreds of employees. He couldn't possibly know all of them, and yet she had a feeling he did.

After introducing her to Josh, Aiden took her arm and turned her toward their suite. Looking over his shoulder at the guard, he said, "You know the rule."

"Yes, sir, I do."

Cordie stopped in the middle of the hall. "What rule?" she asked. Aiden was trying to get her into the suite, but she wasn't budging.

Josh didn't seem to notice the struggle and answered her. "You can't leave this floor unless you're with Mr. Madison."

She looked up at Aiden as he dragged her into the suite. "I can't leave the floor unless I'm with you?"

"He was speaking English, Cordelia. You heard what he said." He picked up a folder from the table and turned to go back to Walker's suite.

She followed him to the door. "I have to know."

"Know what?"

"How come you're so nice to everyone else and so rude to me?"

His answer didn't please her. He laughed.

"You're driving me crazy, Aiden."

She didn't wait around to hear if he had anything to say about her comment, knowing it would probably set off her temper. Aiden was arrogant, bossy, and a know-it-all. And she was still hopelessly in love with him.

Crap.

Cordie spent the rest of the day with Sophie and Regan. Her friends had taken some time off from work to be with her. She knew they were worried about her, and she tried her best to calm their fears. She kept insisting she was on the mend and was safe. She also insisted that soon Alec and Jack would come up with a brilliant plan to get the man who tried to kill her.

Regan surprised her and Sophie with spa treatments. Since Cordie couldn't go down to the spa, the spa came to her. Regan handed her a pamphlet and told her to choose the treatments she wanted. Cordie didn't know what half of them were, so Regan made the choices for her. While she and Sophie had facials, Cordie's hair was shampooed, trimmed, and styled. She was also waxed everywhere, it seemed. After that, she was plucked and then slathered with the most wonderful scented lotion. Last but certainly not least, she was given a lovely pedicure with Mula Red polish. While she was most appreciative, she couldn't help but feel like a car up on a rack getting a lube job. When she made the comment aloud, Regan wanted to know what kind of car, which instigated a whole other conversation among the friends.

As they were sitting quietly waiting for their nails to dry, Sophie wanted to hear the details of Cordie's near-death experience once more.

"Don't make me go over it again," Cordie begged. "And FYI, it wasn't a near-death experience."

"When I write about it for my newspaper, it will be," Sophie said.

"You do the cooking column," Regan reminded her. "Which I still find hilarious. How are you going to work in the near-death angle?"

"That's easy," Sophie said. I'll write something like: 'When you eat this chocolate soufflé, you'll think you've died and gone to heaven . . . and speaking of dying, my friend Cordie . . .'"

"How do you come up with new recipes, Sophie?" Cordie asked. "We know you can't cook."

"That's not true. I'm getting better. But I have a secret weapon."

Regan guessed. "Your husband."

"Yes," she said. "He loves to cook, and he's really good."

Cordie was feeling so serene she sat back against the soft cushions of the sofa with her feet propped up and dozed off while her friends chatted around her. She woke up when Sophie nudged her.

"Do you?"

"Do I what?" Cordie asked, startled from her slumber.

"Do you think Regan's brothers will ever get married?"

She thought about it for a minute and said, "Spencer will. Of the three, he's the most compassionate. Walker . . . maybe. He's vulnerable now, and I think it would be difficult for him to trust anyone outside his family."

"And Aiden?"

She shrugged. "I don't know about him." She did know, though. He was too driven to settle down . . . too busy.

"I don't think he'll marry," Sophie surmised. "But then, I didn't think I'd ever get married, and look what happened."

Regan smiled. "Jack happened," she said.

Sophie blew on her fingernails and tapped one to make sure it was dry. "How are you getting along with Aiden?" she asked Cordie. "Is it weird sharing a suite with him?"

"Look how big this place is," Regan said, throwing her arms wide. "There's plenty of room for both of them."

"We get along just fine. He's rarely here, and I hardly notice him when he is," Cordie asserted, knowing full well that wasn't true. Now she was lying to her friends, and the more questions they asked about Aiden, the more lies she would tell. Not wanting to continue the conversation, she jumped up and reached for the hotel phone. "Let's order room service. I'm starving."

"Great idea," Regan said. "I'm suddenly in the mood for a chocolate soufflé."

TWENTY-FOUR

Cordie decided she was going to have to give up sex. To be more specific, sex with Aiden. Not that being specific mattered. Before Aiden, she hadn't had sex with any man in such a long time she thought there must be something wrong with her. Had she turned into a female eunuch? Or had her hormones taken a sabbatical?

Saying no to the sexiest man alive . . . how hard could that be? She'd given up sugar and caffeine for Lent last year, and she'd gotten through the forty days without cheating. Granted, the first week had been rough. She'd had a horrid headache, and the boys at school ran the other way when they saw her coming, but she'd gotten past it.

This wasn't at all the same. She'd already given up on her "I'm over him" mantra. How could she possibly get over the man while she was living with him? She could walk away from him, though. She could go into her bedroom and shut the door.

Oh, who was she kidding? Just thinking about the way he touched her made her breathless. The erotic words he whispered in her ear were so hot.

She had it bad, all right, and she didn't know what in the world she could do about it. He hadn't given her any promises, and she didn't have any expectations of a future together. For him it had just been raw sex, and she was okay with that.

It was closing in on midnight when she gave up trying to sleep. She'd been tossing and turning so many times she felt as though she were on a trampoline. It was all the caffeine she'd had today, she decided. That was the reason she couldn't doze off. It had nothing to do with the fact that Aiden wasn't home yet. Home? She was calling the suite home now?

She went into the living room and turned on the television. She had a game plan. She would channel surf until she found something boring, like golf or fishing, and that would make her sleepy.

Who knew learning how to gut a walleye could be interesting? The next program did the trick, though. *Fishing with Larry* was exactly what Cordie needed. Everyone on the show whispered so they wouldn't disturb the fish. It was incredibly boring. She drifted off but woke up sometime in the middle of the night. She was wrapped in Aiden's strong arms and sleeping in his bed. He smelled so good, and his body was hard and warm, and oh, did she want him. All she had to do was kiss the side of his neck, just under his ear, and whisper his name. He did the rest. He was gentle with her, taking care to protect her injured arm, yet he was forceful, pushing her to the brink and then pulling back until she was writhing in his arms and begging. He was more out of control this time, and when he climaxed, she was there with him.

Cordie slept soundly in his arms all night long, and when she awoke, Aiden had already left the suite . . . most likely to go down to his office, she supposed. She went into her bedroom, put on her robe, and padded to the bathroom to brush her teeth. Nurse Patty knocked on her door a minute later, and Cordie was thankful the woman hadn't found her in Aiden's bed.

"Mr. Madison will be back here to pick you up at twelve thirty," Patty announced. "He said to tell you that he and two FBI agents will be taking you to the doctor today."

"Jack and Alec are good friends. You've met them."

"Yes, I have, and I'm sure they'll watch out for you. They won't let anyone push you into traffic today. I don't think you really need them, though, not with Mr. Madison around. I know he doesn't carry a gun, but he could take on anyone who tried to harm you. He plays sports, you know." She added with a nod, "He's quite competitive and strong."

Cordie knew how strong he was. She'd caressed and kissed nearly every inch of his magnificent body. She had trailed her fingertips across his chest and shoulders and down his upper arms. She had felt the heat from his muscles, the sinewy strength just below the surface. Thinking about him made her pulse race. She realized she was holding her breath and slowly let it out.

Patty stared at her with a quizzical expression. "What were you thinking about just now? You had the sweetest look in your eyes."

Cordie wasn't about to tell her the truth. "I was thinking that normally I can take care of myself. Aiden taught Regan and Sophie and me a few tricks."

Patty helped her put the plastic sleeve over her cast so it wouldn't get wet while she showered; then she gathered the soap and shampoo and towels and placed them within easy reach, keeping up a constant chatter as she worked. An hour later Cordie was dressed and ready for the day. She wore a simple white blouse and a blue-and-white skirt with ballet flats. Patty helped her brush her hair and then left to tend to Walker. There was still some time left before Cordie had to leave for her doctor's appointment, so she set up her laptop on the table. While she ate a bowl of yogurt with fruit and granola, she worked on answering e-mails. There were several from her former students, and she replied to them first. She might no longer be their teacher, but she didn't want to lose touch.

Aiden came into the suite ten minutes early. He gave her the once-over and asked, "Are you ready?"

She shut down her computer, picked up her purse, and walked to the door. "What about Alec and Jack?"

"They're waiting in the lobby." He turned her toward him and adjusted her sling. "You stay close to me," he ordered.

His hand was on the doorknob, but he stood there, waiting. She assumed he wanted her agreement. "Yes, I will."

Before she could guess what he was going to do, he leaned down and kissed her. It was a long, thoroughly hot kiss, and when he pulled back, she sagged against him.

"Let's go," he said in his brisk, abrupt voice.

He obviously wasn't having quite the reaction she was. She straightened away from him and walked by his side around the corner to the elevator. The guard was holding the doors open. When they emerged in the lobby, she spotted Alec and Jack standing in front of the hotel's tall revolving doors. She moved closer to Aiden, trying to look at every face as they crossed the lobby. Was someone waiting to grab her? Unless he wore a sign, she wouldn't be able to tell if anyone was there to make trouble. She didn't know what to look for.

Jack drove them, and Aiden sat next to Cordie in the backseat. He put his hand on top of hers and asked, "Are you nervous?"

"Why? Do you think the doctor will give me a shot?"

It took a couple of seconds for him to realize she was teasing. "That's not funny, Cordelia. I was asking if you were nervous being outside. This is serious . . ."

He was getting angry, and she could feel the tension in him. "I'm not nervous, because I'm in good hands. You did say you wouldn't let anything happen to me, and I believe you."

"All right, then." He was appeased.

Alec turned toward them, noticed Aiden was holding her hand, but didn't comment of course. He said, "Cordie, I talked to Liam last night, and he wants you to get a DNA test as soon as possible."

"Did he explain why?" Aiden asked. "Does he have a plan in mind?"

"He's working on it."

"The only reason for a DNA test is to legally prove I'm related to that witch. What's he going to do with it? I don't want or need proof," Cordie protested.

"But you'll get the test anyway, won't you?" Alec asked.

"I don't think I want to—"

"It will be quick and easy," Jack told her.

"Over before you know it," Alec added.

"In other words, I'm getting the test, aren't I?"

"That's my girl," Alec said.

"I never really had a choice, did I?"

Alec told her the truth, but he said it with a grin. "No."

Cordie stared out the window. It was a beautiful sunny day and as hot as the devil, which she loved. She tried to sit back and calmly watch the passing scenes on the street, but she couldn't. There were too many thoughts racing through her mind that needed to be sorted out. She was about to have a DNA test. What did Liam plan to do with it? What was the connection to the man who tried to kill her? Was he still out there, and would he try again?

She could feel her stomach tightening, and she leaned into Aiden's side. Just being close to his strength and his confidence was comforting. He was getting one phone call after another, and usually he would be on his phone nonstop doing business, but today he let the calls go to voice mail. The texts were also piling up, but he ignored those as well. It suddenly occurred to her that she had assumed he would go with her to the doctor. Now, why had she done that? He had to know she was safe with Jack and Alec, yet he'd either canceled or rescheduled his appointments to go with her. It was so thoughtful of him, so caring. Her mood lightened, and she suddenly wanted to kiss him. Unfortunately, the feeling didn't last. Aiden ruined it when he said, "It won't be long before this will all be over, and we can get on with our lives."

Had they been alone, she would have told him he could get on with his damn life right this minute. She wasn't his responsibility or his obligation. They weren't alone, though, and she knew Alec and Jack were listening to the conversation. She chose a more subtle response. She moved away from him and turned to look out the window again.

They were in and out of the specialist's office in record time. The waiting room was packed, but as soon as the receptionist saw two armed men with badges, she quickly ushered all of them into an exam room. Cordie felt ridiculous sitting on the exam table with three big men surrounding her.

"I'm safe here," she told them. "Why don't you all go sit in the waiting room."

"I'm not going out there," Jack said. "I might catch something."

Alec nodded in agreement.

Cordie laughed. "Broken bones aren't contagious."

Alec looked skeptical, but he relented. "We'll be right outside the door."

Jack followed him, but from Aiden's stance it was apparent he wasn't going anywhere. He stood with his back to the wall and his arms folded across his chest. He stayed with her while the doctor, who didn't have a humble bone in his body, looked at his handiwork and praised himself for the fine job he'd done. He ordered an X-ray, was pleased with the film, and told her she would be in the cast another four weeks. Next came the DNA test, which was quick and easy. They were on their way back to the hotel in a matter of minutes.

Jack pulled up in the circle drive, parked in front of the hotel steps, and motioned to the guard who was waiting just inside the doors.

Alec got out of the passenger seat and opened the door for Cordie. "We're going to check in with security before we take off," he said. He was about to say something else, but his cell phone rang. "Sorry, I've got to take this," he said.

Aiden wouldn't let Cordie stand there any longer. He took hold of her arm and pulled her along. Once inside the doors, he motioned to the security guard, and the two men flanked her sides as they crossed the lobby. Cordie appreciated the protection, but she was beginning to feel like some paparazzi target being shuffled away from the crowd. The hotel guests stepped aside as the men rushed her through the lobby. She did her best not to look conspicuous, but it was difficult.

Even though she was walking at a fast clip, she spotted Patty near the bellman desk talking to a man holding a huge vase of calla lilies, and she wondered which one of Walker's admirers had sent the impressive get-well surprise. The arrangement was spectacular, so large the deliveryman had to hold it with both his arms around the vase. She couldn't see his face, but she could see Patty's clearly. It was flushed. Was she flirting? It seemed so. The nurse was so wrapped up in keeping the man's attention, she didn't notice Cordie waving to her. Cordie stepped into the penthouse elevator, and as the doors were closing, she heard the man's booming laughter and smiled in reaction. So he was flirting, too. Ah, the power of love. Did most men and women want to fall in love? she wondered. Opening their hearts and becoming vulnerable made them either very brave or stupidly naive, and at the moment she believed she belonged in the stupidly naive category. Loving Aiden was god-awful painful, and she had had enough.

When the elevator doors opened onto the penthouse floor, she turned to Aiden. "Thank you for taking the time to go with me today. I know how busy your job is."

"You are the job right now," he said.

The guard on duty opened the door to the suite for them, but Aiden didn't follow her in, explaining that he needed to check in at his office. Before he left her, he said, "I have to go out of town to-morrow, but you can't be alone, Cordelia. We'll work out a schedule tonight."

The door closed before she could protest. Did he think she still needed a babysitter? He was being ridiculous. Once she was inside the suite, she was as safe as could be. Time for another talk, she decided, and this time she would make him listen. She dropped her purse on the sofa, then reconsidered and took it to her bedroom. She didn't want Aiden, Mr. Neurotic, to hyperventilate if he saw it. She took out her cell phone before setting the purse on a side table and checked her messages. There were five texts in all. She sat on the edge of the bed and scrolled through them. Four were from contractors in Boston. One was from Sophie asking about her doc-tor's appointment, so she called her to give a report. Ten minutes later, they were still chatting. Sophie was filling her in on the fish-ing trip she and Jack had just taken.

"I can teach you how to gut a walleye," Cordie offered.

Sophie was taken aback. "You . . . what? When did you learn that?"

"The other night I was . . . oh, never mind."

After the conversation ended, Cordie went back to her texts and discovered one from Alec, sent a few minutes ago. He said he was just leaving the hotel and realized he forgot to ask her if she was up for dinner tonight with Regan and him. She decided to call him right away. Dinner with her friends would cheer her up.

He answered on the first ring. "Hi," she said as she walked back into the living room. "Dinner sounds great. Make sure Jack and Sophie . . ."

Her head was down, but out of the corner of her eye something caught her attention. Her head snapped up and she saw the flowers. Then she saw him. Immediately she recognized the angry determination in his eyes, the scowl, the Fu Manchu mustache. She did the only thing she could do. She screamed bloody murder. He dropped the flowers—the vase shattering into a thousand pieces—and came at her fast as the door to the suite was closing behind him. She kept screaming. She knew she had to get to the hallway to get help. If she ran into the bedroom, she would be trapped. She circled the table and made a run for it, but he caught her before she reached the door, his hands on her throat, cutting off her air supply.

Jack had just put the car in drive when he and Alec heard her scream through the phone. He slammed the gear back into park and was out of the car and up the steps in record time. Alec was already ahead of him.

Aiden also heard her. He had just stepped off the elevator when Cordie's ear-piercing scream hit him like a lightning bolt. He raced to get to her.

Cordie was not going to die without a fight. She made a fist and punched the man as hard as she could in his Adam's apple. It slowed him down, but not for long. He gagged and released his grip for a split second, then grabbed her again. Realizing she was no match for his strength, she went limp and slumped to the floor, but he had such a strong hold on her, he pulled her back up. Time slowed in her mind, and she was about to black out when suddenly he was ripped away from her. Gasping for air, she slid down the wall. The world was spinning, but all she could see was Aiden, and she was terrified he was going to get hurt. When she finally could focus, she realized Aiden was pounding the hell out of the attacker. Good God, he was going to kill him.

Time was suspended in her mind. Suddenly Alec was there, and Jack was right behind him. She watched Alec pull Aiden off her attacker while Jack lifted her and carried her to the sofa.

"Let's have a look," Jack said. "Are you hurt anywhere?"

"No," she answered. Her voice was so hoarse she didn't recognize it. "I'm fine."

The second he let go of her she jumped up and lost her balance. Her legs had turned to rubber. Grabbing Jack's arm, she took a deep breath to calm herself. She couldn't stop staring at Aiden. The look in his eyes was chilling. If Alec had let him, she thought Aiden would have beaten the man to death. It wasn't temper she was seeing, or anger. It was fury.

While Alec was handcuffing him, the man said something Aiden took offense to. Aiden tried to grab him, but Alec blocked him with his shoulder.

"Go ahead. Call her a bitch again. See what happens," Aiden taunted, his voice deceptively calm. When he tried again to push Alec out of his way, Jack moved in front of him—no small trick, to be sure—and began to pat down the man while Alec recited his rights.

"What's your name?" Jack asked. The man shrugged and didn't answer.

"He's one of the men who was with Simone," Cordie said. "His name is . . ."

Alec finished her sentence. "Arnold Jenkins."

"How did you know—" Cordie began.

"Liam," Alec answered.

Cordie was too shaken to think it through. Everything was happening so fast.

"Is your buddy Charles Kendrick with you?" Alec asked.

Jenkins's response was obscene. Alec had had enough of his filthy mouth and slammed him into the wall. "Stop talking," he ordered.

Jack searched Jenkins and found no identification, just a hotel key card in his back pocket. He pulled a fierce-looking knife out of his left boot. There was a small pistol tucked in the other. As soon as he held up the weapons for Alec to see, Jenkins demanded a lawyer.

"Who do you want to call first?" Jack asked. "A lawyer or Simone?"

Jenkins looked at him blankly for a second and then grinned up at him with an arrogant smirk. The action was not lost on Jack and Alec, who exchanged a what-was-that-all-about glance.

Aiden went to Cordie and put his arm around her. She could feel him shaking when he gently pulled her down to sit on the sofa.

"Did he hurt you?" he asked her. "We should get a doctor here to look at you."

"I'm fine," she insisted. "He just choked me a little."

"Choked you a little?" Aiden was so inflamed he could barely get the words out.

Jack crossed to the sofa and squatted down to look at Cordie's neck. "It's not bad," he said. "His neck looks worse than yours."

"I hit him in his Adam's apple with my fist," she explained.

"Good girl."

Alec had pushed Jenkins into a chair by the door and was on the phone. He finished the call and said, "Jack, five, maybe ten, minutes away."

Jack explained. "Alec has a couple of agents swinging by to get Jenkins. We'll instruct them to lock him in isolation until we get around to interrogating him and letting him call a lawyer."

"Is that legal? Putting him in isolation?" Cordie whispered so Jenkins wouldn't hear.

"Processing a suspect takes time," he replied. "And Alec and I don't like it when someone hurts one of our own."

They considered her one of their own. She was touched and suddenly feeling very emotional. She wiped a tear from her eye. "Make him sweat," she said.

Jack laughed. "That's a given." He patted her hand, then walked over to Alec and said, "You've got this. I'm thinking I'll go ahead and ride with Jenkins, make sure he's put where I want him."

"When you interrogate him, I want to be there," Aiden said.

Alec shook his head. "Sorry, but no."

An argument started and didn't end until Jack left with Jenkins in tow. As he was walking out the door, he told Aiden, "You better figure out how he got up here."

"I'm going to do that right now," Aiden assured him. "Alec, are you staying here?"

"For a little while. Then I'm heading over to Jenkins's hotel room with Jack. The crew should already be on their way."

"Wait until I get back," Aiden told him. "Walker and his nurse must have heard Cordelia. I want to tell them she's okay." His voice turned hard. "And I want to find that guard." He paused at the door to smile at Cordie. "You've got a wicked scream."

After the door closed behind him, she asked Alec, "Was that a compliment?"

"I think so."

"Will you excuse me a moment?" She didn't wait for permission but went into her bathroom to splash cold water on her face. When she looked in the mirror, she was pleasantly surprised. The skin on her neck was red, but she didn't think there would be much of a bruise. Her sling was torn. She couldn't remember that happening.

Jenkins must have grabbed it when he tried to drag her up to her feet. The memory was way too fresh. She pressed her back against the wall and took several deep breaths. She was her father's daughter, she reminded herself. No time for tears or tantrums. She needed to stay tough, to keep it together. She could break down tonight when she was alone.

She took a few minutes to clean up. After tossing the sling into the trash, she changed into a new blouse, combed her hair, and applied a little lip gloss. At the moment, that was the best she could do. She sat on her bed for a while, willing her heart to stop racing, and when at last she felt composed, she took a notepad and pen from the nightstand drawer and returned to the living room.

Aiden was already back and standing at the bar talking to Alec. She went to the dining table, pulled out a chair, and sat down.

"Cordie, would you like something to drink?" Aiden asked.

"Diet Coke, please." Her voice was still raspy, and her throat was sore from the man's hands squeezing it closed.

"Are you sure you don't want something stronger?" Alec asked.

Aiden filled a glass with ice and poured the drink for her. He put it on the table and pulled out the chair adjacent to her while Alec took the seat across from him. Both men were studying her. Cordie was acting as though nothing out of the ordinary had happened, and Alec was impressed by how she was able to hold it all together. Aiden, on the other hand, was worried. He knew she needed to let out her feelings, not squelch them.

"What's the paper and pen for?" Aiden asked.

"I thought I'd make notes and write down Liam's phone number. I want to call him." She picked up the pen and looked at Alec. "May I have his phone number?"

He had the number memorized and rattled it off to her. It was only when she started to write the numbers that she realized her predicament. She was left-handed, and unfortunately her left arm was in a cast. She wasn't ambidextrous, but she tried to write Liam's name with her right hand, giving up after three letters. The scribbles looked like a preschooler's work.

She pushed the paper and pen to Alec, who said, "Where's your phone? I'll program Liam's information in."

"I don't know. I had it when he—" She stopped suddenly, took a breath, and asked Aiden to call her cell phone.

They found it under a chair. After adding Liam's contact information, Alec handed the phone to her. "I want to know why you want to call him," he said, "but you can explain later. Right now I want to hear what happened. Did you let Jenkins in? Did you open the door for him?"

"No. He was walking into the suite when I came out of the bedroom. I saw the flowers . . . then him." Frowning, she looked around the room. "What happened to the flowers?"

Alec pointed to the foyer. The flowers were strewn all over the marble floor, and the vase was in scattered shards. She thought it odd that she hadn't noticed the mess until now. Had he thrown them? She couldn't remember. She'd been busy at the time trying to keep the maniac from choking her to death.

"How did he get past security?" Alec asked.

Aiden had the answer. Patty had gone to the lobby on her break to make a few personal calls. Jenkins approached her with flowers and asked if she knew where the penthouse elevator was located. He was dressed in navy pants and a navy shirt with the name of the florist shop on the back, and he also wore a baseball cap with the florist's logo. She offered to carry the flowers up but realized the vase was too heavy for her. Without thinking, she took him up with her. That was the first mistake.

The second mistake was made by the guard on duty. Walker was pitching a fit because he couldn't get into the wheelchair without help. The guard left his post in front of the elevator and went into the suite to help.

Third mistake: Patty rushed to Cordie's suite and opened the door for Jenkins, not realizing Cordie was back from the doctor yet. Telling Jenkins to just put the flowers on the table, she ran around the corner to help Walker.

Aiden wanted to fire everyone, including Walker—if that were possible—for being impatient and demanding everyone's attention. He wasn't thinking like a businessman now because he was still having an emotional reaction to almost losing Cordelia. He wouldn't allow himself to acknowledge why he was out of control when it came to her, or why just thinking about anyone hurting her sent him into a rage. He found it impossible to be reasonable.

Cordie talked him off the ledge and saved a few jobs in the process. She pointed out that yes, while mistakes were made, everyone would now be more vigilant. In the end Aiden compromised to keep the peace. He would let Patty continue to take care of Walker and to help Cordelia when she needed her assistance, and he would transfer the guard to another less stressful position in the hotel. He told Alec, if he had to hire his very own SWAT team to keep Cordelia safe, then, by God, that's what he would do.

"Do you remember when Regan was in trouble?" Alec asked.

"Of course I remember," Aiden said. "She was being stalked, and you investigated. Once the nightmare was over, we were stuck with you."

"At the time she was temporarily living at the hotel, and you posted a guard."

Aiden nodded. "Yes, I did. I was worried about my sister."

Alec was walking to the door as he continued. "You were upset, but you were in control. It's different with Cordie, isn't it?"

The door closed without an answer.

Jenkins had been staying at an upscale hotel, but his room was a pigsty. There was a *Do Not Disturb* sign on the door, letting house-keeping know they were not to enter. His clothes were on the bed, the chair, and the floor. There were a few items hanging in the closet. Wet towels covered the bathroom floor, and carryout containers spilled out of every trash can. They found a Glock hidden under the mattress.

Jack held it up and asked, "Where did he get this?"

"We'll have to ask him," Alec said.

On the desk in plain sight were three Testor burner phones. Two were fully charged but hadn't been used. The third was just a shell.

Alec showed it to Jack. "How much do you want to bet he was using this one to call Australia?"

Gloves on, they went through all the trash hoping they'd find the guts of the phone, but they didn't. It would have helped their case to have evidence of a link between Chicago and Sydney, to hit redial and see who answered. No such luck. Nothing about this was easy.

TWENTY-FIVE

Before heading to pick up carryout, Alec and Jack dropped their wives off at the hotel. The men had told them what had happened to Cordie, and Sophie and Regan wanted to see for themselves that she was all right. Cordie answered all their questions while they helped her change into comfortable yoga pants and a top.

"How come you have so many workout clothes, and you don't work out?" Sophie asked.

"I'm going to start as soon as I get settled in Boston. I used to get such a workout at St. Matthew's running up and down the stairs a hundred times a day. Now I sit like a blob."

"You don't work out, Sophie," Regan reminded her as she was brushing Cordie's hair.

"I do now with Jack. I'm actually starting to like it."

Regan and Cordie laughed.

"No, you're not," Regan said.

"You're such a bad liar," Cordie added.

Sophie shrugged and nodded in agreement. "I really am."

Cordie stood. "Leave my hair alone, Regan," she said, taking the brush from her hand. "I'm starving. When will Alec and Jack be here?" she asked as she headed to the living room.

"Anytime now," Regan answered. "They're bringing carryout. Alec wouldn't tell me where they're getting the food. He just said it was something exotic and we'd love it."

"Pizza." Sophie and Cordie said the word together.

Regan nodded. "Yes, pizza."

"Jack told me they're getting healthy food."

"Pizza," Cordie said again as she took a seat on the sofa and folded her legs under her. Sophie kicked off her heels and joined her, and Regan curled up in a chair across from them.

"You should have seen this place earlier. There was glass everywhere and flowers. Housekeeping made it spotless again." When she saw her friends exchange a fearful glance, she quickly added, "Let's not talk about what happened."

Regan nodded in agreement. "I've got a huge favor to ask you, Cordie."

"She'll do it," Sophie said confidently.

"Do what?"

"The Summerset Ball."

"We always go together," Sophie insisted. "The Summerset Foundation helps a lot of people, and the ball is their big event. Regan's working on the committee this year."

"When is it?"

"And you have fun, don't you? It won't be the same if you aren't there."

"When is it?"

"In a month. You could stay here that long, couldn't you, before you move to Boston?" Regan pleaded.

Sophie patted Cordie's knee and said, "A month isn't long at all, and didn't you tell us you were having work done on your Boston town house before you moved in?"

"Yes, but—"

"Alec told me they haven't even started refinishing the floors. Something about a union fight. Nothing to do with your town house, but that was the reason for the delay. I guess the dispute is still going on, and they won't go back to work until it's settled."

"Besides, you can't go anywhere as long as people are trying to kill you. Right?" Sophie said.

The reminder was given in such a blasé voice, Cordie began to laugh. "Right," she agreed. "But that will be resolved soon."

"You sound confident," Regan remarked.

"What about the Summerset . . . ," Sophie began.

"If I'm already in Boston, I'll fly back for it."

"Where's Aiden?" Regan asked the question and looked around the room as though she expected her brother to pop up from behind a chair.

"He's not here," Cordie said. "So you can stop looking for him."

Her comment set them off, and Alec, Jack, and Aiden walked in to the joyful sound of laughter. Jack carried a stack of pizza boxes from Tony's Pizzeria. Alec had beer. Aiden was taking off his tie. He took a bottle of beer from Alec, opened it, and took a long swallow.

"Where's Spencer?" Regan asked.

"Meetings," he answered but didn't embellish. "How are you feeling?" he asked Cordie.

"My arm's a little sore, but I'm fine, thank you. You should go get Walker."

"He's busy."

"Doing what?"

Her question made him smile. She'd sounded so suspicious. "He's just busy."

"He loves Tony's pizza. You should take him a couple of slices."

"Cordelia, he's with someone, a female someone."

She didn't understand why, but the realization that Walker was entertaining a woman embarrassed her, probably because Aiden had to spell it out for her.

"Oh."

Aiden laughed. "You're blushing."

"Cordie," Sophie called. "Alec brought Kelly's root beer. I know you love it."

Kelly's was a locally owned company, and their root beer was hugely popular. Jack opened a cold bottle for Cordie and handed it to her.

"My boss, Mr. Bitterman, is addicted to the stuff," Sophie said.

Aiden followed Cordie to the table. "When is Liam calling?" he asked Alec.

"Ten o'clock. I'll set up the computer so we can see him."

"I don't need to see him," Aiden said, his irritation obvious in his voice. "I want to know what the hell he's doing."

Cordie understood Aiden's frustration. "Maybe he'll have made some progress."

"Some progress? I want to hear that there've been arrests and confessions."

"Aiden, you should be more patient," Regan said.

"The hell with that. Has Jenkins said anything yet?" he asked Jack.

"Not yet, but he will."

"How can you be so sure?" Cordie wondered.

Alec answered. "He's being charged with attempted murder. We're letting that fact settle in his mind, and when we next talk to him, we think he'll want to make a deal."

"You mean, he'll give you Simone for a lesser charge?" Cordie asked.

"Something like that," Alec said.

Aiden knew that Alec and Jack were excellent at what they did. They had the commendations to prove it, but he still wanted to take over and tell them what to do. None of his suggestions were legal, though, but in his mind, after seeing that bastard's hands on Cordelia, he didn't think that mattered.

"Cordie, where's your sling? Shouldn't you be wearing it?" Sophie asked.

"It was torn up when Jenkins . . . you know."

"I'll get you another one," Aiden promised. He had his phone to his ear as he walked into the bedroom.

Dinner was relaxed. There was no more talk of Simone or Jenkins, and Cordie was thankful. She ate two slices of veggie pizza and listened to Alec as he enthusiastically explained how he was going to remodel the basement of his and Regan's new home. It seemed the only thing he wasn't putting in was a basketball court.

"Have you signed the papers yet?" Sophie asked Cordie. "Because if you haven't and you still own the house, Jack and I would like to make an offer to buy it."

The stunned look on Alec's face made everyone laugh.

Sophie patted his arm. "I was just teasing."

"We really ought to get things moving and transfer the money," Regan said. "The papers should be ready tomorrow afternoon. If you could go with us to the bank . . ."

Alec shook his head. "We'll bring the papers to you, Cordie."

"When do you get the cast removed?" Regan asked her.

"A month."

"Oh, that's perfect. Since you have to stay to see your doctor, you might as well go with us to the Summerset Ball."

"I've heard there are doctors in Boston," Cordie said.

"You should stay," Sophie urged. "You shouldn't bounce around from doctor to doctor."

"If I have to go to that ball, you should have to go," Alec said.

"You look so handsome in a tux," Regan told her husband. "And you love going. You . . ." She sighed then. "Okay, I can't sell it."

Alec laughed. "I go because it's important to you, sweetheart. And that's why Cordie will go."

"We'll see," Cordie said in the hope her friends would be appeased.

She felt trapped, trapped in paradise, and she was beginning to feel sorry for Aiden. He would go nuts if she continued to stay in the suite after arrests were made and the threat was over. She didn't want to think about that now. Her friends were here. She was having a wonderful time, but fatigue was beginning to take over and her arm was starting to throb. She excused herself and went into her bathroom to get a Tylenol. When she opened the door, Aiden was waiting in her bedroom with a new sling.

"Where did you get that?" she asked.

"It was just delivered," he answered. "Stand still and let me fix this thing."

Once the sling was in place, he moved her hair out of the way. His hands stayed on her shoulders as he stared at her. And then he said something that shocked her.

"You're beautiful, Cordelia."

She didn't know how to respond. He kissed her then, but once wasn't enough. His mouth covered hers again, and he pulled her into his arms. The kiss wasn't at all gentle, but raw, carnal in its intensity, and she was so aroused that, when he pulled back, she desperately wanted to rip his clothes off and fall into bed with him.

Sophie's laughter from the living room pulled her back to reality. Cordie realized her hand was on the zipper of Aiden's jeans. She jerked back and took a deep breath. She wagged her finger at him, patted her hair as though that would straighten it, and all but ran into the living room. She tried to ignore him the rest of the evening.

A few minutes before ten, Alec looked at his watch. "It's almost time to hear from Liam." He went to get Aiden's computer and set it on the coffee table so everyone could see.

Liam checked in at ten on the dot. He appeared on the computer screen wearing a T-shirt that said *Bob's Beer and Babes Bar* on it. The background wasn't in focus, but it appeared he was sitting on a deck or patio with waves lapping at the shore behind him. He asked who was there, and Alec identified everyone and quickly introduced him to Regan and Sophie, who stepped away from the computer screen and mouthed the word *wow* to each other. Liam's good looks had obviously impressed them, because they gave Cordie the why-didn't-you-mention-how-hot-he-was look. She shrugged in response.

Jack watched the silent exchange. Fascinated, he whispered to Sophie, "What are you doing?"

"Talking to my friends," she answered.

Liam greeted the group. His demeanor was courteous and businesslike, and it irritated Aiden that he could be charming and polite to Sophie and Regan, but he'd been a lecherous flirt with Cordelia.

Alec had already talked to him about Jenkins's attack on Cordelia, and Liam wanted to see for himself that she was all right.

She stood in front of the computer screen. "I'm okay," she said, smiling.

"Do you have any more information for us?" Alec asked.

"Hold on," Aiden interrupted. "What about the other man who was with Simone? The one who tried to drag her out of the hotel?"

"Charles Kendrick." Alec supplied his name.

"Where is he?" Aiden asked.

"He's still here in Sydney," Liam said. "We're watching him."

"Anything to report?" Jack asked.

"As a matter of fact, I do have something interesting. Documents," he said. "I've e-mailed them to you, Alec. I think, once you've read through them, you'll understand why I can't stop smiling."

"That good, huh?"

Liam nodded. "Yes, that good. It's dry reading but worth it. Just don't ask me how I got them."

As soon as Liam ended the call, Aiden suggested that he, Jack, and Alec go down to his office to print out the e-mail and start reading.

"This will probably take a while," Jack told Sophie.

"The hotel limo driver will take both of them home," Aiden offered.

Jack and Alec kissed their wives good-bye, then waited at the door for Aiden, who had crossed the room to Cordie.

"Don't you dare leave this suite," he ordered.

"What?" She acted shocked. "But we were going pole dancing."

"That's not funny. I mean it, Cordelia. You stay put."

"Yes, sir."

And he was gone.

"Your brother is like a general. I know he means well, but he's beginning to get on my nerves," Cordie said.

"He's been on my nerves for years," Regan said.

Sophie spoke up. "I love him. He can do no wrong as far as I'm concerned."

"We all love him," Regan conceded. "Cordie and I just recognize his flaws."

Sophie was in a nostalgic mood. "I never told you what happened to me when I was nine years old. It was pretty awful. Aiden became my champion."

"What happened?" Regan asked.

"My dad was in trouble with the law . . . again. I was home with the housekeeper when two scary-looking men with guns and badges came in and took me to the police station. I was so frightened. This one detective kept threatening to put me in foster care, and no one would ever know where I was. He'd make sure of it."

"Why was he threatening you?"

"He wanted me to tell him where my father was. I didn't know the answer, but even back then, if I had known, I wouldn't have told. He also wanted to know if there was a safe hidden in my house. The questions went on and on. To this day I don't know how Aiden found out what was happening. Maybe the housekeeper called him. I asked her, but she insisted she hadn't."

"What did he do?" Regan asked.

"He saved me," she said. "When I saw him, I started crying and ran to him. He put his arm around me and told me everything was going to be all right. He brought a couple of attorneys with him, and he threatened the detectives with all sorts of things. He swore if they ever came near me again, he'd have their badges, and from the way the attorneys were backing him up, I think he could have done it."

"Why didn't you want us to know?" Regan asked.

"Back then it was because I cried, and I thought you two would think I was a baby. Time passed, and I just never got around to it."

"Do you realize how young Aiden was? He couldn't have been twenty yet," Cordie said.

"I wish you had told me when it happened," Regan said. "Talking about it would have been therapeutic."

"I knew," Cordie said.

"How?" Sophie asked, surprised. "Aiden promised me he wouldn't tell anyone, so I know you didn't find out from him."

"We were having a sleepover at Regan's house, and back then I had such a crush on Aiden. Remember?"

Both Sophie and Regan laughed. "We didn't know," Regan said. "Not then. Not until you told us."

"I heard the housekeeper tell Aiden he had a phone call from his family's law firm. I was such a worrier, like you two were, and I thought Aiden might be in trouble, so I listened to the conversation. That's how I found out."

"Why didn't you say anything?" Sophie asked.

"I don't know. I guess I figured that if you wanted me to know, you'd tell me."

"The driver will be here in a minute. Why don't we help you get ready for bed before we go," Regan suggested.

Cordie appreciated the help, and while they were in her bedroom, they continued to chat.

"What's the deal with Liam?" Sophie asked as she turned down the comforter.

"He and Alec have been friends a long time," Regan said. She opened a drawer and brought out a pair of pajamas. "I think Alec arrested him once. That might be how they met. I still haven't gotten the whole story."

"Cordie, don't you think he's gorgeous?" Sophie asked. "Did you notice how he smiled at you and how his voice softened when he was talking to you?"

"No, I didn't notice, and yes, he is good-looking."

"I love his accent," Sophie said.

"He lives in Australia. Would you like me to move there so I can go out with him?"

"Of course not. Make him move here. You're worth it."

There was a knock on the door.

"There's our driver," Regan said. "Let's go, Sophie."

The friends gave Cordie a hug and left.

Cordie was exhausted. She settled into the soft bed and turned on the television. She scanned a few channels and found *Fishing with Larry* on one of the cable stations. Cordie thought the show would put her to sleep, but she actually became interested. An hour later, she decided Larry was turning her into a fisherman.

She heard the outer door open and the men laughing as they came in. Curious to find out what was going on, she got out of bed. It took her a few minutes to put on her robe and sling, but by the time she padded barefoot into the living room, they were opening beers and toasting one another. Aiden dropped a stack of papers on the table in front of them.

"What's so funny?" she asked.

All three looked at her and smiled.

"Do you want to tell her?" Jack asked Alec.

Alec pulled out a chair for her to sit. "As it turns out, there's more than just a scandal driving Simone to get rid of you."

They started laughing again. "Aiden, you explain," Alec suggested.

He pushed the papers toward her. "When we're done with the Taylors and the Rayburns, you're going to own their company."

TWENTY-SIX

You're the firstborn," Aiden explained.

"What does that mean?" Cordie asked.

"When you turned twenty-one, you inherited twenty percent of the Merrick company stock. It was in Merrick's will." He shook his head and continued. "I've never seen anything like it. I can't imagine why Merrick set up his inheritance this way. I guess we'll never know."

"Twenty percent doesn't sound like much," Jack said, "but in fact it's huge. It's worth millions. Simone inherited her shares of Merrick Enterprises from her mother, Alice. Simone wanted the perks, but she didn't want the responsibility, so she handed over the management to her father. According to the will, you now own twenty percent of her share, which is just enough for her to lose majority control."

"And that's why Simone or someone else in the Rayburn family wants you out of the way," Alec reasoned.

"Someone else in the family? No," Cordie said. "Simone wouldn't have told anyone about me. She used a fake name when she married my father. She was Natalie Smith back then."

"She was pregnant with you when she married your father, wasn't she?" Jack asked.

"Yes."

"You're lucky she didn't try to abort you," Alec said.

Cordie sat on the edge of the chair, her back ramrod straight, with her right hand fisted in her lap. Thinking about Simone made her sick to her stomach.

"She told me she wanted to get an abortion, but she was too far along. She was past five months."

No one said anything for a long minute; then Alec commented, "It's a good thing she didn't stay around while you were growing up. I can't imagine what your life would have been like."

"I don't understand why your father couldn't see what she was," Jack said.

"He wore blinders, I guess," Cordie replied. "He loved her almost to the day he died."

"Sounds more like an obsession," Jack remarked.

"Simone's sons seem to adore her," Cordie said. "And she doted on them when they were at the ball." She smiled when she added, "Until I ruined her night."

Aiden laughed. "You did do that."

"The sons are still in their teens, but they're already being groomed by the patriarch, Julian Taylor," Alec said. "Obviously he thinks the older one is the firstborn."

Jack tapped on the printed pages lying on the table. "The way I'm reading this convoluted document—which, by the way, reads like it was written in the Middle Ages—when you turned twenty-one, you not only rightfully owned part of the company, you completely changed the power structure."

"But am I a legitimate heir, since she was using a false identity when she married my father?" Cordie wondered.

"There's no stipulation for it in Merrick's will," Aiden told her. "Firstborn simply means the first child born to Simone."

"Her sons don't inherit it?" she asked.

"Nope," Jack answered. "I'm sure they'll get property and a lot of cash, maybe other assets, but no Merrick stock."

"You can't sell it or give it away," Alec told her. "You're stuck with it."

"What if I don't claim it?"

Aiden answered her question. "There have already been two attempts on your life. Do you think they'll stop? You could run and hide, or you could walk into Julian Taylor's office, drop the DNA results on his desk, and tell him you're going to destroy him and his entire family. I'll be real happy to help you do that."

"And Simone gets away with hiring someone to kill me?"

Alec shook his head. "Let us worry about her."

Jack stood and stretched. "Liam did have a suggestion to speed things up," he said. "He's waiting for the right time. We'll talk about it then."

She wanted to talk about it now, but Alec and Jack were ready to go home. Aiden walked them to the door, made sure the dead bolt was in place, and then followed her into her bedroom. She was removing her sling so she could take off her robe when he turned her toward him and said, "Let me help you get ready for bed."

"I am ready for bed," she told him.

"No, you're not."

He removed her robe and began to unbutton her pajama top. In seconds it was on the floor with her pajama bottoms. She was stark naked, and he was fully clothed. She wasn't at all self-conscious, though, because the way Aiden was looking at her made her feel beautiful. His hands caressed her heavy breasts until the nipples were hard. He kissed her, slowly, leisurely, acting as though he had all the time in the world. He felt her tremble and whispered, "Now you're ready. Get into bed, Cordelia."

She lay down and tried to pull the sheet up around her, but he wouldn't let her. She watched as he removed his clothes and then covered her with his body. His skin was so hot.

Aiden groaned with the contact of his body pressing into hers. "I've thought about this all day. You make me crazed." His arms slid under her knees, and he lifted her. "I'm going to make you as hungry for me as I am for you."

He kissed every inch of her stomach before moving lower. His day's growth of whiskers rubbed her sensitive inner thighs. He made good on his promise and proceeded to drive her out of her mind. She begged for him to let her climax, and only when she threatened to hit him over the head with her cast did he give her what she wanted.

Aiden was just as greedy. Cordie lost count of the number of times during the night that he reached for her.

"You're going to miss me when I'm gone," she whispered.

A long while passed before he answered her. "Yes."

Aiden didn't go out of town the next day. She assumed there was a business reason for the cancellation. She didn't see him or anyone else except the hotel staff for the next four days and nights. She knew Aiden was still around because she heard him leave in the morning, and late at night, she heard him come in. He slept in his own bed. Maybe he had decided to distance himself from her. She should mentally do the same in preparation for Boston, shouldn't she?

Sophie and Regan were both swamped at work, and she didn't want to bother them. It wasn't their job to entertain her. She did talk to Alec a couple of times. Still no news from Australia. He'd told her Liam had a suggestion for speeding things up, but he still hadn't told her what it was. She decided if she didn't hear something today, she would call Liam and ask him.

She was beginning to feel like a caged animal. The walls of the suite were closing in on her, and she was fantasizing about all the ways she could sneak outside for a few minutes.

There were a few diversions. The swelling had gone down in her fingers, and she was now able to type with both hands. She received an e-mail from one of the doctors at the Garvan Institute, telling her he had read her dissertation and was quite impressed. He asked her several questions about her research, and a spirited debate resulted, which was fun and challenging. In the end she'd more than proven her thesis, and when he conceded, he offered her a job.

Jayden Martin was another diversion. He called her in a panic. After several weeks in a summer school class, he was certain he was going to fail chemistry again. How did he know? she asked. His reply was direct: The teacher told him so. Cordie, knowing that Jayden was a very smart young man but lazy, was about to ask him if he had even bothered to open his chemistry book when his mother got on the phone to plead on her son's behalf. Cordie couldn't say no to her, and the first tutoring session was scheduled for the following afternoon at five. In preparation Cordie called the concierge and requested a few items she would need, including an *Introduction to Chemistry* textbook.

Jayden, like a lot of other teenage boys, never went anywhere alone. He and three other young men showed up at her door fifteen minutes early for the session. Each of them had a book in hand, and each of them needed help.

Aiden had been in meetings the entire day, and all he could think about was getting home to Cordelia. He had barely had a minute to himself the last few days, and he wanted to spend some time with her. Just knowing she was there made him breathe easier. He told himself it was concern for her safety that made him want to be close to her, but lately even he couldn't buy that one.

He got back to the suite a little after six. He walked through the door and came to a quick stop. There were four teenage boys sitting at the dining table with papers and pens and books strewn in front of them. Cordelia was standing at a portable chalkboard. She introduced Jayden's friends to him, and after saying hello, he went into his bedroom to change. He was smiling as he walked away. The boys were hanging on Cordelia's every word, and it sure as certain wasn't because they loved chemistry. They looked so enamored he wondered if anything she said was sinking in.

By the time he returned to the living room, the boys had left. The chalkboard had been tucked in a corner, and Cordelia was organizing all the supplies and neatly stacking them inside the credenza.

Alec arrived a minute later. "I just talked to Liam," he reported. "Here's what he suggested. Julian is taking Simone and Craig to dinner Friday night at the Shade House. Liam is going to be there with gun and badge, and when they get up to leave, he's going to make sure Simone sees him take a clean cloth and very carefully pick up her water glass. He wants her to see him put it in a plastic bag. He said to tell you he's going for dramatic CSI stuff. If Simone watches any television at all, she'll know why he's taking it."

"It will send her into a tailspin," Aiden predicted.

"Let's see what she does," Alec said.

"What about Jenkins? Is he talking yet?" Aiden asked. The picture of the bastard's hands around Cordelia's neck flashed through his mind, and his entire body tensed in reaction.

"He wants to make a deal."

"What kind of deal?"

"All charges dropped, and he'll tell us everything he knows."

"And?" Aiden prodded. He knew Alec would never go for such a deal.

"We laughed."

"I was thinking . . . ," Cordie began.

"Yes?"

"I have to get out of here for a little while."

Aiden shook his head at her. It wasn't the thing to do at the moment. She turned to him and grabbed hold of his shirt. "I'm losing it," she said. She let go of him and took a step back. "Stop smiling. I mean it. I'm really losing it." She raised her hand in front of his face and put her finger and thumb close together until they were almost touching. "I'm this close to writing Larry a fan letter, for God's sake. This close, Aiden."

"Who the hell is Larry?" Alec asked.

She whirled around to face him. "Larry the fisherman." Her tone suggested he should already know that.

Alec put his hands up in surrender. "Okay, we'll figure something out."

His promise calmed her. "Thank you," she said with as much dignity as she could muster.

TWENTY-SEVEN

Aiden was standing in the doorway of his office reading a printout his assistant had handed him when he happened to look up and see Cordelia walking past. He did a double take, dropped the paper, and rushed after her. "Cordelia."

She turned around just as Alec caught up with her. "Yes, Aiden?"

"In order to get here you had to take the private elevator to the first floor, cross through the lobby, and take another elevator to the third floor."

"Yes, that's exactly what I had to do."

The muscle in his cheek flexed. "Who let you out?"

"Let me out?"

Alec could almost see smoke coming out of the top of Cordie's head. "I let her out," he said. "I promised her."

"For the record, this isn't out," she argued. "I'm still inside the hotel. I would like to go outside."

"That's not going to happen," Aiden snapped.

"This is a compromise," Alec explained. "Until it's safe. Come on, Cordie. Let's go find Regan. She should be in her office."

Aiden walked down the hall with them. "Let me know when Cordelia is coming back upstairs. I'll go with her." He grabbed her hand and pulled her toward him. Frowning intently, he stared into her eyes. He acted as though he wanted to say something to her, but he kept silent.

"I'll come get you," she promised.

He let go of her, nodded, and went back to his office. He walked past the paper he'd dropped on the floor, seemingly unaware that it was there.

"I'm making him crazy," Cordie whispered. "I almost feel sorry for him. He likes a calm, peaceful, uncluttered environment when he's at home, and since I've been here, it hasn't been calm or peaceful. It's been chaotic."

"He's going to miss you when you leave."

She didn't believe that nonsense for a second. Maybe he'd miss the sex . . . the mind-blowing, incredible sex. "When will I be leaving?"

"Soon," Alec promised. He looked at his watch. "It's ten in the morning in Sydney, and tonight Liam will be busy at the restaurant trying to shake things up with Simone. He'll put on quite a show pretending to collect her DNA. I wish we could see it."

"Will she know what he's doing and why?"

"Oh, she'll know. The only reason to get her DNA would be to match it to yours and prove you're her daughter. Unless she's a complete moron, she'll know."

"Liam told us he already had Simone's DNA and the results. How did he really get it?"

Alec opened the door to Regan's reception area. "I didn't ask, and he didn't tell. It's better that way."

"Liam's CIA, isn't he?"

Alec laughed. "No."

She knew he wasn't going to volunteer the information, but that didn't stop her from prodding. She put the issue of Liam's job aside for now and said, "Simone's going to freak out."

"That's the hope."

"Do you think we'll see an immediate reaction?"

"Yes, I think we will."

As it turned out, he was right. There was an immediate reaction.

Aiden shook Cordelia awake at seven in the morning to tell her Alec was coming over with some news, but before he could say anything, he became distracted. He hadn't touched her in what seemed an eternity, and when she rolled over and moaned, still more asleep than awake, he couldn't resist the temptation. She wore a little silk-and-lace nothing that barely covered her, and he desperately wanted to tear it off her. He turned into an animal with her. There was no control, no discipline. He pulled the sheet back, stripped out of his clothes, and made love to her. She more than matched him with her wild and uninhibited response.

After he caught his breath, he leaned up on his elbow. Looking down and tracing the contented smile on her lips with his finger, he said, "Alec should be here anytime now."

She sat up, pushed the hair out of her eyes, and asked why.

"He said he has some good news for you." There was a knock on the door. "That's probably him now."

She flew out of bed. "Put some clothes on," she said in a furious whisper. She picked up his jeans and tossed them at him. "Do you have any idea . . . We shouldn't have . . . I don't want him to know that we . . . you know." She took a quick breath. "Do you have any idea how frustrated I am?"

He pulled on his jeans but didn't bother to close the zipper. Ignoring another knock at the door, he walked around the bed to where she stood. "Frustrated? How many times did you come? Two? Three times? If you're still frustrated, then we need to get back in that bed and—"

She put her hand over his mouth and started to laugh. "Not *that* kind of frustration. Go open the door."

Fortunately Alec wasn't at the door. Room service was delivering breakfast.

Aiden called out to her, but she was already in the shower. She had become a pro at showering with the use of only one hand. By the time she was dressed, she was starving and ready to take on another day in paradise prison. Later, as she was drinking a glass of orange juice and sitting across from Aiden, who was buried in what looked like a stock report, it suddenly occurred to her how surreal it all was. They were behaving like an old married couple.

Alec arrived a few minutes later. He took the cup of coffee Cordie offered and sat down at the table. "I've got some good news," he said. "Charles Kendrick is on his way to Chicago. Liam reported that he boarded a plane in Sydney using the name Charles Ford and is carrying a passport with that identification."

"And that's good news? I'm assuming he's coming here to kill me. Right?" Cordie asked, trying to keep the panic out of her voice.

"Right," Alec agreed.

"We won't let him get near you, Cordelia," Aiden assured her.

"I know that." She took a deep breath. "So what's the plan?"

"Jack and I are going to be at the gate to welcome him to Chicago with a gift . . . handcuffs," Alec said. "We're taking him in as soon as he steps off the plane."

"Shouldn't you catch him in the act? You can't charge him with attempted murder if he doesn't try."

"For the love of God," Aiden muttered, appalled by the idea.

"No, we have enough to get what we want," Alec said. Once again he refused to expound, and no matter how much she nagged, he wouldn't elaborate.

Aiden could see how discouraged she was. Living day to day with the unknown was unnerving. After Alec left, he tried to cheer her up. "It won't be long now until you can go anywhere you want."

"That will be nice," she said, appreciating his optimism but almost afraid to hope.

"Tonight we'll have a good dinner and watch a movie."

"Sorry. I can't."

"What do you mean, you can't?"

She picked up a bagel and tore it in half. "I've got plans. What did I do with my orange juice?"

"You drank it. What plans? You aren't going out. Stop messing with me."

"I'm playing cards with Walker."

"You couldn't have just *said* that?" he demanded.

Of course she could have, but it wouldn't have been nearly as much fun.

Charles Kendrick wasn't happy to see two FBI agents waiting for him. As soon as he got over his shock, he became surly. Alec thought the man believed he could bluster and intimidate his way out of an arrest. They put him in an interrogation room and let him sweat while they went through his duffel bag. In one of the pockets, wrapped in socks, were three Testor phones. One of them already had a Sydney number programmed in. To Jack and Alec, the find was better than Christmas morning.

Liam had already gone through all the phone logs on every cell phone, home phone, and business phone owned by the Rayburn family, and there weren't any calls to or from Chicago, which meant the number programmed into the phone they held most likely went to another burner in Sydney. The only way to find out whom it belonged to was to call.

Jack led the interrogation. He sat across from Kendrick at a metal table in a small, windowless room. Wanting Kendrick to feel closed in and trapped, Jack had handcuffed him to the table, and Alec leaned against the wall behind him, observing. Every once in a while he'd circle the room and stand behind Kendrick, all but breathing down his neck. Kendrick fidgeted in his seat. Sweat trickled down his forehead, steaming up his round Harry Potter glasses. The first words out of his mouth were expected. "I've done nothing wrong."

Jack sat back in his chair and couldn't have looked more easygoing. "You have a unique opportunity here, Charles. You can help yourself by giving us the name of your boss. All we want to know is who hired you to kill Cordelia Kane."

"Are you crazy? No one hired me to kill anyone," he blurted. "I'm just here to see the sights."

"Oh, I misunderstood," Jack said apologetically. "Well, now that you've cleared that up, you can be on your way."

A flash of relief crossed Kendrick's face before he recognized the sarcasm in Jack's comment. He slumped down in his chair.

Alec moved to stand close behind him again. "It would save time if you told the truth."

"I am telling the truth."

"Let's go back to this unique opportunity," Jack suggested smoothly. "If you tell Detective Buchanan and me now, if you work with us, we'll help you."

"I'm not telling you squat," he muttered. "Lawyer. Get me a lawyer." There were beads of sweat on his forehead.

Jack acted as though he hadn't heard his demand. "It's a sweet deal," he said. "But here's the thing. There's a time limit. Once we call the number you have programmed into the burner, we won't need your help. The deal goes away then, and Detective Buchanan and I will do all we can to make sure you get the maximum sentence."

"For what? You've got nothing."

"Let's start with a forged passport," Jack said. "That alone will put you away. If you don't cooperate with us, we'll see that you go to prison for a very, very long time." He pushed the chair back. "I'm going to go get you a lawyer now."

Alec followed him to the door. He turned back and said, "You've got five minutes before we make the call."

They left Kendrick to sweat—and hopefully panic—and headed to another interrogation room, where Jenkins waited. They'd had him brought up to the fourth floor so they could have another chat with him . . . or, as Alec called it, round two. The plan was to play one suspect against the other.

In the hall Jack said, "Five minutes? You gave him five minutes to decide what he wants to do? Where did that come from? We agreed to tell him he had twelve hours, remember?"

"Yeah, I remember, but five minutes sounded more dramatic. Twelve hours didn't have the same kick."

Jack laughed. "You're right."

"I want to call that number now."

"Me, too, but we have to wait. We're working blind here, but doesn't it make sense that Kendrick wouldn't call his boss an hour after landing? He wouldn't have anything to report. So we wait a little longer, maybe five or six hours. If the boss is spooked and doesn't answer the phone, we're screwed, and easy becomes hard."

"Unless Kendrick and Jenkins tell us what we want to know."

The rest of the day Alec and Jack rotated between the two interrogation rooms, hoping to wear down one or the other of the two suspects, but neither Jenkins nor Kendrick was giving up anything. Threats of longer prison sentences for their crimes didn't seem to faze them. As though they had rehearsed their denials, each separately insisted they were not taking orders from anyone.

Jack was the last to question Kendrick. When he walked out of the room, Alec was waiting for him. "The tech is ready."

A minute later they stood next to a technician as he played a recording that sounded like electrical static. "Will that work?" he asked them.

"Perfect," Jack told him.

"Kendrick's going to cry entrapment, you know," Alec said. "This will never fly in court."

"That's true," Jack admitted. "But it might give him the motivation to open up."

"Time to make the call," Alec said as he picked up Kendrick's burner phone, touched the screen, and laid the phone in the center of the desk so everyone could hear.

The men hovered over it, listening. One . . . two . . . three . . . four . . . five . . . the phone kept ringing. They glanced at one another. No one was answering. Six . . . seven . . . eight . . . Alec shook his head and was about to pick up the phone when suddenly there was a click. A few seconds of silence followed, as though whoever was on the other end was waiting for the caller to speak first. Finally, the silence was broken.

Julian Taylor answered. "Is it done?"

Jack and Alec couldn't wait to have yet another chat with Charles Kendrick. They were both smiling as they entered the interrogation room. Kendrick was sitting next to his attorney, a forty-year-old man with a sour face and a disposition to match. His posture was that of someone who had been beaten down by disappointments.

"I'm not telling you anything," Kendrick stated defiantly. "My lawyer here, Mr. Kale, says I don't even have to talk to you."

Alec and Jack pulled out chairs and sat facing them. Kendrick's smug expression was about to change.

Addressing the attorney, Jack said, "We're going to be adding to the charges."

"What charges are you adding?" Kendrick demanded before his attorney could say a word.

Alec answered. "We know you came here to kill Cordelia Kane, and we can prove it."

Kendrick leaned forward. "How?" he asked with self-righteous indignation. "How can you prove it?"

"Glad you asked," Jack said. "We called the number on your burner and talked to Julian Taylor."

Kendrick didn't look so cocky now. "He talked to you? I don't believe it. He talked to you?" he repeated.

Jack answered. "He didn't actually talk to us."

"No, he didn't," Alec confirmed.

Jack explained. "He thought he was talking to you. He made the assumption, and we didn't correct him."

Kendrick seemed confused. "You're lying."

"We're FBI agents," Alec stated authoritatively. "We never lie." He was somewhat surprised he got that out without laughing.

"We recorded the conversation," Jack told the attorney. "Would you like to hear it?" He put the phone down and pushed the button.

Julian's voice was loud and clear. "Is it done? Is Cordelia Kane dead? Answer me."

Static muffled the answer. "No . . . not yet."

Kendrick's eyes widened when he heard a response. "You should have told him who you were. You tricked him by not identifying yourself."

"We sure did," Jack said. "I guess you could say we're tricky."

He pushed the button again to continue the recording.

"You're not getting the rest of the money until that gold digger is dead. It needs to happen fast. I thought I conveyed the urgency here. They collected my daughter's glass for her DNA. Get it done." He repeated the demand in a near shout. "And if you run into that coward Jenkins, tell him he's fired."

The conversation ended.

"The static we put in there helped sell it, don't you think?" Alec asked.

"It will never hold up in court," Kale blustered. "Never. It's entrapment."

"Maybe, maybe not," Alec said. Since they had no intention of using the tape, they didn't care if it would hold up in court or not. They wanted Kendrick and Jenkins to talk.

"I know the law," Kale snapped.

"So do we," Jack replied.

"I'll file a motion—"

"Go ahead."

"We also have Arnold Jenkins. He's giving you up, Charles. He's answering all our questions. We already played the call for him."

"He seized the opportunity. You didn't," Alec said.

"I think we're through here." Jack picked up the phone and stood to leave.

Alec followed him. They walked out into the hallway, and just as the door was closing behind them, they heard Kendrick yell, "Wait a minute."

TWENTY-EIGHT

The news shouldn't have surprised Cordie, but it did.

"You're certain it was Julian Taylor on the phone?"

Alec nodded. "Liam confirmed it, and so did a lot of other people. It was Julian."

"It makes sense," Aiden said. "With Simone's shares, Julian now controls fifty-one percent of Merrick stock. He can overrule the board whenever he wants. As soon as twenty percent is transferred to you, Cordelia, his power is gone."

"But if I weren't around, he would lose it to Simone's son when he turned twenty-one," she pointed out. She walked over to the bar where they were standing and sat down on a stool.

"Simone gave Julian her shares to control, and I'm sure he could get his grandson to do the same thing."

Both Aiden and Alec were being very calm and matter-of-fact about this latest development. Cordie, on the other hand, wanted to start screaming. She now understood why children had tantrums. It was a thoroughly satisfying way to let out pent-up frustration. She wanted to pick up objects and hurl them across the room. Nature seemed to empathize. The weather complemented her mood. A hard rain was pelting the windows of the suite, and every other minute a clap of thunder could be heard rumbling in the distance. The wind was gathering momentum.

"As soon as Kendrick and Jenkins found out we knew who they were working for, they understood they'd lost their leverage. We can't get them to stop talking now. They've turned on each other and on Julian, both trying to get a deal."

"They were with Simone when she confronted me at the hotel in Sydney. I assumed they worked for her."

"They did work for her, but they also reported everything she did to her father. That's when he found out you were back in the picture. According to Kendrick, Julian has known about you for a very long time."

"How long?"

"Since you were a baby."

"What?" She all but fell off the stool. "This just keeps getting creepier and creepier."

Alec was rummaging through the refrigerator behind the bar. He took out a bottle of Kelly's root beer and opened it. "There are some real serious trust issues in that family," he said.

"He spies on his daughter. Why would he do that?" she asked.

"He's protecting his interest," Aiden explained.

"Kendrick was more of a confidant than Jenkins was," Alec said. "He would sit and drink straight vodka shots with Julian a couple of times a month. That's when Julian would talk about family. One night he told Jenkins that Simone had run away when she was a teenager. It took him some time to find her, and when he did, he got the shock of his life. He couldn't believe what she had done."

"Did she know she would inherit stock when she turned twenty-one?" Cordie asked. She looked to Aiden for an answer.

"I'm sure she did."

"That might be another reason she used the name Natalie

Smith," Alec said. "I don't think she had any intention of staying with your father. She gave birth, and a short time later she took off."

"Julian told Kendrick he was about to send a couple of men to drag her back to Australia, but it wasn't necessary. She came home, apologized for making him worry, and went on with her life. She never mentioned you or your father to anyone."

"What happens to Julian now?"

"He's been arrested," Alec said.

"I wish I had been there to see him taken in," Aiden said.

Alec agreed. "When the Australian press gets hold of this, they'll have a heyday. I've got a strong feeling Simone won't win Woman of the Year again."

"Dear God, I'm genetically linked to those people," Cordie declared. "I wish I had never started this, but at least it's over now. Right?"

"Not quite," Alec told her.

"Oh, come on. Who else wants to kill me? Simone? Her husband? The teenagers?" She grabbed a long swizzle stick and slid part of it under her cast.

"Cordelia, what are you doing?" Aiden asked, looking appalled.

She pulled the swizzle stick out. "It itches," she explained before turning to Alec again. "Who's after me now?"

"No one that I know of, but we are going to continue to be cautious until the stock is officially transferred to you, which will be in a couple of days."

"Julian will try to stop it."

"He won't be able to," Alec assured her. "Liam has your DNA results now. He has people who can make it happen."

She absentmindedly reached for the swizzle stick again. Aiden stopped her. "You could lose one of those in there."

She didn't think it was a good idea to tell him she already had.

TWENTY-NINE

Congressman Mitchell Ray Chambers was prepared to dazzle his constituents. He had set up a press conference a week before the primary to remind the good people of Fallsborough that he was saving their town by working so diligently for the past year to get the Hamilton Hotel and Resort to Rock Point.

He hadn't signed the contract Walker Madison had FedExed to him. He had cleverly scheduled the signing for a week after the primary was over. Chambers had agreed to accept a ridiculously low offer and had, in fact, suggested the amount, but he had no intention of ever signing the contract. He still believed he could get a considerably higher price, and now that Walker Madison was involved, he was more confident than ever. It was going to be much easier to manipulate the youngest brother. All Mitchell needed to do was convince his constituents that he had been willing to do whatever it took to make Fallsborough wealthy and prosperous. Then, once he had the primary in his pocket, he would do whatever it took to make himself wealthy and prosperous. He was absolutely certain, with the Madison brothers back at the negotiating table, he could bargain his way into a sweet deal.

His constituents didn't need to know any of those particulars, however.

Mayor Green didn't stand a chance against him now, and he was assured of a reelection victory in November. Politics was all about manipulation.

He didn't have to worry about his cousin Lester whining and complaining or embarrassing him in front of the cameras, because he'd bought him out and was now the sole owner of Rock Point. The high price he'd paid Lester was going to be well worth it.

He dressed in red, white, and blue for the press conference: a navy suit, a crisp white shirt, and a bright-red tie. He pinned a tiny American flag on his lapel and was ready. The press conference was choreographed in his mind. He had worked out how he would make his grand entrance, where he wanted the podium placed, and, most important, where the flag would be positioned. He wanted it behind him and a little to the left so that on camera the flag would be in every frame with him. He had even practiced a couple of different expressions in front of a mirror. He needed to look humble yet at the same time stately and intelligent. He would brag, of course, but it would be veiled behind his explanation of how hard he'd worked to get the hotel. He was sure he had it all figured out.

The double doors were open to the campaign office. Aiden stayed in the lobby out of sight, but he could see Chambers up on a small stage. A large crowd had gathered to hear what he had to say. Microphones and cameras were capturing every word. Aiden planned to wait until the questions began before walking in. He wished Cordelia were with him. She'd be as disgusted as he was with the congressman's antics, trying to look self-deprecating while taking credit for everything but inventing the Internet. As he spoke, he kept putting his right hand inside his suit jacket over his heart. Was he trying to look like Napoleon? Worse than his phony smile was his speech. Every word out of his mouth was a lie. Every damn word. If Cordelia were standing at Aiden's side, she'd want to challenge Chambers with facts and figures.

As Aiden stood there listening to all the empty campaign rhetoric, he couldn't help but think how much the congressman and Julian Taylor were alike. They were both controlled by power and greed. Julian had proven he would do anything to hold on to his empire, and the congressman was proving he would do anything to get reelected. How long had he been dealing with people like Chambers? he wondered. It made him tired just thinking about it.

The congressman was ready for questions. Mayor Green pushed forward and raised her hand. "Congressman, we are all wondering if you have signed the contract with the Madisons for Rock Point." Before he could answer, she continued. "Or is it going to be like the last time when you changed the terms and pulled out?"

His tone was condescending when he said, "I don't know where you got that information, but it's wrong. You should check your sources, Mayor, before you make accusations."

He took another question on the other side of the room, determined to avoid eye contact with the mayor. The questions were all about the hotel and resort. How many jobs did he think would be available? How long did he think it would take to build?

Aiden could see the desperation in the local residents. Spencer was right. These hardworking people needed a break. He was amazed by some of the congressman's answers. Chambers acted as though he'd drawn up the plans for the hotel and could even give them the dimensions for each of the rooms. He spoke with such authority.

The mayor drew his attention once again. She was now in front of the crowd, demanding with her hand waving in the air that he acknowledge her. "You haven't answered my question," she blurted when he had to stop talking to take a breath.

"What question did you want answered?" He sounded weary.

"Have you signed the contract with the Madisons? Last time we heard you changed your mind. It was on the news."

"You can't believe everything you see on television," he said.

"Answer the question," someone called out. "Did you sign it? Are we getting the hotel?"

"Of course you're getting the hotel," he scoffed.

"Did you sign the contract?" the mayor demanded once again.

The smile plastered on the congressman's face was beginning to crumble. "No, I haven't."

The crowd turned on him in a heartbeat. Bolstering the smile again, he put his hands up and said, "Hold on, hold on. I've read the contract, and everything is in order. Walker Madison and I have decided we should meet in person and both sign. It's the right thing to do. I let Walker set the date at his convenience. I know you all heard about his terrible car accident." He abruptly stopped, swallowed loud enough for the microphone to pick up, and finally lost the plastic smile. Eyes wide, he watched Aiden Madison walking toward him.

The look on the congressman's face was priceless, and Aiden once again thought that, if only Cordelia were here, she would be laughing now. She would also love what was about to happen.

"That's it for today, ladies and gentlemen," Chambers blurted. "I've got to hurry back to Washington for an important vote."

Aiden stepped up to the microphone and promptly captured the crowd's attention. They all knew who he was.

"My name is Aiden Madison, and I have a great surprise for you and for the congressman." He scanned all the curious faces and glanced over at Chambers before continuing. "I have the contract with me, and you'll get to watch both of us sign. My brothers and I are anxious to get started on this project, and I know you are, too."

The cheers were deafening.

The congressman put his hands up to silence the crowd and said, "No, no. I promised Walker that I—"

Aiden cut him off. "Walker has already signed, and so has Spencer. It's up to you and me to finish this." He took a pen from his breast pocket and shoved it in front of him. "Why don't you sign first, Congressman?"

His mind racing, Chambers tried to think of a way out of this fiasco, but he drew a blank. He was trapped, and he knew it. The crowd's cheers grew louder as they began to chant his name. The people were looking up at him almost adoringly, they were so grateful for what he was doing for them. Maybe there was some good to come from this disaster after all. He had them in his pocket now. Every one of them would vote for him because he was their savior. With a flourish he took the pen, bent down, and signed his name.

Only Aiden could see the anger in his eyes when they shook hands. The man was seething, which, all things considered, was an expected reaction.

The congressman was patted on the shoulder a dozen times and had to shake hands with most of the people there on his way out the door to go back to Washington for his important vote. He wanted to linger and lap up the adulation, but he worried they'd catch on that he'd lied about having an important vote. He had no idea what he would say if they asked him what the vote was for. Losing the fortune he could have made from Rock Point definitely stung, but despite it all, he was actually feeling good about the future. He wouldn't need to spend much money on additional campaigning now. He'd just won the hearts of the voters.

Kalie, the young reporter who had talked to Aiden and Spencer the last time they were in town, waited outside the doors. She had her microphone in hand and a cameraman behind her as Aiden approached.

Mayor Green intercepted him. "Thank you again for the generous donation to my campaign," she said, "but after the congressman's press conference, I don't think I have much of a chance."

"You're the woman for the job," Aiden said, motioning for Kalie to start recording. People gathered around as he looked into the camera and said, "Mayor Green cares about the people of this town. If it weren't for her, the Hamilton Hotel and Resort wouldn't be built here. Although your current congressman is taking credit, he had nothing to do with it. Your mayor worked for more than a year, calling and writing and sending photos of this beautiful area, to convince us to build here. She should be your next representative in Congress. I certainly would vote for her if I lived in this district. Just like she fought to get the Hamilton, she'll fight for you in Washington. Do the right thing. Vote for Mayor Green."

He turned to Mayor Green and began to laugh. She looked flabbergasted. Fortunately, Kalie had just given the cameraman the signal to stop taping.

An hour later Aiden was back on the plane and on his way home. He hadn't seen Cordelia in more than a week. He couldn't believe how much he missed her. He knew her cast had come off three days ago, and he'd heard from Regan that the doctor wasn't happy to see a swizzle stick stuck inside.

He felt travel weary. He'd flown from San Diego to Houston and then up to Rock Point. Months ago he had made up his mind to slow down, to stay home more, but it wasn't until he had to deal with the congressman and other men just like him that he realized how tired he was.

He wanted off the fast track. And he wanted Cordelia.

Thanks to Liam's connections and hard work, along with a top attorney and the court in Sydney, Cordelia was now the owner of Merrick stock. It was expected that she would go back to Sydney to meet the board and sign additional papers. Aiden told her there was no way he would let her go there without him. He'd learned then not to use those exact words. Telling her he would "let" her do anything set her temper off. He smiled thinking about it.

He'd heard Julian Taylor's arrest had started a firestorm in the press. Liam told him Simone and her family were on holiday, which he translated to mean they were hiding until things calmed down. Simone's past was such a juicy story, Liam didn't think that would happen soon. So far, they were leaving Cordelia alone. Aiden knew they would eventually want to interview her. He also knew she wouldn't talk to any of them.

It was closing in on one in the morning by the time Aiden got back to the hotel. He went to Walker's suite first. His brother was a night owl. He was going over notes Spencer had left for him when Aiden walked in, dropped the contract in his lap, and said, "It's all yours and Spencer's. He'll take the lead and show you how it's done."

"You don't want to run it?"

"No."

He wasn't worried Walker would screw up. The team wouldn't let him. They had been doing this long enough that they had gotten rid of the wrinkles. It was a well-oiled machine now. "I'll tell you all about the congressman's press conference tomorrow. I'm beat. I'm going to bed."

He went down the hall and opened the door to his suite. It was spotless. There wasn't anything out of place. No phone under a chair, no scarves draped across the sofa, no chemistry books. No Cordelia.

She'd left a note propped up against a vase of flowers on the table telling him she was leaving and thanking him yet again for his help. He held it in his hand as he stood in the doorway of her bedroom. It was just as spotless and sterile as the living room. He didn't know where she was or what she was doing. There was only one certainty. He wanted her back.

Coming to terms with his misery took time. He paced around the living room, and at two o'clock he called Alec. He was sound asleep, of course. It was the middle of the night.

Alec stirred at the sound. He carefully eased Regan off his shoulder so he wouldn't wake her and fumbled for the phone. "Agent Buchanan," he answered.

"Where is she?"

"What? Aiden?"

"Where is Cordelia?" He repeated the question in a firm voice.

Alec yawned. "She's sleeping in the guest room."

"So she didn't leave for Boston?"

"No, she didn't."

Long seconds passed before Aiden spoke again. "She's all right?"

"Yes. She's fine."

"When is she leaving for Boston?"

"Two days," he answered. "Tomorrow is that Summerset thing, and she leaves the next morning."

"Okay, then." Aiden sounded relieved.

"I'm glad you finally figured it out," Alec said on a long, drawn-out yawn. "I'm going back to sleep now."

THIRTY

Cordie had just taken a grueling two-mile ride around her old neighborhood with Jayden Martin in his new used car. He didn't mention that it was a stick shift until she was in the passenger seat, nor did he mention that he didn't know how to drive a stick shift. She had whiplash before they rounded the first corner.

He was proud of his car and wanted her assessment and approval. She was diplomatic as she went over the repairs she thought he needed. First was the muffler. It was about to fall off. Then there were the tires. They were as bald as an eagle's head and needed to be replaced. She also mentioned that he needed someone with experience to teach him how to drive a stick shift because he was stripping the gears.

By the time she got back to the house, she was late getting ready for the Summerset Ball. Alec and Regan officially owned her house now, and it felt strange to sleep in the guest room. Since her bed fit in it perfectly, she decided she would leave it and buy a new one in Boston.

Cordie had deliberately been crazy busy all week so she wouldn't have time to think about Aiden. Once she was on the road, she could cry her way to Boston if she wanted, even though her father wouldn't approve of that behavior. Crying upset him, and whenever he saw tears, he would tell her to man up, which, all things considered, didn't make a lick of sense.

There were a few good things she could concentrate on. The students she was tutoring suddenly figured it out. At first she could almost see the confusing chemistry problems tumbling around in their minds, and when things actually clicked, she felt a rush similar to euphoria. That "got it" moment was the reason she became a teacher. She would still be doing her job at St. Matthew's if it weren't for Aiden, but she was desperate not to follow in her father's footsteps and long for someone she couldn't have. Life was too short to waste, and she was ready for a fresh start.

"Why aren't you in the shower?" Regan stood in the doorway of the kitchen with her hands on her hips. Her hair and makeup were done, and she wore her robe. "You're not ready."

"*You're* not ready," Cordie countered.

"All I have to do is put on my dress. Hurry up, Cordie. You're going to have fun tonight."

Cordie rinsed her glass and put it in the dishwasher. "How do you know I'll have fun?"

Regan shrugged. "No one's going to try to kill you. That'll be fun."

"There is that," she said.

"You've got grease on your face."

"I know." Jayden had popped the hood and wanted her to look at the engine and check the connections. "I'm getting in the shower," she promised and hurried up the stairs.

She wasn't in the mood to pretend to be happy and smile and make inane conversation, but she was going to do exactly that, and no one, not even her best friends, would know her heart was breaking.

The sapphire blue gown she'd worn in Sydney had been cleaned and was hanging in the closet. Unfortunately, Miss Marie wasn't there to oversee Cordie's makeup and hair. She smiled thinking about the bossy woman and hoped one day she'd see her again.

After she'd dried her hair, she put on a little makeup—nothing as artful as Miss Marie's work, but at least she looked more like herself. She left her hair down because the only other option she had was a ponytail, and she didn't think that would be appropriate. When she was ready, she stood in front of a full-length mirror to check that everything was tucked in. Miss Marie was right, she decided; the gown was the exact color of her eyes.

Regan and Alec were waiting for her in the foyer. Regan was fixing Alec's tie. They both turned as she came down the stairs.

"You look beautiful," Regan said.

"You look beautiful, too, Regan," she replied. It wasn't an idle compliment. The deep burgundy gown was stunning on her friend.

Cordie was quiet on the way to the country club where the charity ball was being held. She sat in the backseat watching Alec tug on his collar.

Regan noticed. "Twice a year, Alec. You only have to wear a tux twice a year, so suck it up."

Her husband laughed. "Suck it up?"

The mood lightened, and by the time they walked into the country club, they were all ready to have a good time.

The club was one of Chicago's older establishments, but it had recently been remodeled, and the ballroom had been expanded to nearly twice the original size. It was beautifully appointed in a contemporary design. Two-story-high windows overlooked the lake and golf course. Crystal chandeliers shaped like glistening waterfalls hung from the ceiling and cast a soft light on the guests who mingled on the dance floor in the center of the room. Round tables decked out in white linens and gleaming crystal and silver lined the perimeter.

The band was tuning their instruments on the stage at the far end of the dance floor. Quite a crowd had shown up, and the laughter and champagne were flowing. It was a festive occasion, Cordie reminded herself, and time for her to stop being melancholy and get with it.

Alec found their table. Cordie thought she would sit and watch the couples dance, but that didn't happen. As soon as the music started, she was pulled onto the dance floor by one of the most aggravating men. His name was Elliott, and he had chased after her all through college. He didn't know how to take no for an answer, and like a pesky rash, he wouldn't go away no matter how many times she tried to excuse herself. Forcing a smile, she tried to pay attention to what he was saying, but the romantic song the band was playing kept intruding.

The music finally ended. She stepped away from her partner and, politely refusing another dance, turned to go back to the table. She suddenly froze. Aiden was there, in the doorway talking to Jack and Sophie. Aiden in a tuxedo—there wasn't anything in the world that could take her breath away like Aiden in a tuxedo. She stood in the center of the dance floor, all alone, watching him. Her mind was telling her to turn around and walk—or run—but her legs weren't cooperating. She had thought she'd be able to get out of town without seeing him again. It had actually become a hope.

No such luck.

She could do this, she told herself. She would thank him yet again for taking such good care of her, kiss him on the cheek, and run like lightning. It seemed like a good plan of action until she reevaluated. Being a coward wasn't such a bad thing, was it? Maybe she should just run now.

The music began—another romantic song, of course—and Elliott was back asking for one more dance. Before she could answer him, Aiden was there telling him no and taking her into his arms. Pressing his body to hers, he glided her away.

One dance. She could do one dance. Then she'd run.

"How is your arm?" he asked.

"Good. It's good."

He pulled her closer. "I've missed you."

"You'll get over it."

His reaction was puzzling. He laughed and released his hold so he could look in her eyes. "You know what else I miss?"

"No, what?"

She was totally unprepared for his answer. "The sounds you make when I'm inside you."

"Oh God . . ."

"And when you're begging me to let you come—"

Her hand covered his mouth. "Stop talking like that," she whispered. "People will hear."

Her blush delighted him. "You know what else I miss?"

She buried her face in his chest. "Don't you dare say it . . ."

"I miss the way your nails dig into my back, and I miss the way you say my name when you're writhing in my arms."

She groaned. "Please stop."

He couldn't resist. "I've never heard you say that."

Her knees were going to buckle. Fortunately, he was holding her up. She realized she needed to get the upper hand.

"We have established that you like sex. I don't need to hear any more reasons why."

"I like sex with you. No, that's not right. I love sex with you."

She tried to push away from him. "You like skinny blondes," she blurted.

"I . . . what?"

"You like skinny blondes."

He was looking at her as though he thought she'd lost her mind, and she was beginning to think she had.

"I'm leaving for Boston in the morning," she said.

"No."

They were swaying to the music now, unaware that the band had stopped playing.

"No? What do you mean, no?" Did he think she needed his permission?

"I can't let you go."

"*Let* me?"

He could have sworn he saw sparks in her eyes. "I went to Congressman Chambers's press conference."

Her eyes widened. "You did? What did you do? Was it good?"

He laughed. "Yeah, it was."

When he told her what had happened, she was ecstatic. "The mayor had no idea?"

"No," he answered. "The only person who knew I was up to something was the reporter, Kalie. I told her to be ready."

"Do you think the mayor could beat him in the primary?"

"I think she has a chance."

"I wish I had been there to see it."

"I wanted you there with me," he admitted, his tone serious now. "Cordelia, I need to talk to you . . . to tell you . . ."

"Yes?"

"Come back to the hotel with me. We'll have privacy there."

She shook her head. "No, Aiden. I'm going to Boston tomorrow, and if I go back to the suite with you, we both know what will happen."

"I can't let you leave." He sighed. "Yes, I heard it. I meant I *won't* let you leave."

He tried to kiss her, but she turned her head. "We're in public, for Pete's sake. Behave yourself."

"You won't go with me to the hotel where we could have privacy," he reminded her. "So I guess we're going to do this here."

"Do what?" she asked suspiciously.

"If we were in my suite, first I would kiss you, and then, if I could keep my hands and my mouth off you long enough, I would tell you I love you."

She was so stunned, it took her several seconds to react. "No, you don't. I was just convenient. Yes, convenient," she insisted when he looked so incredulous.

"What goes on in that mind of yours?"

"You don't love me," she insisted.

"Yes, I do, Cordelia." His smile was filled with tenderness. "I love you. Do you love me?"

"I'm going to Boston." She was shaken and was having trouble holding a thought. He loved her? When did that happen?

"Do you love me?" he asked again.

"I've bought a town house. I have to move there."

"Cordelia, answer me. Do you love me?"

"Yes." It was a whisper, but he heard her. She poked him in the chest. "That town house was expensive."

"Then I'll move to Boston with you."

"You can't move to Boston; your whole life is here," she said.

"Where you go, I go," he said. "That's how marriage works."

"Marriage?"

"What are you not understanding here? I love you, Cordelia." He wrapped his strong arms around her and kissed her so passionately her whole body went weak.

When the kiss ended, Cordie, still wrapped in Aiden's embrace, looked around. "The band's not playing," she whispered.

"I know," he said, leaning in to kiss her again.

She put her fingers on his lips to stop him and nodded her head to the side, motioning for him to look at something. He turned and smiled. Regan and Sophie were standing there staring at them with their mouths open in shock.

Aiden laughed. "I'll let you explain."

"*Let* me?"

EPILOGUE

Cordelia and Aiden were married at St. Matthew's Church three months later. Neither of them wanted to wait, and although there hadn't been much time to plan, they managed to pull it off without any glitches. Sister Delores was so happy Cordie had decided to come back to St. Matthew's to teach and so grateful for the scholarship fund Cordie had set up in her father's name, she actually got teary-eyed during the ceremony. The newlyweds honeymooned in Australia, and Cordie got to see all the wonderful places she had read about. Julian and his daughter couldn't ruin her love for the country, but she avoided Sydney until it was time to meet the board and sign the papers. She didn't want the stock, yet according to the will she couldn't give it up.

"What are we going to do with it?" she asked Aiden.

"We'll figure out something," he assured her.

When they reached Sydney, they stayed in their suite at the Hamilton, of course. According to Liam, the scandal of the year was finally dying down. He went with them to the company headquarters to meet the board. He wore his weapon on his hip, but Cordie didn't see a badge.

"Do you expect trouble?" she asked. She walked between Aiden and Liam up the steps to the entrance of the office building.

"Just a precaution," he explained.

The board members were waiting for her. There were eleven at the long table, all men, and all of them trying to mask their unease. The twelfth board member, Craig Rayburn, was noticeably absent, and Cordie was thankful she didn't have to be in the same room with him. The men stood when she entered.

"Miss Kane is here," the man at the head of the table said.

"It's Dr. Madison." Aiden made the correction.

"Doctor?"

"Yes." There was a hard edge to Aiden's voice, and Cordie presumed he was telling them to respect her.

Each board member introduced himself. She didn't shake hands with any of them. Aiden handed her a pen. She appreciated that her husband had gone to law school, because only after he had read over the documents did he allow her to sign. Liam, acting like a bodyguard, stood watch behind her.

"Do you plan to be active . . . with your stock? Will you be voting?" the man in the chairman's chair asked.

"Perhaps," she answered.

Thirty long minutes later, Liam was driving them back to the hotel, and Aiden was trying to talk him into having dinner with them as a thank-you for all his help.

"I appreciate the offer," Liam said, "but I have to be in Melbourne tonight. There's a . . . situation I have to clean up."

"Liam, may I ask you a question?" Cordie asked.

He looked at her in the rearview mirror. "Sure you can."

"Who do you work for?"

Grinning, he said, "Depends on the day of the week."

"Okay, today who do you work for?"

"The government."

"Which government?"

"That's a good question. If you don't mind, I'm going to drop you off at the hotel and be on my way. I have a plane waiting for me," he said, effectively putting an end to the topic of his employment.

Giving up, she turned to Aiden. "What did you think of the board?"

"I haven't made a judgment yet. Not enough information."

"I don't think they liked me."

"What makes you think so?" Liam asked.

"I can tell when I'm being played," she said with authority.

Liam thought that was quite funny. "You can tell, huh?"

"Yes, I can. I'm used to people trying to con me. I teach high school boys."

"Then you knew all those delays on the floors of your Boston town house didn't really happen. Alec was scheming up one excuse after another to keep you in Chicago . . . but you figured that out, right?"

"He what? Why would he want to keep me in Chicago?"

"According to him, you two were clueless. Those were his words, not mine. He thought Aiden needed time to figure it all out, and so did you."

She was astounded. She had been played. "Then the floors . . ."

"They were finished the first week."

That devil. "I'm going to be having a little chat with him when we get home."

She was still thinking about Alec's tricks when Liam pulled up in front of the hotel and got out to say good-bye. "It's been a pleasure," he said, shaking Aiden's hand.

When he turned to Cordie, she hugged him and said, "Thank you so much for everything you've done."

"Anytime," he said. He winked at her and got back in the car.

As he was driving off, Aiden took Cordie's hand. "I could use a drink. How about you?"

"That sounds lovely," she replied.

They entered the lobby and were heading to the bar when Aiden asked, "Do you see her? Simone is here."

Cordie looked at the far end of the lobby and spotted Simone sitting stiffly in a wingback chair near the bank of elevators. "What does she want?" she asked.

"You don't have to talk to her, Cordelia."

"I don't think she'll go away. Let's get it over with."

They continued into the bar, conscious that Simone was watching. When she stood and followed them, Cordie felt as though she was heading for a showdown at the O.K. Corral. Taking a seat at one of the tables, she waited.

Simone didn't try to hide her anger. There was a round table between them, and for a second Cordie thought the woman might lunge at her.

Simone's voice shook. "Do you know what you've done to me? To my family?"

"I don't believe I'm the one who did anything. It was your father who tried to have me killed. He belongs in prison, and I'm not so sure you don't belong there, too, but unfortunately, it's not a crime to be a coldhearted bitch."

Simone couldn't restrain herself. Her hand flew at Cordie, but Aiden grabbed her wrist.

"Why did you come here?" Cordie asked.

"I wanted you to know the terrible, terrible thing you've done to me. You've destroyed me and my family."

"How have I done that?" she asked quietly.

"We can't hold our heads up, thanks to you. The shame . . . the humiliation is too much to bear. I've been asked to resign from every board, every charity. I'm being shunned and cut out of every social function in the city. Your hate did that to me."

"I don't hate you. I feel sorry for you. The scandal will fade, and in time it might even be forgotten. I promise, you'll never have to worry about seeing me in the future. And you can forget all about me once again."

Cordie's promise seemed to calm Simone. She nodded and, without another word, walked out of the bar.

Leaning into Aiden, Cordie watched her leave. "She was very young when she had me."

"Is that an excuse for her behavior?"

"Maybe," she said. "I do feel sorry for her. She made me realize how very lucky I am. I was raised by a loving father, and I doubt Simone got much affection from her father. Julian was more interested in keeping her in line." She put her arms around Aiden's neck. "You're going to be a wonderful father."

"You think?"

"I know." She kissed him and whispered in his ear, "Shall we go upstairs and get started?"

A **150**-YEAR PUBLISHING TRADITION

In 1864, E. P. Dutton & Co. bought the famous Old Corner Bookstore and its publishing division from Ticknor and Fields and began their storied publishing career. Mr. Edward Payson Dutton and his partner, Mr. Lemuel Ide, had started the company in Boston, Massachusetts, as a bookseller in 1852. Dutton expanded to New York City, and in 1869 opened both a bookstore and publishing house at 713 Broadway. In 2014, Dutton celebrates 150 years of publishing excellence. We have redesigned our longtime logo-type to reflect the simple design of those earliest published books. For more information on the history of Dutton and its books and authors, please visit www.penguin.com/dutton.